'It's time you had a husband to teach you better manners.'

Marietta was forced to react to that with a look of undisguised contempt. 'I have no wish for a husband, my lord.'

'I thought that's what every woman wanted. Marriage. Bairns,' Lord Alain replied.

Her irritation surfaced again. 'You are mistaken. It is what every man *thinks* that every woman wants. But I am not every woman and I allow no man to make my decisions. I have a mind of my own!'

Juliet Landon lives in an ancient country village in the north of England with her retired scientist husband. Her keen interest in embroidery, art and history, together with a fertile imagination, make writing historical novels a favourite occupation. She finds the research particularly exciting, especially the early medieval period and the fascinating laws concerning women in particular, and their struggle for survival in a man's world.

THE KNIGHT, THE KNAVE AND THE LADY

Juliet Landon

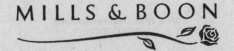

MILLS & BOON

All the characters in this book have no existence outside the imagination of the author, and have no relation whatsoever to anyone bearing the same name or names. They are not even distantly inspired by any individual known or unknown to the author, and all the incidents are pure invention.

First published in Great Britain 1996
Harlequin Mills & Boon Limited,
Eton House, 18-24 Paradise Road, Richmond, Surrey, TW9 1SR

© Juliet Landon 1996

ISBN 0 263 80018 0

Set in 10 on 11pt Linotron Times
04-9702-90498

Printed and bound in Great Britain
by BPC Paperbacks Limited, Aylesbury

CHAPTER ONE

THE richly embroidered curtains across the back of the travelling carriage parted just wide enough to allow the passage of a small brown and white terrier, wriggling frantically against the grip around its middle, its short legs scrabbling helplessly in the air way above the dusty track. Already, a hot stream of liquid had begun to leak down the arms of the maid who held it, causing a hint of irritation to colour her plea to the rider beyond.

'Here, Master Bruno, please. . .quickly. . .grab it!'

Bruno leaned forward over the stallion's neck.

'Here, catch its rope.'

But it was too late. The yapping creature had already half leapt from the restraining hands and Bruno, not wishing to be wetted like the maid, had released it before being able to snatch at the cord dangling from its jewelled collar. He watched in exasperation as it disappeared like a white rat between the horses' hooves, across the track and on up the bank into the field beyond, scattering sheep and lambs, yapping frantically, pausing to lift a leg tantalisingly out of reach and then on again as it discovered an irresistible trail.

'Oh, Master Bruno. . .please, don't lose it!' The maid's voice was a wailing whisper. She turned to peep into the carriage and then at him again. 'My mistress! She'll. . .'

'I'll get it! Damn stupid animal! C'mon, you lot!' He turned to the young grooms and pages who rode behind. 'Give me a hand,' and pulled away in front of them, not looking to check their response.

His command had not included his sister, but after riding soberly along the highway since dawn, she longed for a few moments of excitement and saw no reason to be excluded from the chase. Without waiting for her ladies, Marietta followed, digging her leather-clad heels into Dulzelina's dapple-grey flanks, taking the high bank in two easy strides, ignoring the shouts of alarm behind her.

From the corner of her eye she saw her father in the distance at the head of the cavalcade, still unaware of the diversion, too far away to hear. Well out of range, her stepmother's huge carriage rocked and jolted its occupants over the pot-holed track, the maid's face a mere pink blob of anxiety like a button on the curtain's opening.

The mare's legs stretched across the field in an easy rhythm, her snorts and swishing tail signalling that this escape was long overdue; as the riders sped to overtake the terrier's tiny white form, Marietta smiled in antici-pation of her parents' reaction. Her father would, she was sure, try hard to hide the twinkle in his eyes behind a stern expression and a slowly shaking head, as much to convince Lady Alice of his disapproval as herself.

Her stepmother would see Marietta's behaviour as just one more reason to support her argument that the girl was unmanageable, unladylike, un-everything, and that she should have been married years ago. Why Sir Henry had allowed his daughter to turn down so many good offers she would never understand.

As though to exacerbate the forthcoming disap-proval, Marietta pulled her gold circlet from her brow and slid it over her wrist, then pushed the white linen wimple down into folds around her neck, allowing her long thick braids to stream behind her like coils of brown rope. How could one be truly free, even if only for a few moments, she thought, unless her hair was free too?

She shook her head and laughed at the merry grins of the grooms, but her laugh turned to a puzzled frown at their shouts of alarm, their sudden check as they wheeled away. The terrier was still ahead, rooting into a rabbit hole, its white rump and wagging tail waving like a mast above the ground.

Her brother, dismounting and ready to throw himself upon the terrier, turned at her arrival and shouted a warning, pointing to something behind her and making a grab at her bridle. But, for the second time, his efforts came too late; the mare's head jerked away, not from him but from two large wolfhounds that bounded between them, startling the horse by their silent and explosive approach.

Had Marietta not been a good horsewoman she would undoubtedly have been thrown off to one side. Instead, she clung to the rearing mare, riding out its terrified plunging and doing her best to calm it by the sound of her voice. But the two unruly hounds would not let well alone. Having seen the effect of their presence on the mare, they leapt alongside, clearly enjoying the event, then, as they spotted the white terrier once more in flight, gave chase as cats after a mouse, their jaws dripping with saliva.

For Dulzelina, however, that was not the end of the episode—she was convinced that the yapping beasts were still at her heels and, taking the bit hard between her teeth, she set off across the open field as though all the demons of hell were after her. Even the heavy thud of hooves behind them made as little check on the mare's speed as her rider's hands, for she refused to respond to any sound, and Marietta's efforts to turn her away from the coppice ahead went unheeded.

Thinking that the pursuing horse was a servant's, Marietta yelled at him to stay aside as she saw a fallen tree across her path at the entrance to the shadowy coppice and, knowing that her mare could not feel the pull on the reins and dreading the ache in her arms as a sign that she couldn't hold on much longer, she wondered whether the jump over the tree would be a parting for them both.

With a feeling of mixed irritation and fear, Márietta realised that the pursuing rider had not understood her warning to give her a clear run and, as they approached the barrier, she let out a final yelp to keep away. It was all she remembered before the ground and the trees unexpectedly changed places and the grass came crashing down on top of her.

It was by no means the first time she'd ever dismounted so rudely and her fingers were well disciplined to hold onto the reins and prevent the escape of her mount when she needed it most. But at one point beyond her vision, something wrenched persistently at her shoulders and a voice was growling through a haze of whirling images. Briefly, for an instant, she wondered if the trees were talking to her.

'Let go, lass! Open your fingers. Let go!'

'Bruno!' She struggled to get up. 'I told you to....'

'Open your fingers, woman! God's wounds, Will, cut the reins, will you?' The voice turned to one side, obviously exasperated.

'No! Don't you dare!' Marietta yelled, pushing at the hand enclosing her wrist. 'Bruno!'

'It's not Bruno. Open your eyes, lass. Come on, open them and look at me. That's it. Now, let go the reins, or we'll all be trampled to death.'

'Who're you?'

'Let go, damn it!' he shouted at her.

Bruno would not have yelled at her like that. She unclenched her fingers and heard the exclamation of relief, her senses doing somersaults as she frowned at the unfamiliar face peering down into hers. 'Who *are* you?' she repeated.

'Never mind.'

Two strong hands slipped beneath her armpits and heaved her backwards to lean against the log. The sky and trees came to rest and a head moved about in front of her, a dark head, older than her brother's. This was no mere lad of sixteen summers, but a man more like thirty, his voice authoritative, his shoulders even wider than her father's. What's more, no one had ever spoken to her in that tone before, nor had anyone ever felt at her shoulders and arms in such an intimate and probing manner.

'No broken bones here, anyway. . .' His words came to an abrupt halt as Marietta's arm swung back and made a lightning arc through the air towards his head. But it was caught well before it made contact with his ear and held out of the way while a hand gripped her chin, the strong fingers turning her head this way and that under the gaze of two laughing dark eyes. 'Nothing wrong with the arms, either. Now, any bruises? Uh-huh! A few grazes on the cheek and forehead. Scratched nose. Not too serious, I think, eh, Will?'

She snatched her face out of his hand and saw Bruno running. 'Go away!' She sucked in her breath at the effort. 'My brother's here. He'll attend me. Let me *go*!'

The man turned, released her wrist and stood to face Bruno. Even from this angle, she could see the difference in their height and width, though her brother, at sixteen, was no weakling. The man waved a hand over to the distance. 'Get those hounds off that white thing, will you? And hold them. Will, give the mare a quick check over. . .her legs.'

Bruno bent over his sister. 'Is she all right, sir?'

'Yes, lad. She's all right. You're her brother, are you?'

'Yes, sir. Bruno Wardle.' He pointed to the track where the cavalcade still wound its way down towards the village in the distance. 'We're on our way to Monksgrange just down the hill yonder. We were after my mother's terrier, but. . .' He swung round to survey the bloodied heap now lying lifeless in the grass some distance away.

The man looked Bruno up and down, noting the well-bred appearance and noble bearing in spite of the dusty clothes. The lad was well built and honest looking, dark-haired, like his sister and father. 'So, you're Sir Henry's lad, are you?'

'Yes, sir. I'm to be squire to Lord Alain of Thorsgeld Castle from tomorrow.' He could not contain the unsolicited information; he was proud of the new connection and this man would surely be impressed, though he realised that this was hardly the time or the place for such a display of vanity.

'Well, well! And here's your father. . . Sir Henry.'

Marietta saw the figure of her father canter towards them across the field and struggled to rise, but before Bruno could come to her aid, the man bent swiftly towards her and swung her easily up into his arms, ignoring her protests and moving her head away from her brother so that she could not see him. 'Put me down!' she yelled. 'Put me. . .' A pain shot through her head.

'Ah, Sir Henry,' he called.

'My lord! Is she. . .?'

Bruno ran to hold his father's bridle. 'Yes, Father, she's shaken but not badly hurt.'

In spite of her protests, she was pinioned helplessly against the man's chest, furious that he was taking charge of her, not even asking how she felt but taking it upon himself to find out as though she was a horse. 'Father, Father, get someone to attend the mare, please.' She winced at the pain.

'Yes, lass. What happened to bring you off like that?'

'Two great hounds and a fallen tree. But tell this oaf to put me down! Tell him!'

'It was my fault, I'm afraid, Sir Henry. My hounds

saw the terrier, and your daughter's mare took exception and bolted. . .'

'It did *not*, Father. I was in control. If this fool. .'

'I managed to catch her just in time. . .'

'. . .had not chased after me. . .'

'. .and she came off with quite a thump. . .'

'. . .I'd have stayed on and brought the mare. . .'

'. . .perhaps she needs a few lessons, sir.' He smiled down at her infuriatingly.

'. . .back to the track! Let me *go*!'

Sir Henry Wardle looked sideways at the man as they turned to walk back. 'Lessons, my lord? It's taken me eighteen years to get this far. . .' he nodded to Marietta's struggling form '. . .and still some way to go.'

'Then a change of hand is what's needed, sir.' The two men exchanged grins, noting the two half-undone plaits hanging over his shoulder and arm, the loosened wimple and torn gown.

Marietta's angry face was still beautiful, despite the red and soiled graze on her cheek, her large dark eyes still sparkling with embarrassment at this unwarranted handling of her by a stranger. But his tight grip told her quite plainly that she was not to be released, and his long easy stride at the side of her father and brother seemed not to affect his conversation in the slightest. Obviously, he felt her to be no weight at all, rejecting both Sir Henry's and Bruno's offers to take turns at carrying her.

'Did you say "my lord", Father?' Bruno asked, incredulous. 'It's not Lord Alain, is it?' The thought that their neighbour could be here at this time suddenly seemed to be quite a possibility. The town of Thorsgeld was, after all, only across the valley from Monksgrange.

'Yes, lad,' said Sir Henry, 'you've run into your future master sooner than you expected. I was to have brought my son to you tomorrow, my lord.'

'Then I shall spare you the journey, Sir Henry. I fear

I owe someone a new terrier. Was it Lady Alice's?' He glanced across at the limp form in the arms of one of the grooms, its jewelled collar and bloodstained cord hanging from its ripped neck and badly mauled body.

'Holy saints, man!' Sir Henry barked at the unsuspecting servant. 'Don't let Lady Alice see it like that or she'll pass out before we get there. Take that collar off and bury the body under those bushes before we get to the carriage. Hurry!'

So, this was Lord Alain, the man with whom Bruno would be living for the next five years, the man he'd talked about incessantly since his return from Sir Robert Finch's household where he had been a page since he was seven. Marietta peeped through her lashes, knowing that Lord Alain would certainly be aware of an open stare, his cheek being only a few inches away from her nose.

The soft green velvet under her cheek now took on a new significance and, even while retaining her anger at being held so closely against the rich stuff, its clean newness and well-tailored cut told her what she might have noticed earlier, that this man with the commanding manner was someone of importance. Through half-closed eyes, she allowed herself to note the comfortable folds of the fur-edged hood around his wide shoulders and the row of tiny gold buttons on the sleeves from elbow to wrist, the strong lean fingers around her knees.

His jaw was square and strong, clean-shaven; thick swathes of dark hair fell in layers over his head, jutting out over his forehead after the exertions of the afternoon. Marietta thought his mouth firm, too firm for kindness, though she could make out a dimple at one corner as he smiled at her father's remark. Well, she wished her young brother joy of his new master. She doubted if he'd find any softness there, but perhaps that was something her brother would regard as a good thing. A challenge. At least *she* wouldn't have to see any more of the arrogant brute.

'Put me down, sir!' she growled again, squirming.

Lord Alain looked down at his new squire's sister, still fuming, as they drew level with the track once more where carts were still moving. A group of ladies and grooms awaited them, clearly relieved to see that there was no cause for alarm.

'Ready to find your feet, damoiselle?' he asked.

'I could have walked, my lord, if I'd been allowed,' she snapped, suddenly even more aware of how close their faces were to each other. She squirmed again, straining away from him, seeing the grins on the faces of those who waited and suspecting that he held her deliberately longer than need be, just to thwart her attempts. 'Let me down,' she hissed.

'Certainly, damoiselle.'

Had she timed her demand more accurately or even made it sound more like a request, she might have spared herself an undignified gallop into the bottom of the ditch and a scramble up the other side onto the track. Though willing hands were there to aid her, her bruised limbs and torn gown became the source of humiliation before the gaze of so many, especially that of Lord Alain, who stood above her in the field, quietly laughing at the sight of her struggles.

She heard his chuckles but refused to look, shrugging off the hands, clambering up the lowered tailboard of her stepmother's carriage and disappearing inside with a sigh of relief. Now she must bear the petulant and scolding tongue of Lady Alice, who had wanted to be among the first to arrive at the manor, not the last. But even this well-rehearsed tirade was preferable to being manhandled by that man, lord or no.

'A fine way to begin, I must say,' Lady Alice grumbled, removing the tangled wimple from around Marietta's neck and handing it to a maid. Her own cauled and braided hair was still immaculate, even at the end of the rough journey, her plump pretty face contrasting sharply with the grimed and fierce beauty of her stepdaughter. She pursed her lips, as Marietta knew she would. 'Just when we wanted to make a good impression.'

'Well, I don't have to make an impression, Mother,' she replied. 'You can still do that without me, thank goodness. You've got until we return home after harvest. That should be long enough for anybody.'

'I only hope you're right, Marietta. It's just as well your father met Lord Alain before this. . .at least he knows what *we*'re like. And you've lost the gold circlet your father gave you.' She dabbed gently at Marietta's grazed face.

'No, I haven't. Bruno's got it safe.'

'Did he catch Sugar?'

'Er. . .yes.' Not a time to tell the whole truth, she thought, coming so soon after this. 'They've got him back there, somewhere. They're keeping him safely out of the way.'

Fortunately, Lady Alice accepted the explanation as being perfectly reasonable, for there'd be enough to do as soon as they reached the manor after a day's journey of almost twenty-five miles.

They made the move to one of their four manors several times a year to keep them tended and in good repair, to see to the needs of their tenants and villeins, to hold manor courts, to check on accounts and sales, workers and lands. They were all quite used to it, though it was always easier to travel down the dale than to return to Upperfell in September for the winter.

Such moves took days to organise and sometimes a week to prepare for, food to pack, bedding, furnishings, hangings and arms, everything from the kitchen, the offices and the chapel. The staff and members of the closer household numbered over one hundred, including Sir Henry's knights and esquires, yeomen men and personal officers as well as those who served Lady Alice.

Some of them, mostly kitchen and household servants, had come down a few days in advance with Sir Nicholas Bannon, Lady Alice's younger brother, to make the place habitable. But even so, it would be far into the night before everything was unloaded from the wagons and installed once more into its rightful place.

'Nearly there!' The youngest maid turned back into the carriage; her bright face reflected their relief.

Lady Alice rolled her eyes heavenwards at the news; even in a sumptuous carriage like this, lined with tapestried covers and feather-filled cushions to ease the jolts, even so, they were glad that the village was now in sight. She had been pleased when Sir Henry had announced that they would spend the summer months at their newest manor, for Monksgrange had only recently been purchased from nearby Bolton Priory. Reluctantly, the Augustinians had let it go in a lean year after the pestilence and the drought of more recent times.

It had hit everyone hard, it seemed, though the monks had escaped the worst effects, thank God. But the landscape already showed signs of change. Now fields were enclosed by stone walls and full of sheep instead of crops, small hamlets were emptied of villeins, woodland was less tended and harbouring larger bands of outlaws and thieves.

It was most convenient, Lady Alice thought, standing up to peep through one of the flaps in the sides, that they could bring Bruno to begin his new life at nearby Thorsgeld Castle, something they'd not thought possible two years ago when all that had been arranged. Then, Lord Alain had been married. But his young wife had died of the pestilence and Lady Alice was eager to discover whether he was looking for a suitable replacement.

If he was, she had two fair and pretty daughters, at least one of whom would gladden any man's marriage-bed. She looked sideways at Marietta's grazed cheek and angry frown. A far cry, this one, from her own gentle two, for they would never have gone tearing across fields like that or been brought back torn and bruised under the stares of half the household. She tightened her lips again: the eldest she may be, but no nearer finding a husband at eighteen than she'd been at three, when Alice herself had been a bride of fifteen marrying the widowed Sir Henry.

It had been difficult, taking on a wilful babe of three and the newly born Bruno, especially when her own two had followed on so soon, but Sir Henry had been a good catch and had made her life as comfortable as any woman had a right to. Except for Marietta, who'd always needed a firmer hold than her father was willing to exert, in spite of a steady stream of offers to take her off his hands.

She sighed as the heavy carriage rumbled to a standstill. 'Wait there, Marietta. I'll get Sir Nicholas to carry you in.'

'Oh, no, thank you, Mother, I'll walk.' And she disappeared over the tailboard before Lady Alice could insist, determined to deprive her uncle of that joy, above all else.

The courtyard was already crammed with wagons, carriages, horses and people, shouting orders, waving arms, laughing and exclaiming at their first-ever glimpse of the newly acquired manor house. The smell of new woodwork lingered in the cool passageways and the sounds of the carpenters' hammers echoed off the stone walls where doors were still being hung. Maids, grooms and officers of the household swarmed from the wagons, dusting down long gowns and helping the older ones to stagger, stiff-legged, indoors.

Hereward, her father's household steward, greeted the family. It was his responsibility to allocate and prepare their rooms, an onerous job, for Monksgrange was far larger than some of the other properties they lived in, and here they could have rooms with more privacy than anywhere else. 'Come, mistresses—' he bowed to Marietta and her maids '—I've saved the sunniest room for you.' He had a soft spot for Sir Henry's eldest daughter and she for him, for he was rather like an indulgent grandfather.

'We want to know what he's like,' whispered Anne, the elder of the two maids, giggling as they followed Hereward along the upper balcony around the hall.

'Who?' Marietta said, innocently, though she knew who was meant.

'Lord Alain,' the maid replied, round-eyed. 'He carried you, didn't he? What's he like? He looks so strong, so courteous...'

'Courteous, my foot!' snarled Marietta, under her breath. 'It was his hounds that caused the mare to bolt. And as if that wasn't enough, he had to come chasing after us to make matters worse. The fool should have left me be. I'd have managed better without him.' She limped up the stairs.

They were shown into a fair-sized and pleasantly sunny room at the back of the house that overlooked the kitchen-gardens, a view that Hereward knew would please the young mistress. The windows had recently been glazed with new green glass, which let in a fair amount of light though not quite clear enough to see through.

The large bed was already being assembled by a group of carpenters and assistants and the bed-hangings lay in neat piles ready to be fixed. In through the open door chests and panniers were being carried, rugs lay in rolls near one wall, tapestries drooped in narrow tubes over a trunk, while tables, stools and the priedeiu stood in one corner.

'This is your private solar, Mistress Marietta,' said Hereward, beaming, 'and look here, your own private garderobe.'

He opened a tiny door to a closet where a wooden seat was fixed to the wall and where hooks were ready to receive her furs. 'And here. . .' he opened another door off the main room '. . .here is a small room for your maids.'

This was luxury, indeed, for not only had she always shared a room with her maids but with her half-sisters and their maids, too. Now, she could be quite alone whenever she wished, a rare treat indoors, for privacy was a rare commodity unless one could go out alone, a risk she'd been warned over and over not to take. Naturally, she defied the warning, for to be alone was one of Marietta's addictions; her frequent escapes were a release from the imposition of too many people in too small a space.

As if to take instant advantage of their seclusion, Anne and Ellie tended their mistress's grazed face, her bruised thigh and shoulder. The mare had caught her with its hooves and dragged her hard along the fallen log, scraping the skin off her elbows and leaving semicircular imprints on her leg. The numbness had now begun to wear off, leaving a painful ache as the stiffness set in.

Her face felt hot and tender, in spite of their applications of witch-hazel, and the dull ache in her head pounded across her eyes, leaving her light-headed and nauseous. She was never ill and had little patience with those who were, so fought against it, clenching her teeth against the throbbing pains and brushing away her maids' suggestions that she should rest. There was exploring to be done first.

Sounds of high-pitched voices floated along the passageway towards them and two younger girls stood in the doorway, their eyes round and pale blue like forget-me-nots, their hair in long flaxen plaits.

Emeline, at almost fifteen summers, was so well developed that her eighteen months' lead over her sister Iveta looked more like twice that. She was exceedingly pretty, an indication of how Lady Alice must have appeared to Sir Henry at the time of their marriage, quiet, grave, and yet with a certain vague recognition of the impact her looks were having on the men of the household, the delicious feeling of power when heads turned for her, as they always did for Marietta.

Iveta, at well past thirteen, was set to become just as pretty, though her expression was kinder. She was more aware of others than of her effect on them, more animated, less self-centred, and found it easier to talk to Marietta than Emeline did, for Emeline saw her elder half-sister as a rival, which Iveta did not.

'You've got a pretty room, Marietta,' Iveta piped, clearly pleased for her. 'Ours isn't as large as this, is it, Emmie?' The question was quite without guile, but it received a stony stare from the other forget-me-not eyes.

'No, we have to cram four of us into our room.'

Marietta ignored the pettish remark and took Iveta's outstretched hand. 'Come and look out here. We can see the garden, and look, there are two gardeners already digging it over. See. . .the beeward's already at the hives.'

'Where?'

'Over there. Shall we go down?'

Together, they turned and saw that Sir Nicholas stood in the doorway directly behind Emeline, his hand gently resting on her shoulder, his forefinger slowly moving up and down her bare neck, a seemingly innocent gesture. But Emeline had flushed bright scarlet and was powerless to move away.

His finger dropped as Marietta glared at him, both of them fully understanding that the caress had the double effect of wielding a power over Emeline while sending a clear message to Marietta of his desire for her. He was as aware as the rest of the family of Marietta's dislike of him and, from time to time, their antagonism flared before reverting to polite atonements on his part, for the double game he played was finely balanced.

'Shall we all go down?' he asked, bending his head to Emeline, 'or shall I show you my room first?'

'Where is it, Uncle Nicholas?' Iveta asked.

'Next door to this one.' He cast a sideways look at Marietta. 'Isn't that convenient?' He laughed and led the two girls out.

It was obvious why Emeline adored him, for he was handsome in a brown and blond way which set his grey-blue eyes and white teeth glinting like pearls in sand. Like his sister, Lady Alice, he had come to live in Sir Henry's household when she married, and at twenty-five years old he was still landless and desperate for property.

With no household of his own, he was in no position to marry, despite his attractive appearance and his knighthood, and though he was given a certain amount of responsibility and duties by his brother-in-law in return for his keep, he looked forward to the time when his plans for the future would materialise.

'Is there a lock on this door?' Marietta whispered to her youngest maid Evie, who was already bustling about the new room. 'Just check, will you?'

'Bolts, mistress. Top and bottom.'

'Good. We'll have them drawn into place every night. Will you all remember? To prevent intrusions.'

The maids understood without the need for further

explanations; they had been with Marietta for upwards of six years and knew her ways well. Anne took a look at her mistress's pale face and frowned. 'I think you should lie down for a while, love. Your bruises are getting to you, aren't they?'

Marietta nodded. Yes, they were. 'But where...?' She spread her hands helplessly; the pages still carried panniers in and the carpenters had not finished with the bed.

'Stay there,' the maid said, 'I'll be back in a moment.' She returned in the blink of an eye to lead Marietta slowly into a large solar two doors away, where the workmen had finished erecting the large curtained bed and where now all was quiet and orderly. Marietta hardly noticed. She felt dizzy and the ache was beginning to spread from her buttock down to her knee. Knowing almost nothing of how she got there, she allowed Anne to help her onto her parents' bed and to tuck her underneath the soft furs, then to draw the curtains to keep the painful glare of sunlight at bay, easing her into sleep.

It was the sound of quiet sobbing that woke her, and for some moments she lay in the warm cocoon of the furs, attempting to marshal her senses into order. Then her father's voice added a second layer of sound and she understood where she was, though the light was now fading.

'It didn't stand a chance, love, against those hounds. It wouldn't have felt a thing. Don't be upset, lass. There...there...'

More sobs followed, mixed with incoherent words.

'Yes, of course, he said he'd find you a replacement. He's to come over tomorrow and take Bruno back with him at the same time. Saves me the ride, though I might go over some time.' He turned away so that the rest of his words were lost.

'Tomorrow? He's coming here?'

'Yes, I told you.'

'Henry, why on earth didn't you say before?'

'Why, love. . .?'

'Well. . .' Marietta could almost see her stepmother splaying her hands in an attempt to make her point, a common enough gesture she used to indicate that an explanation would only be required by a half-wit. 'Well, you know I want him to see the girls. . .no, not Marietta. . .I can't see that *that* matters, but especially Emeline.'

'Marietta's the eldest, dear, you know. . .'

'Yes, dear, but she's obviously not interested. . .never has been. . .look how many offers. . .already turned down. . .'

At the distinct 'Sshh. . .' Marietta turned onto her back, knowing how such a sound was invariably followed by a revelation of importance.

Lady Alice continued, 'It's just that he's already seen her and he'll think they're all as. . .as wayward—' Marietta smiled at her stepmother's search for the kindest word '—as difficult as *she* is, and I want him to see how well behaved and pretty Emeline can be. You know how *you* fell for me when I was that age.' And in the silence that followed, Marietta could imagine how Lady Alice was wheedling her husband with pretty sidelong glances. A low chuckle confirmed his reaction.

Looking up at the canopy of the large bed, Marietta felt the loud thud of her heart, not so much for being an eavesdropper, but at the thought of *him* being here, tomorrow. Lord Alain, here, at Monksgrange. Well, she could think of no reason why she need be anywhere in evidence at that time; she could say her farewells to Bruno beforehand and keep well out of the way until they'd gone, for it was quite obvious that Lady Alice wanted him to see the younger girls, not her.

Lord Alain himself would certainly not miss her after

shouting at her so rudely and taking the force of her own discourtesy, and she was quite sure she'd be happier somewhere in the garden, anywhere, than near such a person as that. He had not even apologised for allowing his hounds to unsettle Dulzelina and for causing her fall.

She feigned sleep as a shadow approached the curtains of the bed and made a convincing return to consciousness as her father roused her gently. It was time for supper, he told her. Did she feel easier now that she'd rested? Would she come down to the hall to eat on their first night at Monksgrange? Or would she prefer a tray in her room?

Stiffly, she sidled down the stone staircase to the great hall, feeling that it would be a pity not to do justice to the feast which had been specially prepared. Earlier, in the privacy of her own solar, she had twisted round to see her bruises, finally getting Evie to hold a mirror to one side so that she could see the full extent. Sure enough, her thigh was slowly turning purple from hip to knee and was now so painful that she was obliged to sit lop-sided on the hard bench at the high table.

Later, back in her own chamber, she sat with her father for a few precious moments, discussing what would have to be done on the estate in the days and weeks ahead, how she would need to begin checking the stores and ordering more stocks from the local markets and from York. These were things Lady Alice preferred to leave to Marietta, aware of how she enjoyed the management of the household affairs, the tending of the garden and the beehives, the making of salves and potions for her medicine cupboard and the ordering and buying of supplies.

It was true that Hereward was highly efficient, but he had taught Marietta far more about housekeeping than Lady Alice had and appreciated her attention to detail. It would be no hardship to be fully occupied tomorrow, or any other day.

They wandered slowly around the room. Marietta pointed out where the tapestries would be hung on the morrow, identified a chest that was in the wrong room, showed him where she would place her possessions and her bowls of flowers from the garden.

Later still, as she wriggled into the dark warmth of her feather bed, listening to the strange sounds outside, of servants calling to each other and the distant crash of a last piece of furniture being brought in, her hands crept spontaneously over her bruises, retracing the path of that man's fingers over her shoulders and arms, recalling the memory of his grip beneath her knees, his glinting eyes close to her face. Too close.

He had refused to allow Bruno or her father to carry her but that, she was sure, was because he was amused by her anger and wished to infuriate her more. Yes, he'd much prefer pretty Emeline, one he could intimidate without a murmur on her part. And then she slept, disturbed by aches, no matter how she turned.

CHAPTER TWO

THE silk cote-hardies and brocade surcoats lay on the bed in a pile so high that they were in imminent danger of falling off. Iveta sat to one side, sulkily fingering the fur edgings and embroidered borders, watching from beneath lowered lids the maids who fussed around her sister. Lady Alice Wardle directed the transformation from a stool by the window. Emeline was getting the full treatment early in the day, for none of them knew at what hour Lord Alain of Thorsgeld would come to collect young Bruno. Even if Emeline had to sit still all day, she would be ready for that event.

Indeed, as the long golden hair was combed out around her pale blue neckline, she was a model of patience, gazing with empty acceptance at the pretty surcoat edged with marten-fur over the silk cote-hardie. The narrow front panel was deeply cut away at each side and sat so low on her hips that the dainty gold girdle was quite exposed, though Lady Alice would allow only her gold circlet as jewellery.

'Your turn in a moment, dear.' Lady Alice smiled at the younger beauty. 'We'll have you dressed in no time.'

That was not exactly what Iveta wanted to hear; she would have liked as much time lavished on her as her sister had, but it was no use pretending that she'd look like that, even so. She gazed somewhat enviously at her sister's profile, allowing her eyes to rove furtively downwards to the swell of the breasts under the silk. Could they not see the clear outline of her nipples? Did it not matter that they showed? Was that the idea? She examined her own flat chest; no matter what gown

she wore, she would never look as interesting as
Emeline or as lovely as Marietta, she mused.

At a mere thirteen summers, Iveta was not to know
that it was not only an interesting silhouette which
decided the amount of approval but an animated
expression and liveliness, which she had in plenty. The
simple cream surcoat she was given to wear echoed the
colour of her hair, and the compliments of her mother
and maids were gratifying, though Uncle Nicholas's
stares made her blush.

'Heavens, Nicholas! How long have you been standing there?' Lady Alice turned sharply, noting Iveta's
reddened cheeks.

Sir Nicholas lounged inside the doorway, his slow
perusal well under way long before his sister had
noticed her daughter's blushes.

'Long enough. I have a message for you, sister dear.
Your guest has arrived. Sir Henry wants you to greet
him in the great solar, if you please.'

The excitement was almost tangible. 'He's arrived?
So soon? Emeline dear, come. Iveta, you too.'

'Wait,' Sir Nicholas said, pushing himself away from
the door. 'You take Iveta in. I'll bring Emeline.' He
stared at his sister's hesitation. 'Go on, I'll bring her in,
in a moment.'

Iveta frowned. 'Why can't she come with us,
Mother?'

'Hush, child.' Lady Alice took her hand firmly and
drew her to the door. 'Come now, don't forget. . .your
best courtesy,' and with a last smile at Emeline, she left
the room, bustling the maids out ahead of her and
ignoring their glances of disapproval.

Sir Nicholas sauntered across to where Emeline
stood, biting her lip and burning with confusion.
'You're not going to get far with the old goat if you
stand there and bite your lip, you silly wench,' he said,
softly, touching her neck with his fingertips. 'Are you?'

Emeline looked away, her blushes spreading down her neck and over her shoulders. She wished her mother had not left her here alone with Uncle Nicholas. 'He's not old, is he?' she whispered.

'How do I know, lass?' Sir Nicholas drew his fingers around her neckline, pulling it a little wider over her shoulders. 'I've never clapped eyes on him. Anyway, it doesn't matter a toss whether he is or not. He's a widower, and you know what *they* look for, don't you?' He slipped his hands under the fur edges of her front panel and pulled her a step nearer.

For a moment, she was puzzled and resisted his pull, but his pale eyes held hers and eventually she moved forward, flustered and surprised by the closeness of his hands.

He leaned his face to hers. 'Listen to me, Emeline,' he whispered, 'this is important. The first impression has *got* to work. He's got to want you. . .do you understand me, lass?'

Her big blue eyes stared into his. She understood his words and yet she had no way of knowing what she was supposed to do. Then she felt his hands move down the fur as though he caressed its softness, allowing his fingertips purposely to brush past the peaks of her breasts as he did so in a flagrant gesture of intimacy that took her breath away.

'Stop!' she whispered, grabbing at his wrists.

'Let go. Let go of my wrists,' he commanded, softly.

With not a streak of rebellion, she obeyed, watching his narrowed eyes and quivering under the movement of his hands which slid up and down the fur over the silk cote-hardie. 'Uncle Nicholas. . .!' she gasped.

'Understand me, wench. When you get what *you* want, I get what I want. So look lively, as though you know what you're about. Wet your lips with your tongue. . .go on, do it! And part your lips. Now, let's have a look at you.' He held her back and looked intently at her heavy lids over the darkened eyes, her flushed cheeks and then, more directly, at the place where his hands had lingered. 'That's better. Perfect. Now, are you ready?'

She nodded, quite speechless. And on trembling legs she was led into the great solar as though in a trance.

Marietta's quick peep in the polished steel mirror verified the presence of a red-streaked graze over one cheek, on her forehead and on the tip of her nose. All the other more painful signs of her mishap were hidden beneath the comfortable loose-fitting kirtle and green bliaud, tied around the waist with an old plaited leather girdle. Rejecting any attempts to dress her hair, she had insisted there was no time if she wanted to find Bruno where she could speak to him in private. Instead, the glossy brown curls had been bound up on top of her head with braids. It would have to do.

Certain that the rest of the family were occupied with their guest, Marietta slipped through the busy hall, still teeming with servants putting the place in order, carrying in the last of the household goods from the wagons, hanging the tapestries and hauling up the great wooden candle-brackets towards the beamed roof.

Sneaking through the stone-flagged screens-passage and out through the heavy door at the back of the house, she flattened herself against the stone wall as a page passed close by, his arms laden with clanking shields, swords and belts, heading towards the armoury. He caught her wary expression, her defensive posture, and grinned cheekily, then skirted round her very slowly in an exaggerated arc, looking over his shoulder as she relaxed.

He was as old as Marietta. 'Feelin' better, mistress?' She laughed at his overreaction. 'Thank you, Ben. I'm well enough. Where's Master Bruno?'

'Gettin' ready to go, mistress. Upstairs.'

'When you've taken that, tell him I'm in the garden, if you please.'

The lad nodded politely and went about his business, though he took time to watch Marietta disappear into the cobbled courtyard.

Through the arched gateway at the side of the stables, Marietta passed into a more peaceful world of greenery and lush spring growth where two men pushing wheelbarrows moved silently along straw-covered pathways. From this large kitchen-garden, she could see across a deep valley to the hillside beyond, where patches of light and shadow rippled across the woodland.

Set high up above the trees, she saw the great stone Thorsgeld Castle, looking for all the world like an outcrop of sculptured limestone grown up from the forest floor. She would be able to see Bruno, if he hung a red banner from one of the battlements. The idea made her smile. She would miss her brother again.

At the side of one of the high white-washed walls, an arbour was lightly covered with new leaves and, over in one sunny corner, the lids of cold-frames yawned like open mouths, waiting to receive new supplies of cucumber, specially brought down from Upperfell Manor by her father, who loved it. He had bought her a plant in London some years ago and insisted on it being grown in all his manors.

She looked around her, nodding in satisfaction; the monks who had lived here previously had been gardeners, too, for new shoots of spinach were showing and fruit trees had been trained along one wall. It looked as though she'd have to do something about the herb-plot, though, for many gaps showed that they'd taken those precious plants away with them.

Arching her back and wincing at the pain in her shoulder and legs, she heard Bruno approach. He pointed to her green bliaud. 'Had a job to see you in that,' he grinned. 'If it had not been for the white kirtle, I might have mistaken you for a tree and gone without you.'

Marietta laughed. 'Silly. Are you ready to go, now?'

'Yes, love. I was told to go and get cracking, so we'll be off as soon as they've said their farewells. Lord Alain's in Mother's good books now; he's brought her a pup like the one his hounds ate.'

'Oh, Bruno! Don't say that. They didn't really eat it, did they?'

'As good as. They'll eat anything that yaps and pees all over the place like that one did. Serves it right. Doesn't it hurt you to laugh?'

'Yes, you dolt! It does!' she gasped, holding her ribs. 'I shall miss you, dear one.' She linked her arm into his and lowered her voice. 'I wish Emeline was going instead of you.'

'Well, by the way she's trying just now, it won't be too long.' He jerked his head towards the house. 'You should just see. . .

'I'm glad I can't. Is she trying hard?'

'Hard? Lord Alain will have to be blind not to see what she's offering. I'm glad he knows we're only half-related.'

'My bruises were a good excuse to stay out of the way. Lady Alice didn't want me to appear, anyway. Not after yesterday.' She placed a hand over her cheek and looked away, mentally trying to evade the picture of Emeline simpering before two dark eyes.

'He asked about you.'

'Who did?' There was an instant thud in her breast.

'Lord Alain. He asked where you were.'

Marietta turned to her brother, her heart now leaping. 'And they told him. . .?'

'That you were in bed, quite poorly. I went to your chamber to look for you, but Ben told me you were here.'

Noting her expression, her pained frown, he put his arms around her and bent his head to draw her eyes upwards from their study of the pathway. 'What is it, love?'

'Oh, Bruno, they didn't need to make such an elaborate excuse. Really, they must have known I'd be perfectly happy to stay out of the way. I don't mind Emmie getting wed. The sooner the better. I wouldn't do anything to make it difficult for her. And anyway. . . just look at me.'

Bruno knew she meant her scratched face, but he saw only his beautiful beloved sister, her dark eyes bordered with thick lashes, the perfectly boned features and lovely mouth. Her coils of dark hair spilled in wayward strands around her ears and neck and he knew, even in his youthful innocence, that Marietta would need none of Emeline's tricks to snatch a man's heart away.

'I don't think of myself as competition, even at the best of times. . .' she tried to laugh, brushing away a tear with the back of her hand '. . . but, love, you must be going. You don't want to keep your lord waiting today, of all days. Say farewell now. Shall we see you before we return to Upperfell in the autumn, do you think?'

'Yes, love. Sure to. But it should be you they're trying to find a husband for, Marrie. You're the eldest, and the nicest, by far.'

'Oh, love, if you can find me one like Father, let me know and I'll show some interest.' They hugged, carefully avoiding Marietta's bruises, then Bruno stepped back, kissed her knuckles and both cheeks.

'God speed, love. Be an obedient squire and make us all proud of you.'

Without another word, he trotted away up the path, pausing at the gateway to wave, then turned and rebounded into the figure of Lord Alain.

With a noiseless wail of 'Oh, no!', Marietta whirled away into the opening of the arbour. Through the new leaves, she watched the two men pause to speak, saw Bruno point to where he'd left her, then bow and leave Lord Alain to find his way down the path. Silently, she moved away to the far end, expecting to find a way out, but last year's tendrils of honeysuckle had not been pruned back or re-trained and she was obliged to face her unwanted guest with their tangle at her back.

Though her green bliaud gave her some concealment, his slow and purposeful approach signalled quite clearly that she had been spotted. For the first time, she had a chance to see him entirely, to complete her fragmented image of him from the previous day. She saw the almost black hair again, the square jaw and high cheekbones, the powerful neck and shoulders.

This much she had already glimpsed but now she noted the clothes, too, the calf-length bliaud of deep blue figured-velvet, split up the front and back for riding, every edge decorated with an embroidered band of silver and red. Over his slim hips a garnet-studded belt was slung; his sword-belt, resting below it, glinted with silver buckles, finely chased. Deep red sleeves with silver buttons came almost to his knuckles and Marietta saw that his hands were strong and brown, the fingers splayed over his hips as he stood at the entrance to the arbour, eyeing in some amusement her attempt to disappear backwards into the sparse green foliage.

He walked slowly towards her, like a cat. 'Bolting again, damoiselle?'

Marietta glared. There was no reply to that.

'I was told that you were ill. Is this what your mother meant?' He looked up and around him at the green structure.

'No, my lord. It is not. And the Lady Alice is my

stepmother.' She held a hand flat against the graze on her cheek. 'She thought I would stay in bed, but I. . .'

'But you had other ideas?' He laughed, a deep throaty chuckle. 'Yes, I can imagine you would. You seem to have a flair for escape, do you not?'

Irritated by his quick perception, she attempted to turn the direction of her enforced conversation away from herself to him. 'Have you come to apologise, my lord?'

His eyes widened in surprise at that, then creased into laughter. 'Apologise? Do I owe you an apology, then?'

'You must know that you do. It was your hounds that unsettled my mare.' She was careful not to use the word bolt. 'Surely that deserves an apology?'

He kept his hands on his hips, filling up the width of the arbour. 'Very well. You first.'

Marietta frowned and searched his eyes for a meaning. 'Me first what?'

'Your apology first. Ladies first.'

'My apology for what, pray? It was I who received the bruises.'

'For your incivility. You don't remember?' He was laughing at her, she was sure, provoking her again.

'No, my lord, I do not. I remember being extremely civil, in the circumstances.'

'As you are being now.'

'Yes,' she snapped, turning away.

'Then it's time you had a husband to teach you better manners.'

Marietta was forced to react to that with a look of undisguised contempt. 'I have no wish for a husband, my lord.'

'I thought that's what every woman wanted. Marriage. Bairns.'

Her irritation surfaced again. So typical of a man's thinking. So predictable. 'You are mistaken. It is what every man *thinks* that every woman wants. But I am not every woman and I allow no man to make my decisions. I have a mind of my own!'

He flicked one eyebrow, but stood his ground, enjoying her fencing. 'I see. And the other part?'

'What other part?'

'Babies.'

Since he was intent on asking personal questions, she would give him the truth. 'My mother died giving birth to Bruno when I was two years old. She was just my age. I'm not going the same way, my lord. I intend to live longer than eighteen years.'

'And you've staved off marriage for that reason?'

'That's as good a reason anyone could ever come up with,' she retorted. 'The ninety-nine other reasons I have for not wanting a husband are quite niggling by comparison.'

'Such as. . .?'

'My affairs cannot possibly be of interest to you, my lord.'

'On the contrary, they are of great interest to me. I intend to change your mind.'

'Oh!' She threw back her head to let him see the full effect of her grazed face. 'You have someone in mind for me, do you? Forget it, my lord. Find someone else for your favourite retainer.'

'It was not one of my retainers I was thinking of, damoiselle, it was myself.'

Now she knew he was jesting. That remark could never be taken seriously. 'It pleases you to jest, my lord. Kindly leave me now. I am supposed to be in bed, and you were supposed to. . .'

Yes, my girl, he thought. That's exactly where you should be. 'Yes? What was it I was supposed to be doing?'

Marietta was silent, realising that she'd allowed him

to goad her towards indiscretion. Was it possible to redirect the words?

But Lord Alain had already caught the drift. 'I was supposed to do what, damoiselle? Show some interest in your half-sister, was that it? Well, well.' He threw back his head and laughed with a rich bellow of sound, showing his white teeth. 'Thank you for the warning. I had already begun to suspect, though, I must admit.'

'No. . .no. . .you mustn't think. . .' The argument and her pain were beginning to make her feel dizzy and slightly sickened. 'Emmie is a lovely girl, and—'

'And you?' he interrupted, taking her shoulders in his hands. 'Why were you not with them in the solar? Why are you not dressed up to the eyebrows, but out here in working clothes? Is this how they treat you?'

She winced at the pain of her bruises under his fingers, hardly able to think coherently. 'No, my lord, on the contrary. I dress as I please, but I did not wish to. . .I had other things to do.' She floundered further into the mire. No matter what she said, it was going to sound unmannerly. 'Let me go, my lord.' She pushed his hand off her shoulder.

'Yes? You did not wish to meet me? You decided to be somewhere else,' he answered for her. 'And next time I come you'll have bolted again, will you?'

Marietta turned away, desperate to escape and furious at his exact summary of the situation. 'Yes,' she whispered, 'yes, I will.'

But he caught her back by a hand beneath her arm and swung her painfully towards him, holding her immobile. 'Then I am forewarned, damoiselle.' Before she could make any response, and before her fuddled mind could understand what was happening, she was being wedged against his shoulder and her lips were being sought by his without any consideration for her battered state.

She knew what he was saying, that if she chose to

hide away, he would find her and show her no mercy until she'd learned not to. He was relentless and she was in no condition to fight him as she would surely have done at any other time. She merely hung on like a drowning woman, too weak to cry for mercy.

He held her in the crook of his arm, too close for her eyes to focus. 'Bolt as far as you wish, but I shall find you and bring you back until you tire of the game. And now, you are forewarned, too.'

For an instant, she surfaced enough to rebel. 'I suppose that is your apology, is it, my lord?' Her lips tingled with the shock of his kiss.

'No, wench. It's yours.'

She did not see him pass through the swirl of greens and the distorting tears, nor did she hear his receding footsteps over the sound of her first uncontrollable sobs. Hanging onto the trellis-work of the arbour, she shook at it in a spasm of fright, anger and helplessness, endeavouring to shake away the pain of his hands on her bruises and the humiliation of being held captive in his embrace.

Gasping to keep back her tears of rage and to still the waves of pain, she felt again the merciless kiss and the hard pressure of his hand behind her head. Her legs buckled, threatening to give way. If he'd known how ill she felt, would he have tormented her so?

He was for Emeline, not her, and judging by his remarks, he'd seen how amenable her sister could be. Surely, if he was so keen on obedience to his wishes, he would prefer Emeline's certain co-operation to her own prickly manner, so why would he derive any satisfaction from teasing her like that? Unless he enjoyed the idea of playing people off against each other. Did it boost his ego, perhaps? Had he also teased Emeline like that and then tried it on her, to see the difference?

She shook the trellis again and let the sobs gush out,

relishing the ache in her limbs as a distraction from her confusion. Her father's heavy tread gave her warning of his approach and his hands on her shoulders came as no surprise to a body throbbing with the imprint of strong fingers. Marietta turned gratefully into the comfort of his arms and moaned with anguish.

'Hush, little one, hush, it's all right. We'll go in now. Enough, hush.'

'No, Father, I can't. . .can't go in like this.'

'Yes, you can. . .like this. . .put your arms around my neck.' He bent and picked her up in his arms, cradling her against him. 'Turn your face into my chest, lass, and close your eyes. They all know you're not too well. It's no cause for remark.' And he carried her along the pathway, through the courtyard of servants and into the house.

They must both have known that they'd not get far before the sound of Lady Alice's voice assailed them. As it was, they were fortunate to reach the solar stairway in the corner of the great hall. 'Sir Henry, take Marietta to my solar, if you please. I need to speak to her,' she called.

To Marietta's amazement, her father stopped on the lowest step, swung round from his greater height and replied with withering coldness. 'Mind who you speak to in that tone, m'lady. I'm taking Marietta to her chamber because she is unwell after her fall yesterday. And you will leave her in peace and tend her with all heed to her comfort. You have your new lap-dog and this lass still has her bruises. Look you sharp and tend her.'

He continued to the top of the stairs and waited until Lady Alice had passed him and opened Marietta's door. 'And send that hussy to our solar. *I* need to speak to *her*!' He glared at Emeline, who stood behind her mother, her face a picture of apprehension and alarm.

'Now, lass—' he placed Marietta carefully on the bed

as her mother hustled the maids into action. '—you're going to get back into bed and stay there. Understood?'

'Yes, Father.'

'Good. I'll come to see you later on and we'll see how you feel then.' He smiled and touched her sore nose with one finger, then stood to face his wife who hovered at the end of the bed, wringing her hands in uncertainty. 'She's tired, and overwrought, and in some pain. A little more attention in this direction and a little less in *that*. . .' he pointed to Emeline '. . .and I'd be better pleased. See to it!' He closed the door quietly behind him.

Lady Alice turned to her stepdaughter. 'Marietta, dear,' she said.

For the rest of the day Marietta was tended as carefully as any father could have wished, bathed and salved again, warmed and banked up with soft pillows, fed with soothing draughts of feverfew and honey and left to rest in peace between visits from her stepmother, the maids and her father. Compresses of witch-hazel had been placed over her sore face and as soon as one dried, another one took its place. The coolness and the fragrant smell calmed her spirits and helped to remove the vexations of the morning, and when Emeline finally appeared along with the trays of food at suppertime, Marietta was almost relieved to see her.

Nothing had been said about Lord Alain's visit, no information offered and no questions asked, though the new pup had been brought in to see her and had caused the usual hilarity associated with baby creatures, puddling in the rushes and chewing at everything it could get between its tiny jaws. They had decided to call it Comfit.

Now Emeline sat with her sister and they ate together, quietly, though both were a little subdued, Marietta half-expecting to be told of Lord Alain's

reaction that morning and yet not wanting to broach
the subject in the light of Emeline's obvious disfavour
with their father. Had something gone seriously wrong?
she wondered, glancing at her sister's reddened eyes.
She decided to ask.

'What did you think of Lord Alain, Emmie?'

Emeline looked up quickly and lowered her eyes
again, playing with a piece of soft cheese while she
thought of the best words to use. 'He's very charming,'
she said.

'Does Mother think so, too?'

'Oh yes, Mother thinks so. She's thrilled with the
pup.'

'But what, Emmie?'

'Oh, nothing.' She popped the cheese into her mouth
at last. 'Father seems to think I overdid it, but I don't
know what I was supposed to do different. Trouble is,
it's a bit difficult to know when he's being serious.'

'Who? Father?'

'No, not Father, Lord Alain. He says serious things
with a twinkle in his eyes, and then he says funny
things seriously, and I don't know how to tell one from
the other. So I suppose I got a bit muddled and Father
thought I was being silly. But he didn't seem to mind.'

'So you think he'll make an offer for you?' She made
the question sound casual as she looked firmly into her
goblet of watered mead.

'Mother's sure he will. She seemed pleased by the
way things went, but I don't know what Father thinks
about it. He says he's going to check what I wear next
time he comes.'

'He didn't like what you wore?'

'Father? No, not much. He says it was immodest. Do
you think it's immodest, Marrie?'

'No, love. I think you look wonderful.' She had no
time to weigh up the implications of her reply, but even
as it formed she knew that it was not what a loving

sister ought to have said who was totally impartial to the outcome of the proceedings.

This would have been the perfect moment to be helpful, to say that the kirtle beneath the brief surcoat was too sheer, too clinging, too revealing, and that *that*, together with her muddled responses to Lord Alain's remarks, would have been enough to give the impression that she was trying too hard, which her father had deplored.

How strange, she thought, that Emeline and her mother thought it necessary to try at all, in view of Emeline's fair, fashionable prettiness. And how strange, too, that her father should think Emmie had tried too hard and that she, Marietta, had never tried hard enough. Indeed, why should either of them have to try? Were they not acceptable just as they were, without this silly charade?

'Yes, well, I thought it looked wonderful too.'

'And did he say he'd visit again?'

'No, but I expect. . .oh, wait a moment, yes, he did. He said he'd come back when you were better and see how your bruises did. But Mother says he spoke to you in the garden just before they went off. Did he ask you about them?'

'Yes, that's all he wanted to know. Just that.'

'Mother's been dying to know all day but Father said not to ask you.'

'Well, there's no mystery about it. He'd never have known I was there, if Ben hadn't told him where Bruno was and he came to look for him.' She didn't regret the lie. It would not help Emeline to know what he'd said. She had also discovered that he said serious things strangely, and she supposed that when he'd said it was himself he was thinking of as a husband for her, he was jesting. Yes, of course, he was jesting.

Before sleep came and after the events of the day had been turned over in her mind for the hundredth

time, Marietta had to admit that she was no nearer
understanding Lord Alain's attitude towards her than
she was to understanding her own towards him.
Emeline had found him charming; she had found him
arrogant and domineering. His manner to Emeline had
been courteous; to her it had been discourteous in the
extreme.

And yet, she could not help but wonder. Why had he
gone to such lengths to tell her that he would search
for her, and find her, and bring her back if she
continued her avoidance of him? Well, they would see
about that. There must be plenty of places where one
could keep out of the way of another, here at
Monksgrange, and perhaps she'd discover a few of
them in the next few weeks. After all, Lady Alice and
Emeline had decided he was for them, and it would be
a shrewd man who managed to deprive them of what
they sought.

For one night's reflections, that should have been an
end to the matter, but in her memory, his face pressed
close against hers and his lips moved incessantly to
torment her through the darkest hours, and the doves
in the dovecote had begun their monotonous cooing
long before she sank into sleep. And though her father
had peeped into the room twice before she awoke, she
was still sure she had not slept.

From his distant view, Sir Henry was able to understand the cause of her distress better than most. He
had observed her ways with men who would like to
have come close to her and knew that it was less to do
with mere perverseness than a real fear of being
dominated. None of the young swains had been her
match either in intelligence, in courage or in self-will
and it was for this reason that he had let the matter of
her marriage lie, sure that there would come a time
and a place.

Meanwhile, he refused to offer her up to someone for whom she had no respect—there was no need for her to succumb to any but the ablest. And when the time was right, he, her father, would leave her in no doubt.

Now, he had met such a man, and while he had no way of knowing what had passed between him and Marietta, he had seen the effect of their second encounter when the man had obviously asserted his authority. The uncomfortable truth, however, was that Lady Alice had earmarked this man for her Emeline, or so she would have it, and as things had progressed this far in her schemes, he felt duty-bound to foster her cause. But what a waste. What a waste. Perhaps he should leave it to Lord Alain to sort it out for himself.

Lady Alice crossed herself, raised herself from her knees and closed her book of prayers, delaying as long as possible her exit from the little chapel, knowing that her brother Nicholas was waiting for a word. She did not want to face his inquisition today any more than she had yesterday. There was already more than enough expected of her without him, too.

He took her elbow and walked along the balcony and down the stairs to the hall, accepting her excuse not to go into her solar. She was far too busy to take time off for idle conversation, she said.

'It's not an idle conversation I want, Alice,' said Sir Nicholas under his breath, drawing her away from others who waited to speak with her. 'I simply want to know why Emeline was crying.'

'Perhaps you should ask Emeline herself.' She looked away and caught sight of her pantler waving his fingers for her attention. But her brother took her arm beneath the loose sleeve of her gown and gripped it painfully tightly. Alice gave a gasp of pain and turned to him, her mouth open in protest.

'I *have* asked her, Alice. You know bloody well that I have, and that she won't tell me because Henry told her not to. Now *you* tell me, or you'll find that new pet of yours in the duckpond. And then you'll have some explaining to do.'

'Nicholas! You wouldn't do that!' Her face registered horror.

'Yes, I would, dear sister. Yes, I would. Now, tell me!'

'Let go of my arm, please. I'll tell you, but let go.' She pulled it away from his grasp and held it, massaging the pain with her free hand and turning her back on those in the hall. 'Henry scolded her about the gown, for one thing,' she whispered, angrily.

'The gown? What was wrong with it? I saw her beforehand and thought she looked good.'

'Well, he didn't think so. When she came into the solar with you, Henry said she looked so fuddled she could hardly speak a word of sense. And he said the gown was too revealing for a maid.'

'Revealing? She was covered up. What are you talking about?'

Alice lowered her head and looked sideways at him. 'Nicholas, does she. . .has she. . .?'

'Has she what?'

'Has she got. . .you know. . .a lover?'

'Hah! Well, if she has, she hadn't been with him then, if that's what you mean. Why? Did Henry object to her showing that she fancied Lord Alain so soon?'

'Sssh! Yes, I expect he thought it was too obvious. He's not what we expected, is he? Lord Alain, I mean. He's younger than me, not the old man I thought he'd be. Anyway, Henry told her to behave more modestly in future.'

'Well, if I were you I wouldn't care what she does in future as long as she gets married first, old, young, fat, thin, anybody! If that old couple die before then,

Henry'll put somebody else into Beckington Manor and that'll be the end of my plans to live there.'

'No he won't.' Alice didn't sound too convinced. 'It's mine, you know.'

'I know it is, sister dear, but Henry seems to have more say in who lives there than you do.'

'Well, only until I pass it on. . .'

'. . . To the first daughter to get married. Yes, I know all that,' he snapped, 'but if Emeline hangs about much longer, my plans will go for nothing. It's clear the other one's never going to make it, is she? Prickly little bitch! If I wasn't her uncle, I'd. . .'

'Nicholas! Stop it, this moment! Marietta is my stepdaughter—'

'Yes, and you don't know how to handle her do you? Well, I do!'

'Nicholas, for goodness sake. . .we're being looked at. . .'

'It's all right, woman, I won't. But be quick and get Emmie into bed with that mighty lord, will you? Because *I* want Beckington. And I want it soon, otherwise I'll be too old to sire any brats, too.'

'Please. . .!' Alice pushed herself away and turned into the company who waited patiently to speak with her. 'Now, let's see, I must speak with the pantler. . . about today's bread.'

Sir Nicholas sat down hard on the stairway, watching the throng of people around his sister—knights, ladies, yeomen, grooms of the chamber and household servants waiting for instructions, greetings, directions for the day ahead—and thought with a resentment that deepened almost daily of how he should be the owner of such a place as this.

Five manors Sir Henry had, while he had none, being the youngest and landless son of a large family. Alice had married well, for her only dower had been the manor of Beckington, a large estate not far from

Monksgrange, which had always been handed down, since it was built in the twelfth century, from mother to daughter, whichever daughter married first.

In spite of Alice's pleas, Sir Henry had always steadfastly refused to allow her to turn out the elderly couple who managed it and allow Nicholas to live there. Now his only chance of overriding Sir Henry's interference in his wife's property was to remove it once more down the female line to pliant Emeline, who had been well schooled to do his bidding. But it would not be hers until she married, and it was time she was settled.

He sighed and watched the new pup flop unsteadily down over the edge of each enormous step as it came past him to its mistress, and with one hand he scooped it up and lowered it to the floor. He felt a toe between his shoulder-blades.

'If you're not otherwise engaged, Nicholas. . .and if you have the time. . .Emeline will need an escort as soon as she's ready. Only until noon. And then, I have a job for you.'

Sir Nicholas stood. 'Not Marietta?'

'No, not Marietta. She'll be with me,' said Sir Henry.

Not surprising, he thought. I'm the last one she'd want to be with.

CHAPTER THREE

FROM the front, Monksgrange stood foursquare and solid, as though grown from the hillside, rooted for ever in the limestone crags which had given it birth. Even the sloping rooftops were stone-flagged and encrusted with lichens, mosses and houseleeks. But it was not until two days after their arrival that Marietta was at last able to take a good look at the place her father had purchased less than a year ago; not until she had been carried from the house, still too stiff to walk, placed in a horse-litter thickly padded with cushions and taken on a tour of the buildings and village.

Until recently, Monksgrange had belonged to the Augustinian priory of Bolton and was one of a dozen or so satellite sheep farms dotted about over a considerable acreage, supervised by the cellarer and run by lay brothers, reeves and a bailiff. It had been the largest of their granges; not only did it farm more land than the others but served also as a retreat and convalescent house for monks who were old, recovering from illness, or in need of spiritual solitude.

It had more rooms, its own chapel, extensive gardens and a pleasantly sheltered aspect on a hillside, lying on the edge of the village of Ings. From Monksgrange, they could see across the valley of the River Wain to the wooded scars that formed the great plateau where Thorsgeld Castle watched over the valley on one side with the town of Thorsgeld tucked in behind.

Bad times had forced the canons of Bolton Priory to let Monksgrange go; repeated raids by the marauding

Scots, two catastrophic summers and bad crop-yields, followed by the predictable sheep and cattle diseases that had cut their flocks and herds to below half, made it impossible for the monks to eke out an existence. Their tenants could not pay their tithes nor could the wool-clip be sold a year in advance when so many sheep had been lost.

The monks' loss had been Sir Henry's gain. With enough reserves to tide him over the lean years, he had been less convinced than the monks that the Lord would provide and had preferred to provide for himself. With careful husbandry and protection from the Scots' raids up in the highest fells, he had weathered the storm, held onto his assets and expanded.

With Marietta in the litter and a retinue that included the bailiff, reeve and steward among household knights and scribes, Sir Henry went over the wooden bridge through the village to meet the parish priest, the new tenants and the miller, whose mill on the beck ground the corn of the villagers. As they surveyed the fields, many of them now enclosed by stone walls, Marietta pointed to black patches high up on the fell behind them. 'Father, stop a moment, please. Those. . .what are those up there?'

The bailiff answered for Sir Henry. 'Caves, mistress. There's quite a cluster of 'em round theer. Demon's caves. Nobody goes up theer.'

'Demons?' Marietta scoffed, gently. 'Wild animals, more like.'

'Nay, mistress, there's no way o' knowing. No road. Nothing. Village folk always keep away.' His voice took on a dark tone.

Lady Alice might well have swallowed such nonsense with ease, but Marietta and her father were less gullible, neither of them subscribing to such superstitions. It hardly mattered—while Marietta was with her father, she was well out of range of any danger, superstitious or otherwise, and the risk of being discovered again by Lord Alain had all but disappeared.

For the next few days, her expeditions with Sir Henry became a treat, as treasured for her new mode of transport as for the comforting knowledge that, under her father's wing, she could not be provoked by this large and daunting man. Her father allowed her to walk in the mornings, attend to the garden and direct the new planting, then to take a small part in the ordering of stores, checking the malt for brewing and the fish-ponds for the kitchen.

During these days, her bruises moved through a startling spectrum of colours; by the end of the week, most of them had faded to pale green and yellow except for two crescent-shaped imprints on her buttocks which stayed violet for a while longer. On her face, the soreness vanished quickly and eventually the litter was abandoned and she was able to travel further afield and thus make the possibility of meeting Lord Alain even less likely.

Emeline had never been interested in the running of the demesne, preferring to leave such matters to Marietta, so it was hardly surprising that she was easier to find at home on the occasions when Lord Alain came. She was preparing to go hawking one morning when he appeared unexpectedly, a week after his first call. Bruno and another squire accompanied him, showed him round the mews, and together the party went into the hills with the falcons, returning with several wildfowl for the kitchen.

Marietta was secretly delighted to have missed him, for she had been with her father and his bailiff at the new mill on that day, talking about setting eel-traps in the beck. The nearest she came to being seen was well into the second week when Lord Alain rode into the courtyard from the front as she rode away out of the back. Aware of Lady Alice's intention of asking him to share a meal with them on his next visit, there was an unmistakeable smile on Marietta's face as she rode out, knowing that she could arrange to stay out of the way until well after noon, when he would be gone.

It was obvious that Emeline was certain of a conquest; never had she been so gay, so brimful of excitement and chatter, planning for the future and even turning a new-found charm on her sisters. Lady Alice could scarce contain herself and even Sir Nicholas had begun to mellow.

Their uncle caught up with Marietta as she came in at suppertime, breathless and glowing from a ride with her father to see the new stone wall which should last, he'd told her, for a few hundred years. 'Marietta!' Sir Nicholas called.

'Uncle?' She wished he would not think that she enjoyed his sudden attentions. He was no more welcome to her than he'd been before.

'If you need an escort when your father's not available one day, I'd be honoured to accompany you.'

'Where to?'

He was taken aback by her abrupt response. 'Where to? Anywhere.'

'Anywhere?' Her smile was cynical. 'Is your nose being pushed a little out of joint, Uncle? Now that Emeline's attentions are engaged?'

'Not at all. Is yours, Marietta?'

'No. That's why I'm co-operating with Emeline. But I've seen the kind of help you offer and I wouldn't like any of it, thank you. Now, would you excuse me, please?'

Sir Nicholas stood back to let her pass. 'Well, then,' he said, 'watch them carefully at supper, and if you change your mind. . .'

'Them? Watch who?' She had an uncomfortable

feeling that she knew the answer to that already. Was *he* still here?

'Her new suitor, of course. Did you not know?'

'No, I didn't! I thought. . .' She looked away angrily, but it was too late to conceal what her uncle construed as jealousy of Emeline's happiness. It was not jealousy, she thought, as much as a desire to avoid Lord Alain, for he would want to know why and how she'd managed to thrust Emeline at him, in spite of his warnings. But then, perhaps he'd changed his mind since then, after being in her company so often.

'What did you think, Marietta? That he was staying only for midday dinner? Too bad. But you'll want to see Emmie perform, surely? No?' His eyes held a mockery that she would dearly love to have wiped away with a resounding smack.

But common sense came to her rescue and in the instant before she let go of her temper, a better idea occurred to her. Make use of him.

'No, Uncle Nicholas. I'm more interested in my food than in watching Emeline. Make a place for me at your side. I'll go in with you.' Before she could fully appreciate the expression of astonishment on his face, she'd swept her gown away and stalked off.

Too bemused to be angered by her imperious tone, Nicholas watched her ascend the wooden stairs, half-aware that he was being made use of, but having no idea that the alliance was meant to deceive Lord Alain rather than Emeline and the others in the hall. Still, he would go along with it. Even that was better than a total rejection.

Lord Alain's retinue, together with the large household of Sir Henry, made for a merry enough meal during which it was not too difficult for Marietta to put on a convincing show of indifference. Outwardly, she talked and laughed with the guests, even with Uncle Nicholas, avoiding Lord Alain's eyes like the plague and allowing Emeline and Lady Alice to dance around him, leaving no one in doubt that they were honoured by his presence.

Even when they assembled in the great solar before the meal, he could do no more than greet her with a solemn and studied bow before being hauled away by Lady Alice as though any lingering contact with Marietta would be precious time away from Emeline.

Inwardly, Marietta's emotions were by no means as under control as she made it seem, sensing a desperation in her stepmother's and Emeline's manipulation of events that hurt her, even while she went along with it. Disturbed by Lord Alain's manner towards her, she was sure she wanted no more of it, so why did she find it so difficult to put him from her mind? Why did her eyes fail to register any detail of the food before her, and why did she not hear when Uncle Nicholas spoke?

The guests at the high table were entertaining, but her ears strained only to catch the sound of Lord Alain's voice, her eyes glancing sideways at his fingers on the goblet of wine. And when the goblet she shared with Uncle Nicholas was filled, time after time, was it he who drank it all, or her? Was the laughter, indeed, growing louder, the musicians noisier, the room growing hotter by the minute? Was it her exasperation at Emeline's high-pitched giggles that made her want to leave and seek the cool air of the evening?

Her father leaned back from his bench and touched her arm. 'You all right, love?' he mouthed, behind the backs of three people.

Marietta's cheeks were flushed and her eyes sparkled, but whether from laughter or tears not even she could have said. 'Think so. . .Father. . .may I. . .leave?' she mumbled, almost falling backwards off the bench.

Sir Nicholas's arm caught her around the waist and pulled her to him in a gesture part-rescue, part-embrace. He laughed. 'I'll take her, Henry.'

That was not what Sir Henry wanted, but from that distance he could not argue. 'Bring her straight back,' he said.

Sir Nicholas nodded, his expression one of bland innocence.

There was nothing strange about leaving a hall during a meal of such duration but, even so, Sir Henry watched with more than a hint of concern at the sight of his brother-in-law's arm around Marietta's waist as they left through the opening of the carved screen that led into the passage.

Away from the heat and noise and cooled by the draught of air along the passage, Marietta became aware of Sir Nicholas's hand on her ribs as he led her towards the courtyard door. She pushed at the hand, vaguely irritated by its warmth on her, but before he could respond, three pages approached from the kitchen outside, bearing a huge platter between them loaded with sweetmeats and glazed fruits, nuts and tiny pastries to round off the meal.

Nicholas pulled her close up to the wall and pressed himself against her as they passed, needlessly placing his hands over her hips as though to protect her from danger.

'Uncle...Nicholas...!' Marietta twisted away, smelling the hot reek of wine on his breath. 'I can manage... alone,' she said, forcing the words out in the right order. It was difficult, for while the inside of her head seemed to be in perfect working order, her arms, legs and words were disobeying her commands in a most alarming manner.

'It's all right, Marietta,' Nicholas said. 'Come on outside. You need some air. I need some air, too. We'll go together, eh?' His head fell towards her, too close.

'No, Uncle...I'm perfectly lone all right...let you go...now.' She could hear the silly words wilfully confusing her, pretending that they'd said what she meant them to say. What *had* she said?

'Yes, all right, come on then. We'll go now.' He turned her again to face the door.

There was one word she knew could not be misconstrued. 'No!' she yelled.

The voice that replied was much deeper than Sir Nicholas's. 'Sir Nicholas, your brother-in-law requires your presence at the table, I believe. Immediately. I will relieve you of your duty.'

There was no arguing with that tone, even after so much wine. Without another word, Sir Nicholas relaxed his grip on Marietta's arm, clenched his teeth on an oath and left her to face Lord Alain's well-timed interference. If he had heard the suppressed oath, Lord Alain would have laughed.

Marietta would not. Relieved beyond words from a danger she herself had done something to precipitate, this particular form of deliverance from her uncle's company was embarrassing in a different way, one which, in her present state, she had no idea how to handle.

She discovered immediately that she was not required to. Lord Alain took her hand and led her, unprotesting, across the almost deserted courtyard and round the corner into the garden where he had encountered her in the arbour. Slowly and without speaking, they entered the same shelter where the carpenter had constructed a turf seat along one side, facing the herb-patch. At the far end, where the foliage gave them some privacy, he took her by the shoulders and sat her down, seating himself by her side.

The conflicts which had beset Marietta since their first meeting surged forward into an accumulation of futile longings and denials made so much more potent by his nearness. Hardly caring whether he scolded again, or teased, or even said nothing at all, she relished his presence by her side with few of the former inhibitions she had nurtured in defence.

Lord Alain appeared to sense this. 'Does it take four goblets of wine to stop you bolting then, damoiselle? Do I have to get you pie-eyed before we can talk without you snarling like a wildcat? Eh?'

'Don't,' Marietta whispered.

'Don't what?' He took the long dagged tippets of her sleeves between his fingers and held them together like reins.

'Don't talk to me, my lord.' That seemed to sum it up, she thought, hazily.

'Not talk to you? Why ever not? Is it forbidden?'

The truth came out so much more easily, this time. 'You're supposed to be. . .be talking. . .to Emeline,' she whispered, wearily laying her head back against the trellis. If she concentrated very hard, she could just get the words out before they tripped each other up. Giving all her attention to the words made it difficult to remember what her heart and her head disagreed about.

'Aye, well. . .I've talked to your sister Emeline for the best part of two weeks now and, in spite of what I told you, you've managed to avoid me. Where have you been? Do I have to camp outside the gates to catch you before you make a dash for it each morning?'

'Been felping my. . .felping. . .*helping* my father,' she said, focusing her eyes on his strong hands. 'I have to see to stores. . .order food. . .'

'Doesn't Lady Alice do that?'

Marietta shook her head, then wished she had not, for the action seemed to leave her eyes at a standstill somewhere out of focus. 'No. . .me. . .I do it. I like it. Garden, too. . .all this. . .I like it. Haven't been voiding you. . .'

'Don't lie to me, wench,' he said, cutting off her explanation. 'I know damn well you have. Why? Come on, I want to know. And why encourage that uncle of yours? Do you like him?'

'No,' she glared and pulled her sleeve tippets out of his hands. 'No, I do not! I just. . .' She stopped, unable to remember what it was she had needed Uncle Nicholas for.

'Just to show me you don't care. Was that it?'

'I don't know, my lord. Go away, please. If you came here to pick another quarrel, you choose your times very ill. First I'm bruised from a fall and then I'm. . . tired. Emeline says you're charming to her, but to me you're pro. . .provoking.'

'Leave your sister out of it, if you please. It's you we're talking about.'

'And last time you spoke to me alone, you were most ob. . .ject. . .able!'

'Was I, lass? So you remembered that, did you? Is that why you kept well out of reach? So's I wouldn't do it again?'

'Yes. . .yes, it is!' Goaded into an admission, Marietta turned on him in fury, purposely re-introducing her half-sister as a weapon to annoy him. 'Why don't you torment Emeline like that? She'd like it! I don't!' She would have risen, then, and flounced away if she could have trusted her legs to stay rigid under her, but Lord Alain reached across and caught her hands in his, and she could not release them.

'Torment?' he said. He pulled her nearer to him so that her face was only a whisper away, making it impossible for her eyes to evade his. They were dark in the dappled shade of the arbour, but she saw how they roamed over her, lingering on her bare neck and low-cut bodice, taking in every detail of the gold circlet on her brow and the mass of dark-brown curls, her lips and then her eyes. 'Torment?' he repeated. 'You think I should torment her, do you? Like this. . .?'

The world of greenery tipped over her and his head

took the place of the arched bower as all details merged into one sensation of being held close to him, lowered across his lap, submerged as she had wanted to be in her dreams but never was. His wide chest was above her, his shoulders blocking out the gentle golden sunset, his head of black-brown hair framing his face. She felt his breath against her skin. 'Did you tell her how hard my kiss was, Marietta? Did you? Or did you keep it to yourself. . .a secret?'

'Don't. . .please don't, my lord. Please. . .'

'Why, Marietta?'

She could think of no coherent reason except that he'd been earmarked for Emeline and she was not supposed to be any part of that plan. And if he was fooling with her, this was a most despicable and ungallant action for a man to perform if his intentions were indeed directed elsewhere. Yet, *she* was here, not Emeline, and she would only have to scream and make a fuss to bring help, to show him that she meant what she said.

But did she mean it? Did she not secretly want this part of him, this memory to take with her beyond Emeline's marriage? A dream, a slice of reality, a few seconds of ecstacy for the length of a kiss? His head was lowering, not waiting for her deliberations.

'You're for Emeline. . .' was all she could think of to say.

'Aye,' he whispered on her lips, 'that's what you'd all have me believe, is it not? So before I make my offer tomorrow, we'll get one or two things straight, shall we?'

If she wondered what he meant by that, she was given no chance to enquire, for his arms tightened under her back and she was brought up to his mouth and held darkly in his embrace. It was not the cruel punishing kiss of their first conversation but no less positive in its message of intent, and for the second time she felt the strength of his arms and the firm mouth seeking a response from hers.

She had dreamed of kisses, but this was far beyond her dreams. She had seen village men kissing the women in the hayfields, behind the barns, in the darkest corners of the hall, and had wondered why they writhed so, and moaned, and made it look so uncomfortable.

Now, she began to realise, in the hazy recesses of her mind, how one was impelled to search for new surfaces and tastes, to give and then to relax and accept, to accede to the demands of one more experienced and sink below the warm surface of his quest and let him go, and search, and find. Gladly, she went with him, holding his head to hers and sharing every sensation.

When she realised that his hand had found a way inside her bodice and onto her breast, she let out a low cry against his mouth and, placing a hand over his, pushed at it to heighten the sensation. He responded immediately by easing both her surcoat and her cote-hardie over her shoulders, exchanging her lips for her breast and fondling with his mouth so exquisitely that, even though this was a first experience for her, she would have done anything that he'd asked.

He stopped and raised his head, looking for a reaction, but Marietta lifted her arms and drew his head to hers again, riding high on a wave of new perceptions, matching one against the other as though time was running out. Which indeed it was. For the last few moments, she took all he offered and gave all he asked.

Lord Alain held her quietly against him and looked down at her lovely face. 'So, my lovely Marietta,' he whispered, 'you still have no wish for a husband?'

She was sure he taunted her and would have pushed her way off his lap in sudden indignation and guilt if he had not anticipated her rejection by catching her to him and preventing her escape. 'Answer me!' he said.

'It pleases you to play games with me, my lord. You

know as well as I that that meant nothing to either of us.' She winced as he gripped her cruelly tight in his arms.

'Stop it!' he growled. 'That kind of talk does you no credit, lass. Don't try to tell me that that was a game. Even if you *are* inexperienced and tipsy, you can't have pretended that. Tell me truthfully, if you please. Do you still want me to offer for your sister?'

He had asked for the truth, but it was not hers to give. Still utterly confused, still conditioned to put Emeline first in the marriage line, still angry at her own passionate response and fearful of this man who could wield such power over her body, she was in no position to capitulate. Struggling against his hold, she replied with all the anger built up since their first eventful collision.

'Yes! Offer for her! Why should I care what you do? She's willing enough to have a husband. . .she'll be compliant. . .let me go!. . .and do your bidding. . .like a pet lamb! Offer for her. . .you won't have to ask twice. . .let me *go*, my lord!'

Thinking that he might reciprocate in kind, which she could not have borne, she rolled away and sprang to her feet with unexpected agility, pulling at her surcoat and cote-hardie to straighten them. But Lord Alain was not injured by her outburst; on the contrary, he appeared to be somewhat amused and, keeping hold of her around the waist, eased her back onto the seat by his side.

'All right, my girl. . .all right. . .calm down. I can see your feathers are ruffled. I should have known. We both have much to learn about each other. Come, make yourself straight and composed, we must walk back into the hall as though we've been to take the air. No more. Say nothing of this. . .I give you my word I shall say nothing, either.'

He stood and settled her circlet straight on her head

and pushed her hair tidily over her shoulders. 'There, are you ready to go in, now?'

Marietta nodded, absorbing some of his composure.

'Smile?' he whispered, lifting her chin.

She did not smile. 'My lord, pray do not tease me any more.' Her heart still pounded. This must not be repeated, ever; for hers and Emeline's sakes, he must tease her no more.

'The only time I have ever knowingly teased you, my lovely Marietta, was at our first meeting when I insisted on feeling for your bruises to rouse you, to bring you back to consciousness. And I insisted on carrying you because you could not have walked, even though you would have tried, stubborn lass. That was the only time. Since then, everything I have said, or done, has been said in all seriousness.'

'Oh. Then you will make your offer tomorrow, my lord?' She dreaded the reply but had to know so that she could be well out of the way.

'Yes, I shall speak to your father on the morrow. But I do not want anyone to know of this, Marietta. It must remain our secret. Will you give me your word on that?'

A woman's word. Was it worth anything, then? 'Yes, my lord, I shall not. . .not speak of it.'

'Come then. There must be no sign of tears when we return. We don't want to give Lady Alice the wrong idea, do we?' He held out his hand.

As if to add to the interminable discomforts of the night, Marietta struggled wearily into the new day with a pain in her head worse than any she could remember. Stoicism was one thing, but this was blinding. Her maids knew what to do; Sir Henry was the same after too much red wine. 'Here,' Ellie said to Anne, 'lay the cloth out on here and hold it while I spread this over it. We'll soon have her bound up.'

'This' was a mixture of chopped rue and vinegar, one of a variety of remedies which they chose according to the time of the year. Ivy berries were not available yet and plantain roots must be dug up before dawn. The red cloth, soaked with its sour-smelling mixture, was wrapped around Marietta's head and pinned in place while the two bustled about quietly and efficiently to prepare an infusion of vervain and honey for her to sip. It was not like their mistress to drink too much. Had it been Sir Nicholas's fault, perhaps?

They had noticed, for little escaped them, how her uncle had returned alone after escorting Marietta out of the hall, how his expression had betrayed only too clearly that he'd been sent packing by Lord Alain, who had followed them with purposeful steps.

Much more they'd noticed, too, enough to fix a sulk on Emeline's face for the rest of the evening and for Lady Alice to harangue her in ear-shattering spasms until Sir Henry had gone to calm things down. She would not treat Marietta to such a tirade, that was for sure, not if she wanted to come off best. The two maids nudged each other and grinned, having worked out their own version of what the problem might be. Their mistress's sleepless night helped to confirm it.

With the dreadful pain in her head now more under control, Marietta nevertheless revised her plans to ride off to some far-flung corner of the demesne in favour of some work in the gardens. There were three which needed much attention, but the herbs were her special province and she'd be safe enough there from the comings and goings of Lord Alain and his companions.

She stayed in the shade where the bright sun could not hurt her eyes, directing the maids and the young garden lads which plots to dig, to manure and to tidy. The rosemary was already well up and covered with pale mauve flowers, the same colour as her surcoat, which she wore over an undyed linen cote-hardie.

Her hair she'd had plaited and coiled around her head, and a veil hung from its lower edges over her neck, useful, she thought, for keeping flying creatures away. And though she was unable to keep thoughts of him away as efficiently, the green foliage and the gentle industry of the gardeners gave her some peace and space in which to ponder on recent events.

It was Bruno who came to seek her, well past dinner time. He and the other young squire had demonstrated their serving graces on the guests at Sir Henry's table, but Marietta had not appeared, preferring to take a small meal of honeyed oat cakes and milk in the arbour, unable to face real food or the sight of Lord Alain with Emeline.

'I can't stay, love.' He pecked her cheek in simultaneous greeting and farewell. 'I have to go. My lord is waiting.'

'He's still here, then?' She knew, but wanted Bruno to say.

'Yes, he and Father have been closeted up together all morning.'

'And Mother. . .?'

'Lady Alice is in a buzz. . .you can imagine.' He was backing away, anxious to go.

'Emeline?'

'Haven't seen anything of her.' He stopped backing to think more clearly. 'I think she's been told to stay out of the way until it's been announced. You'll be glad to see the back of her, won't you?' His sudden smile after the wicked question brought a gust of dry laughter from her.

'Certainly I will, love. Both of them. Now, hurry. . . or you'll be in trouble.' She waved a hand at him.

'Yes, we've discovered how fierce he can be, Marrie. Everybody jumps when he gives an order. Bye, love. God be with you.'

'And with you, dearest.'

Marietta watched as he ran nimbly along the pathway towards the gate, passing the maids who approached from the house. Their faces were solemn, as she thought they might be.

'Mistress, Sir Henry asks that you attend him in the great solar.'

She knew what he would have to say and that they would all gather there as an outwardly happy family, beaming with joy and relief. She would have to share it with them, pretend to be happy, congratulate Emeline and bear her empty prattle with a good grace. Rinsing her fingers in the water-butt, she shook them dry, tucked a stray lock of hair away, and went in.

Sir Henry indicated a stool by the window-seat where Lady Alice sat. 'You'd better sit down, love,' he said.

Marietta stood inside the large sunny chamber, bewildered by the absence of happy smiling people. Where was everyone? 'No, it's all right, father. . .I think I can guess the news,' she assured him. 'I'm so—'

'You know?'

Lady Alice looked puzzled, scanning Marietta's face, then her husband's.

'Yes, of course. It's Emeline, isn't it? Lord Alain has offered. . .'

'No, dear.' Her father shook his head. 'Look, do sit down.'

Marietta sat, now even more at a loss, and glanced at her stepmother's joyless face. No excitement? He'd not been accepted, then? Perhaps the two men could not reach an agreement, after all.

'Lord Alain has asked me for your hand,' he said.

The room spun slowly round, taking the words with it. She must have misunderstood. 'What?' she whispered.

'He has asked me for your hand in marriage, Marietta.'

Still her eyes registered nothing except the two faces in a void. Surely there was some mistake. 'No, Father. That's absurd. It's Emeline he's to marry. Emeline, surely.'

'No, love. He's to return tomorrow for your answer. I told him the marriage had my blessing but that you'd have to be consulted. You can have until then to think about it, but I think it would be best if we were to discuss it now rather than leave it until then. This is rather a surprise to us—'

'A surprise to *you*? You can't have understood, Father. It's Emeline he's been paying attention to, not me. This is all wrong!' She leapt up and strode to the door.

Lady Alice caught at her hand before she could reach it. 'Child,' she said, unusually quietly, 'child, don't flounce out like that without trying to discuss it. We're all surprised. Think how Emeline feels.'

'You told Emeline first, then?' Marietta's brown eyes blazed in anger.

'Yes, dear. A moment or two ago. She was expecting some news and I couldn't make her wait any longer. She needs time to get used to the idea.'

'*She* needs time? To get used to the idea of not being married? She's had nearly fifteen years to get used to that, hasn't she? And now. . .' she pulled away from Lady Alice, furious at being placed second, even at a moment like this '. . .now you spring this ridiculous news on me and tell me I have a mere twenty-four hours to think about it? And you tell me she needs time? God's wounds, Mother!'

'Marietta! That's enough! Don't speak to your mother so.'

She stood as stiff as a poker. 'I beg your pardon, Mother. But the whole thing is a nonsense, anyone can see that. They've been together for days, enjoying each other's company; the only times he's spoken to me he's been totally uncivil. It was no penance to keep out of his way this last few weeks, I assure you. It was a pleasure.'

'And you?' Her father poured ale into a goblet for her. 'Have you been civil to him? Was that civility you showed him at your first meeting?'

The arrow hit the mark. Bullseye. 'It was his damn hounds that brought me off my mare. He's not apologised for any of that,' she snapped.

Lady Alice shook her head, confused by the turn of events. 'Well, I must admit, I do find it strange, dear. They seemed to be getting on so well.'

Sir Henry handed the goblet to Marietta. 'Perhaps I did the wrong thing by taking you off every day. Perhaps I should not have interfered.'

'It would have made no difference, Father. I would have taken myself off, with or without your help.' She was shaking with anger. The man was playing a game with them, in spite of what he'd said on that first meeting in the arbour. 'You've discussed settlements with him, Father?' If he'd got that far, she thought, he must be serious, for no man would tell another what he was offering in any detail unless he was in earnest.

'Yes, we've spent the morning discussing the business part of it. He brought his clerks to make notes of the transactions and they're to return tomorrow when my proposals have been looked into.'

'*Your* proposals? You've got that far?' She was incredulous.

'Yes, love. He wasn't playing games. He's serious.'

Tasting nothing of the ale, she pushed the goblet back onto the table. 'Mother,' she said, her voice shaking now as much as her legs, 'Mother, I've done nothing to make this happen. Nothing! You've seen how I kept out of the way every single day. I wanted none of this. I still want none of it.'

As her words fell into the quiet room, she met her

father's eyes and knew that he understood the ambiguity of her dilemma, that in her most secret heart she had indeed wanted it but had not expected it, was afraid of it and, for Emeline's sake, would willingly have sacrificed it. Furthermore, she was painfully aware that, to Emeline, it would have all the hallmarks of treachery, even though Marietta had never seen herself as a rival.

Emeline was overtly ripe for marriage, and knew it. Marietta was happy to let her get on with it, for a man's dominance had never been something she craved, though Sir Henry knew better than she did herself that her capacity for loving was as great as any woman's and that her sexuality lay beneath a fine veneer of indifference, waiting to be roused.

What he had secretly wanted to happen had come to pass; obviously the man had seen her worth and made the best choice. But now, she would have to be convinced that this was in her best interests, or she would have to be forced into it. Failing that, Lord Alain himself would have to insist, and Sir Henry could hazard a guess that his strong-handedness so far had both antagonised and aroused her. He wondered how long it would take for one to fuse into the other.

Lady Alice came to sit by her, taking her hand gently in reply to Marietta's cry for help. 'Would you not want to marry him, Marietta?'

'No, Mother.'

'Why not, dear? He's very wealthy. You'd be mistress of a fine castle.' Lady Alice was growing ambivalent about the prospect. The only problem would be to keep her brother Nicholas quiet about Beckington, but that would have to take care of itself. At least she would have a daughter married to a lord. Any daughter. Any lord. 'Why not, dear?' she repeated.

'Because I'm convinced I'm not his first choice,' Marietta said impatiently, revealing some of the internal conflicts her father had guessed at. 'He's playing some clever game with Emmie. I can feel it. And I'm not going to be a part of it. He can think again. He can't come wooing one sister and then calmly offer for the other. It's not done. It's unfair on both of us.'

'Is that the only reason?' her father asked, quietly.

Marietta looked away out of the window across the valley to Thorsgeld Castle; though nothing was clearly visible through the opaque glass, she knew it was there. His arms still pressed across her back and shoulders, the search of his mouth was still on hers, on her body, skillfully persuading. She had been light-headed with wine and he had taken advantage of her lassitude. He had sworn it was no game, that he was not teasing. What, then?

'Let me go to my solar, Father.'

'No, Marrie.'

She sighed, drooping her shoulders, querying him.

'You have not yet asked what your mother and I say about this. Do you think you are the only person involved? Has it not occurred to you what it will mean to us, to Bruno's future prospects, to Emeline's and Iveta's?'

'Father, surely you're not taking this offer against my will, are you? Of what use is it to ask for my thoughts on the matter and then override them with yours?'

'Marietta!' Her father spoke sternly, though he could follow her argument. He smoothed a hand down his figured velvet surcoat, feeling its soft obedience to his touch. 'No one has spoken of overriding your wishes, but you must remember that discussions are between people. I've discussed it with Lord Alain and I assured him I'd discuss it with you. You are duty-bound to—'

'Then why did he not discuss it with me? Why suddenly spring it on me like this, when we all thought it was Emeline? Including her.' But as she spoke the words, she knew the answer.

He had. Of course he had. She had refused to listen when he'd told her and he'd not been fool enough to argue about it but had made her take it from another source. It was her own fault.

'I've already said that perhaps I got it wrong, Marietta. I thought it would help if you were out of the way but perhaps I should have made it easier for Lord Alain to contact you. But what would you have replied to an earlier offer, lass? What have you *ever* replied to an offer for your hand?'

'No.'

'Exactly! Lord Alain's nobody's fool; he's experienced. Thirty years old and a widower. He probably saw from a mile away that you'd say no at any stage in the negotiations, so his best course was to ask me and bypass you altogether. That seems reasonable to me; it's what anybody with any sense would do. He's a different kettle o' fish from all the others who've offered for you so far. I wouldn't have given you to any of them.'

'And you'd give me to Lord Alain, Father?'

'Yes, lass. I would. . .willingly.'

'Because he's a lord, and wealthy, and lives in a castle?' Purposely, she echoed her stepmother's priorities.

It was not lost on Sir Henry. 'Your mother pointed that out because they are the material things every mother wants for her daughter. You would. They make life bearable—no one can deny that.'

'And him? Would life be bearable with a man I don't love?'

He frowned at the irrelevance of her question. '*Love*, lass? For pity's sake, you can't have everything. That will no doubt come later. Respect is more important at this point, and you need an older man. You've always known that as much as I do. A strong man.'

'I don't need any man! I don't need *him*!' she snapped, scared by this talk of strength and experience.

'Yes, you do, dear,' Lady Alice said. She picked little Comfit off her feet to stop him chewing at her slippers and placed the white bundle on her lap. 'All women need men. It's hard for a woman to live without them.'

'I'll not be second choice, Mother! You wouldn't!'

'You are *not* second choice, for God's sake!' Sir Henry glared at her, suddenly exasperated by wave after wave of refusals. 'Stop punishing yourself! He didn't mention Emeline, not once. And even if that had been the case, you still owe it to us to treat this matter seriously. Offers of this kind are not all that thick on the ground, you know, even for eldest daughters. A fair face is one thing, but land and connections carry far more weight.'

'And have you offered him a good deal, Father?' she asked, scathingly.

'No, lass. I haven't. If you really want to know, I made it as hard for him as I could. If he wants my eldest daughter, he can pay dear for her.'

'What?'

'I'm not discussing the details until they're finished, but it will mean that, if he accepts them, he'll have proved that he really wants you.'

'Beckington goes with you too, you know,' Lady Alice offered.

Sir Henry nodded in agreement. 'Aye, there's Beckington. That belongs to your mother's family and goes to whoever marries first. But we've never needed it, have we, so no great loss. Just as long as that uncle of yours doesn't get his hands on it. There'd be nothing left of it in a couple of years.'

Property. Connections. Bargains. She could listen to no more. 'No!' she hissed.

'What?'

'No, Father. I can't. . .I'm sorry.'

Sir Henry turned away impatiently. 'Go to your chamber, lass. It's almost time for supper. We'll talk about it some more later. Go, now.'

Marietta made her courtesies and left, noting how Lady Alice moved into Sir Henry's open arms even before the door closed, laying her head upon his chest.

Sir Nicholas was passing the door of her solar as she approached, but he back-tracked and stood with his hand upon the latch, a slight smile behind his eyes. He was quick to notice the preoccupied expression and the angry flush on her olive-skinned cheeks.

Now, he thought, he was going to have to switch loyalties from Emeline to Marietta if he wanted to retain a chance to acquire Beckington and, after his mistake last night at supper, perhaps he'd better put things on a better footing without delay. He kept his hand on the latch. 'Is that a sigh of resignation or relief, Marietta?' he asked.

She looked at him steadily, only half-remembering what had transpired last evening. 'Resignation if you keep your hand on the latch, Uncle. Relief if you open it for me.'

He quirked an eyebrow and lifted the latch.

'Thank you.'

CHAPTER FOUR

As Marietta had expected, Emeline was alone and every bit as confused as she was herself. Overcoming her first instinct to leave her half-sister alone and to give her a chance to come to terms with the surprise, Marietta could not face the prospect of supper in an atmosphere as close to sisterly rivalry as it was possible to get. She knocked on Emeline's door and entered, having no idea what to say to ease matters. But the mixture of contempt and blatant jealousy which crossed the pretty face as Marietta entered was something never before encountered.

To say that Marietta had instantly lost a friendship in the last few hours would have been stretching the truth, for they had never truly been close friends. Their paths had diverged too much for that: their needs were too different, their characters too dissimilar. Emeline had never possessed either the energy or the rashness to pick a quarrel merely for the excitement and Marietta was far too discriminating to quarrel without the possibility of a good fight.

Now, it seemed, Emeline was indeed in a belligerent mood as never before and Marietta, while seeming to have the advantage, saw herself to be the victim of duplicity, though she had never sought the role of victim or victor, nor did she condone the events that had caused it. Whilst having every sympathy with her sister's plight, Marietta was being obliged to take on the traitor's guise, knowing that Emeline would never believe the innocence she was about to protest and feeling that she wouldn't either, if the same had happened to her.

They sat, facing each other like two farm cats waiting for the other to make first move. Emeline had been weeping; her kirtle was damp down the front and wrinkled where she'd lain on it, sobbing. Her long fair hair was damp at the ends where she'd chewed it, a baby habit of which she'd never broken herself.

'Emmie,' Marietta said, 'did you quarrel with him?' She waited, thinking that Emeline was going to stay silent. 'Please tell me. I'm as mystified and unhappy about this as you are. Did you quarrel?'

'Have you accepted him?' Emeline gulped, petulantly.

'No, of course not. Father says I have to talk with them again after supper. But I don't want to marry him. He was to be yours, not mine.'

'Then why didn't he ask for me, I'd like to know?' She buried her face in her hands as the hot tears spilled over again, sobbing bitterly.

Marietta waited, then asked again, 'Did you quarrel?'

'No, not once. I told you, he was charming.'

'He didn't talk of marriage?'

'No, he wouldn't, would he? Not before he'd spoken to Father.' There was a silence, except for Emeline's sniffs and sobs, neither of them knowing how to alleviate the pain. Then, little by little, the sobs were replaced by angry words, spilling out at random, of how Marietta had always spoiled her plans by her wayward behaviour, how she'd never known what to do with her own suitors but taken the only one she ever wanted, while Marietta sat, dejected and hurt by the abuse.

When the noise of supper preparations sounded from the great hall, Marietta preferred to go and pretend to eat rather than stay and listen to her sister's tirade. Sir Nicholas made a point of sitting next to her again and behaving so courteously that Marietta knew instinc-

tively that something was up. It took little reasoning to
tell her that this latest bout of gallantry had something
to do with her changed prospects.

Once more in her parents' solar, the cresset-lamps
were lit and the scent of beeswax filled the room as
darkness fell early, for the sun had set behind a thick
gathering of heavy clouds, and rain threatened. Lady
Alice put on a display intended to suggest that all was
normal by tugging sideways at one of the long tapestries
on the wall to straighten it, and sweeping her hand
down the wrinkles made during transit.

'You've spoken to Emeline?' Her hands still swept.

'Yes,' Marietta said, watching. 'She's angry with me.'

'Have you quarrelled?' Lady Alice came to the table
and took a sweetmeat from the dish, pushing it across
to Sir Henry.

'No, Mother. But I don't know what to say to her
that she'll believe. I told her it was not my wish.'

Sir Henry pushed the dish back with one finger.
'Then the sooner you're betrothed the better,' he said.
'It's high time you were married anyway, my lass. I said
as much only the other day.'

'Father! Were we not to have discussed this some
more?'

'I've said all I can say about it. You know my
feelings, and your mother's. Those are our wishes. And
now, we have to talk about times. Lord Alain wants to
have the betrothal ceremony tomorrow and I've
already spoken to Father Gilbert. He'll—'

'No, Father. . .please, no!'

'Then it will take a little while before contracts are
drawn up.'

'Father. . .!'

'Meanwhile I'll see that you have a chance to get to
know Lord Alain better.'

Marietta sat down hard on a stool with her back to
her parents, shaking her head in disbelief. He had said

they could discuss some more and here he was, telling her what he'd decided.

Down there in the hall, the subject had been carefully avoided by the closest members of the household, the chaplain, confessor, Sir Nicholas, well aware from the set faces and Emeline's absence that dark clouds had gathered above their heads. They were far too well briefed in matters of this nature to take a happy outcome for granted until it was announced. So much could go wrong.

But up here, where they could talk freely, her father had taken the reins. 'Marietta, come here to me.' He held out an arm, beckoning.

Reluctantly, she went to him, knowing almost word for word what he would say: that he knew better than she did what was good for her, that this was an offer too good to refuse, that it was the best she'd ever get and that, anyway, he had an inkling she was not as averse to this man as she would have them believe.

That touched a raw nerve and her eyes lifted in an instant from a study of his pointed leather-clad toes to his face, wrinkled with wisdom.

'It's true, isn't it, lass?'

She dared not admit it. 'He's Emeline's,' she said, looking away.

'It was a mistake we all made. He had other ideas and decided to act quickly before it went any further in the wrong direction. It's you he's asked for, Marietta. You.'

'She'll never forgive me, Father.'

Sir Henry ignored that possibility. 'Is there someone else, Marietta?'

'No,' she whispered. 'No, there's no one else.' God knew, there had never been anyone she'd reacted to as she'd done with this man. He had been in her thoughts every waking moment since he'd picked her up off the ground. She had felt his hands on her and needed his touch more than she needed food. And yet, she was afraid. Desperately. He was fierce and large, and she had not been able to put him down and dismiss him the way she'd done with all the others, for he had refused to be dismissed.

He was a good tactician, a soldier, and she was no match for him. She had told him that her mother died in childbirth, but that had been a lie to give some credibility to her reasons for not marrying. It sounded impressive, dramatic, but it was not the truth. The truth was that she, Marietta, was a born manager, and to hand her own reins over to a stranger was unthinkable. Madness. She would not do it.

And yet, what had she done last evening? What bliss had she felt as he had taken control? Had that been so very terrible?

'Then I shall tell Lord Alain that his offer is accepted?' Sir Henry took her silence as assent.

Marietta made one last bid to Lady Alice. 'Mother, I don't want this. . .please. . .tell him.'

'Hush, dear. . .' Lady Alice's arms were feather-light '. . .you are taking the only course open to you. There's nothing new in that. We've all done it. Look at me, I was fifteen, but it didn't take me long to fall in love with Sir Henry. And Emeline will have a wonderful time once she gets over the shock. Stop worrying about her and think of your own happiness.

'This is a brilliant match, Marietta. I can't deny that I thought Emeline would attract his attention first because she's more at ease with men's attentions than you are, but you have a different kind of beauty that appeals more to some men. You should be flattered, dear.'

She held Marietta away from her at arm's length and looked into the troubled eyes. 'He's been widowed for two years, had the pick of the north and decided on you, of all people. . .' she caught Sir Henry's raised eyebrows and realised how clumsily she had phrased that '. . . I mean, he's chosen you out of so many other rich and beautiful ladies. . .' She wallowed deeper and deeper into verbal quicksands before Sir Henry came to the rescue.

'You have rare qualities, love. Qualities he's been searching for and not found in others.'

'He told you that?'

'Yes, he told me that. He said he admired your courage and your beauty, your pride and intelligence.'

'Beauty?' She looked puzzled at that. Dark hair was not fashionable. 'What was his first wife like? Did you ever see her?'

'Yes, I saw her once when I went to discuss Bruno's future, several years ago.' His eyes took on a distant look as he remembered that meeting. 'She was a lovely creature. Fair, petite, gay and very vivacious.'

'Like Emmie?'

'Yes, very much like. . .' He stopped abruptly. Too abruptly. Suddenly aware of her quietly spoken prompt, he amended his mental image. 'No. . .not really. . .' But by that time, it was too late. The damage was done.

Like Emeline. Now we're getting to the truth, she thought, he had been looking for someone like his first wife, the one who'd died in the pestilence. Then he'd seen Emeline and fallen in love with her but decided he could not go through with it after all. So he'd grabbed at *her* as a way of escape, suspecting that she wanted him. He'd almost made her confess as much. Not second best, but third best.

Yes, he must have searched far and wide for two such ideal targets within one family; marry her so that he could keep Emeline in his sights, to remind him of the first one.

Hurt and angered by her new discovery, she reached blindly for her father. 'Father, I. . .' she stammered.

'Yes, love?' He turned, thinking she was about to acquiesce.

'I bid you goodnight. . .Mother. . .' She kissed them both and went to her room, too full of distress to talk to her maids, even. And as the night engulfed her in its heavy cloak, she lay in its silence, unable to surface from beneath the black pall of anger and resentment until the first rays of light stole in from the east

The two maids cowered against the wall of Sir Henry and Lady Alice's solar, hand in hand, searching their minds for a scrap of useful information which would calm their master's rising anger.

'I don't know when, Sir Henry. . .we. . .we were asleep. . .an' she must've slipped out. . .like a mouse. . . we didn't hear a thing, honest!'

'God's truth! You're supposed to hear whatever sound she makes. Haven't you understood that, yet? What's she wearing? Have you noted *that*?' Sir Henry knew in his bones that he should have put a guard across Marietta's door last night; this was just the kind of thing she would do. She'd done it once before, years ago, and stayed out all night. They'd had the whole village of Upperfell looking for her. But this was unknown territory. She could be anywhere.

'She was wearing her green bliaud, sir,' Anne said.

'And she took her brown fur-lined mantle, too,' Ellie added, 'and she must have been wearing the leather chausses she uses for riding, cos they're gone.'

Lady Alice sat up in bed, obviously concerned. 'If she's not here when Lord Alain arrives, Henry, what happens then? I might have known she'd lead us a merry dance, one way or the other.' She swung her legs over the side and pulled her robe off the bed. 'Have you checked the stables. . .the kitchen. . .the gateman?'

'No, Lady Alice.'

'Then —'

'I'll see to that, Alice,' Sir Henry barked. 'Get Sir Nicholas in here, you two.' The maids turned and fled. 'He can make himself useful, for once. This is going to look good, isn't it? After all my efforts yesterday.'

'She doesn't know this area, Henry. She can't have got far, surely?'

'She knows which direction Thorsgeld lies, and she's not going to head for there, is she? And look at it...' he pointed to the window where, only yesterday, the sun's rays had filtered in to light up the room '... black as pitch! There'll be mist on the tops. I'll thrash the lass when I get her back here. Of all the times to choose...'

Even Lady Alice tightened her lips and sent a look of exasperation in the direction of Sir Henry's back, meeting her maid's raised eyebrows in a complete exchange of understanding. Trust a man to think that the timing had been Marietta's choice.

If Marietta had heard the last of her father's remarks, she would undoubtedly have agreed with him as she was compelled to dismount in order to see the track through the white wet mist that enclosed her. It had been barely light when she'd ridden out through the gates of Monksgrange, unchallenged by the sleeping gateman, though it was the cloud hanging low over the hillside that made it seem more like March than May.

She had intended to gallop at a steady pace, putting as much distance between herself and Monksgrange as she could in one day, even over country not familiar to her. But past the cornmill, the track dwindled to no more than a sheep-path alongside the beck, leading steeply upwards, diverging and criss-crossing until the beck went one way and the path went the other, and by that time the white cloud had rushed towards her to draw her into its embrace.

Dulzelina snorted and shook her head, but the mist clung on. 'Come on, lass.' Marietta said, cheerfully, 'even this is better than staying there like cooped-up chickens. At least we're free. Come on.'

She led the grey mare on, watching the path, stumbling now and then as it steepened and then followed another ridge or skirted around a boulder. The eerie bleating of sheep and lambs led her on until quite suddenly the path joined the side of a stony track that ran across the hillside instead of vertically up it and where the incline was far less steep. At last, there was something they could follow.

Tucking her green woollen bliaud into her belt, Marietta re-mounted and rode at a slow walk, following the track on and upwards, relieved to see unmistakeable signs of horse dung here and there, an indication that the track was used by travellers, still.

It was a strange sensation, to have no idea of what lay behind, ahead, or to the sides, to be shut off from the rest of the world, hidden from them completely, safe from their machinations. When words had no effect, actions might convince them. They had neither listened to her nor tried to understand her reasons; they had decided it between them, apparently because none of them had expected her to consent. Not at any stage, her father had pointed out.

But consent, she knew as well as anyone, was not a vital ingredient, only co-operation, however reluctant. And if they had been in any doubt before, she would make them aware now that her reluctance was something more than maidenly coyness. She would return when she was ready and, beating or no beating, it would be worth it, just to show them.

The track grew steeper and hoofbeats were muffled, but even so, Marietta could sense that they were passing through a narrow gorge, for the mists thinned in patches and allowed her glimpses of dark, damp, moss-covered rocks. She could hear water, too, splashing downwards as though over ledges. The track was wet and slippery.

Then, ahead of her, the mist grew brighter and thinner, the air freshened into a breeze and in a few more strides, they were out of the mist and into the hazy sunshine, high up above the clouds. Laughing, patting the mare's neck and whooping with joy, Marietta eased the reins over and left the track where it curved away round the hillside, veering up onto the highest grassy bank where the sun's rays were brightest and warmest.

Now, looking down, she knew something of the eagle's power when it soared high above into the clear air. Before her were banks of white fluffy lambswool, filling the valley-bottoms almost to the peaks away in the distance.

She dismounted and stood, straining her eyes to pick out any landmark she might recognise. A white block of light appeared on the hillside, glinting in the sun. Thorsgeld Castle. Gleaming white limestone. High up on her level, its wall-like white ribbon stretched out sideways, watching her, reminding her so clearly of his words. 'Bolt as far as you wish, but I shall find you and bring you back until you tire of the game'.

'Hah!' she yelled, throwing her arms out wide. 'Hah! I'm here! Look, I'm here! Do your worst, my good lord. . . Oh! Saints alive. . .no, Dulzelina. . .come back! Come *back*! Oh, for pity's sake. . .!' Frantically, she ran to the edges of the mist, peering into its thick shroud after the startled mare, cursing and yelling at it to come back here if it didn't want to be fed to the hounds.

But Dulzelina, with not a whit of sense or loyalty, had vanished along the grassy hilltop and down into the swirling whiteness, not even her hoofbeats telling of her possible whereabouts. Her joy and fury coming so hard on each other's heels, Marietta's emotions were all set to take another turn towards fright and sheer

desperation combined with vexation at herself for her
own forgetfulness.

The mare had always been skittish—Sir Henry called
her the stupidest mare he'd ever come across—and
vanity was the only reason why Marietta favoured her
above the others, for she was very pretty, dapplegrey
and charcoal-muzzled, long-tailed and fine-limbed, a
delicate, empty-headed, easily frightened creature.
What was even worse, she carried Marietta's hastily
wrapped food in the saddle-bag, her leather water-
bottle and a blanket. All that Marietta needed to
survive for the day.

'Damn! Damn! Stupid creature!' she yelled. 'Now
what am I going to do?'

The only thing she could do until the mist cleared
was to sit in the sun and wait. But though time passed
and the sun reached its highest point, the mist remained
and eventually obscured Thorsgeld Castle as it rose
higher and higher. Lonely curlews fell silent, the few
remaining sheep disappeared taking their lambs with
them and Marietta was on the point of making a move
towards where she thought the track should be when
she froze, listening into the silence for the repetition of
a sound.

At first, she thought the clink of stone on iron must
be from Dulzelina's hooves and she was about to jump
up and run towards it when a man's shout followed,
then an answering call from further down, then a neigh
and a long snort.

It was them, come to look for her. It must be them!
She was lost, and horseless. Should she allow herself to
be caught and taken back so soon? Wavering between
safety and defeat she hesitated, watching the mist
thicken with every passing moment, puzzled by the
apparent frequency of the calls below her, the neighing
and answering snorts, far more men and horses than
she would have thought necessary.

Travellers, she thought, keeping contact in the mist by calling to each other, not a search-party but travellers on the track over the hills. If she had heard women's voices, too, she would have run down to join them, gone along with them to the next town. But she heard only men, coarse and rough, not a crowd she'd want to ask for protection. They passed, and silence returned.

With the sounds went also the light and Marietta realised how, when there was nothing to see or hear, her hunger became more acute. Cursing the mare again, and threatening her with banishment, at least, she moved carefully downwards through the thickening mist towards the track. It had disappeared. Try as she might to find it, it could have been a hundred miles away instead of a few yards.

A sheer rock-face appeared before her at barely an arm's length, and a rocky floor instead of turf, and further on, where the mists parted, she found herself in the large gaping entrance to a cave, with a fresh pile of horse dung at her feet. It was then that she realised where she was: in one of the caves she'd seen from the village below when the bailiff had told them that demons lived here, that no one ever came here. Well, she thought, he was wrong on both counts. No demons, and travellers aplenty.

Here at least was shelter from the wetting mists that had already dampened her hair and mantle. Here, she would wait out the rest of the day, and the night too, and hope that she would be able to see clearly on the morrow. It would be foolhardy to venture down over the cliffs that she knew to be there.

Here also, she had time enough to think and balance the pros and cons of marrying Lord Alain of Thorsgeld, of being mistress of her own household, of forgetting the griefs and woes of Emeline and Lady Alice, of

pleasing her father. She would be near Bruno too. He
would love that.

It was not until sounds of approaching hoofbeats
broke the utter stillness that Marietta realised how her
place of safety could also be a place of no escape, for if
anyone were to find her here, she would have a hard
task to get out. The travellers who used this route
might be glad to find a woman, alone.

She shrank against the cold stone and waited for
them to pass, but to her astonishment, it was Dulzelina
who appeared at the entrance to the cave and
Marietta's soft cry of delight was in direct contrast to
her earlier threats of the knacker's yard.

'Dulzelina. . .come! Oh, you've come back!' She
slipped down from the shelf of rock and ran to the
mare, throwing her arms around the cold damp neck
and holding onto the bridle with a firm grasp. 'Where's
that food, girl? And my blanket. . .' She groped for the
saddle-bag, laughing with relief.

'Looking for something, damoiselle?' a voice spoke
from the entrance.

'Oh!' Marietta yelped with fright and whirled round,
clasping at her chest and feeling her heart leap beneath
her hand.

Lord Alain led his great bay stallion into the cave,
almost blocking out the last remaining light and leaving
her no room to move away. 'I'll say this for you, lass,
you and this mare of yours spend a lot of time bolting
off together and then parting company, don't you? If I
were you, I'd find a more reliable nag than this.'

'You!' was all Marietta could say. Her eyes searched
beyond him.

'There's nobody else here. Only me. I told you I'd
find you. Didn't you believe that, either?'

With the mare's bridle in her hand, she felt almost
bold again. 'You were not supposed to find me, my
lord. I'm not going to marry you.'

She felt him smiling in the dim light as he began to unbuckle his saddle-bags and to loosen the stallion's girth. 'Did you particularly want to discuss that now, or shall we leave it until we've eaten?' he said, amiably. 'Loosen your mare's girths and let's get that saddle off her.'

'Why take it off? Surely we can go back the way you came, can't we? It's not quite dark.'

He heaved the saddle off the bay and laid it over a boulder, then took the reins and pulled them over its head. 'Yes, tomorrow,' he said, tying them to Dulzelina's.

Marietta placed a hand on his arm to stop him. 'Tomorrow? No, now. . .if you please. I can't stay here all night with *you*!'

Facing her, he placed his hands on his hips, making himself appear even larger than he did already. 'Where were *you* planning to stay, Marietta?'

'Here. *Alone*!' she snapped.

'Well then, damoiselle—' he touched her nose with his knuckle '—you'd better get used to spending your nights with me, because that's where you'll be in the future. Now. . .' he turned back to Dulzelina '. . . are you going to get this saddle off and give the mare a rest?'

'No.'

'Very well. I take it you'll say no to food as well. Am I right?'

'No.'

'Then do it, or you get not a crumb.'

'I'll do it for Dulzelina's sake, not because I care. . .' Her about-face was cut short by his large frame nudging her out of the way, accepting her token gesture of obedience.

'Here, I'll lift it off. Now, unpack that food while I take these two out for water.' He took their bridles to lead them away.

'Are you going to tether them out all night? There are travellers along this road who might take them.'

His laugh was no more than a grunt. 'At night? In a thick mist? Surely not?'

'Yes, in a mist. I heard them late this afternoon coming up the fell when I was on top of the hill.'

Lord Alain stopped, his face serious with frowns. 'You heard them? Did you see them?'

'No. I've told you. They were below me in the mist but there were a good few of them with horses. They passed along the track.'

'Did they see you? These travellers with horses?'

'No, I took care not to be seen. You can tell by the droppings that plenty of them come past here. Look, there's some by your foot.'

He nodded. 'Yes, I noticed. Stay here, Marietta. I'll water them and bring them back in for the night. Look in my saddle-bags, too.'

He must have known that she'd not make a run for it, not even bothering to remind her, but setting her to look for food instead. It was, she thought, the most unexpected turn of events, though whether this was better than being found by her father's men, or worse, she was not so sure.

Certainly he was bent on making her obey him and that was something about which he'd better be put straight, for she obeyed only her father, and even then there were lapses. As for his talk about spending her nights with him, perhaps she'd better make that position clear, too. She had no intention of doing any such thing.

There were oatcakes and cheese, pieces of spiced chicken, bread rolls and apples all hastily scavenged from the kitchen. There was her water-bottle and, in his bag, a huge wedge of venison in pastry and a leather bottle of ale and one of mead. A feast. By the time he returned with the horses, their muzzles dripping,

Marietta was seated cross-legged on a ledge of rock looking at the spread with nose twitching and mouth watering. She was ravenous, glad that he allowed her to eat in silence without questioning her.

It was she who asked the first question. 'How did you find me?'

'A hunch,' he said, briefly.

The light had almost faded now, and she could scarcely see his eyes but knew that he watched her, for all that.

'I found your mare, so I sent my grooms back to Monksgrange to tell your father I had you safe.'

'Had me safe. . .? How could you possibly—?'

'Marietta, if you would stop always losing your temper and *think*,' he barked, 'you'd work it out for yourself.' She was silent. 'The mare had obviously not fallen. I could see that. She's the daftest animal I've ever encountered, so the likeliest explanation was that she shied and bolted *again*!' he emphasised. 'And with your food on board. So you were not likely to have gone far without it, were you? Particularly in this mist and on unfamiliar ground.'

'Do *you* know this land, then?'

'Course I know it. It borders on mine. It's your father's land.'

'They told us these caves had demons in, that nobody ever came near. They must have been kidding. . .'

'Who? Who told you that?'

'The Monksgrange bailiff. I don't know his name'.

'Village nonsense,' Lord Alain said, dismissively. 'Take no notice.'

'I didn't. I wouldn't have been prepared to stay here, otherwise.'

'Alone.' He handed her a piece of cheese on the point of his knife.

'Yes, my lord. Alone. Thank you. You went to Monksgrange, this morning?'

'As you knew I would.'

She looked away towards the open cave mouth. The horses stood to one side, resting contentedly together.

Lord Alain noted her glance. 'What did your father and mother say to you yesterday to make you bolt again?' he asked in a quiet voice. He took a crunch at an apple, and she thought his question sounded more like an enquiry after her health.

'It was not so much what *they* said as what *you* said.'

'That made you run? I thought you had courage.'

'Not courage enough to spend the rest of my life with you, my lord.'

He took another bite and spoke with his mouth full. 'Nevertheless, damoiselle, that is what you will do. With or without courage.'

'No, I think not.'

He continued, ignoring her retort, 'I'm surprised. I thought I'd made it clear to you in the arbour the day after your fall. I could have sworn you heard.'

'I *did* hear. And I was sure that you jested. I told you as much.'

'I never jest about such things. I explained that to you the other night in the arbour. You should have believed me, Marietta, it would have saved you a whole day.'

'You were wooing Emeline. You cannot deny that,' she said sharply.

'I can and do deny it! And if she thought I was, that's because she wanted to believe it. I came to see you, but you evaded me. Now I've caught you and it's no good thinking that I'll take pity on you and let you go, because I won't. It's time somebody took you in hand, lass.'

'And you're the one to do it, I suppose?'

'You've understood that, at least.'

'I do not want to be taken in hand, as you put it.'

'You responded to my hand very well, I seem to remember.'

The man, she thought, was goading her, damn him. And how ungallant to remind her of a time when she'd had more to drink than she was used to. During the day, she'd had plenty of time to reflect on her future and had even come close to thinking there might be just a few advantages in the arrangement, but his arrogance astounded her, his nearness made her uncomfortable. She looked around her. The cave was quite large, she knew, but now, all was black except for the entrance.

'It's no good looking, lass, I know what you're thinking, but you can forget it. I shall take you home tomorrow morning and there'll be a formal betrothal ceremony, just one day later than planned.'

'No!' Her voice echoed loudly inside the cave.

'Good. You can do all the shouting and yelling you like in here. Here, take a gulp of your water.' He passed her the bottle.

She took a deep swig and coughed as it stung her throat. 'Argh! That was mead, not water. . .!'

'Ah, then this must be the one. . .here.' He took a drink and passed it to her. 'Now, before it gets too dark to see what we're about. . .'

While she watched, sullenly, seething with resentment, he cleared away the remains of their meal, spread Marietta's blanket on the large flat shelf of rock and laid his own great cloak over it. Then he came to sit by her side, between her and the horses.

She felt his coolness, the male smell of leather, the brief warmth of his breath as he leaned his head to hers and took her hand. If only that was all there was to it, just his nearness, his arms, the warmth of him, she thought. She could bear that. But she would not be managed.

'We can talk now, Marietta. There's no one to hear

or interrupt. You can tell me what it is you fear, what your objections are.'

How could she voice them? 'You don't realise. . .do you?' she faltered.

'What is it that I don't realise?'

'What a position you've put me in. I did my best to oblige my mother and Emeline, and I thought I was pleasing my father, too.'

'By keeping out of my way, you mean?'

'Yes. Lady Alice had decided, long before I had a chance to—'

'To say what *you* wanted?'

'Yes,' she whispered, aware of how immodest that must sound. 'I heard them discussing it while they thought I was asleep and Lady Alice said then that she wanted you to woo Emeline. So when you did—'

'I didn't. I told you.'

'I can't believe that, my lord.' The words slipped out, inadvertently, but Lord Alain did not take offence.

'Can you not believe, Marietta, knowing what you've been able to discover about me so far, that I am perfectly capable of making my own mind up without help from anyone?'

She could believe it, of course, but what of the reasons for his choice? What of his first wife and her likeness to Emeline? Pure coincidence? She wanted to believe it, God knew she did, but could she? She kept silent.

'Am I right in thinking, Marietta, that you are used to fighting off all suitors, whoever they are?'

That was something she could not deny. 'Yes,' she whispered.

'So you would have hidden, run, evaded me, even if Lady Alice had *not* planned to pass you over. That's true, isn't it?'

'Yes, I would!' The whisper was more rebellious now.

'Why? You told me you feared to die your mother's death, Marietta.'

'Yes, she—'

'She died in a riding accident while she was carrying your brother, did she not? And your brother was delivered after her death, not as you told me.'

'You knew!' She leapt away, angry and ashamed that her major excuse had been exposed. It had been a perfect pretext. Now she could hide behind it no longer. 'Who told you? My father?'

Lord Alain kept hold of her and pulled her back to his side, placing his arms around her like a cage.

'Yes, your father. And now I begin to understand why you're so determined not to be caught. Not because you fear childbirth or that you care so much about Emeline's chances, or that you want to please your parents by staying in the background.

'Nor is it because you think I'm one of the usual weak-kneed youths who've tried their luck in the past. It's because the more they go on about it, the more you'll show them you don't care, isn't it? The more they put you to the gate, the more you'll refuse, just to show them who's in control. That kind of courage borders on pig-headedness, Marietta, because that way you'll get hurt when you find you want to jump and your pride won't let you.'

'You're talking as though I were a horse!' she said, severely.

He smiled. 'When we're married, you'll discover the reason for that.'

'I don't want. . .no. . .put me down! Put me *down*!'

'Yes, that's what I am doing. . .here. . .right here.' He lowered her down onto the blanket and cloak and unclasped her mantle with nimble fingers before she could tell what was happening.

It was dark and impossible to do more than push at his shoulders, but they were wide and powerful and she was scooped up against his warm body, held close in his arms with her head tucked beneath his chin and there was no escape, for a wall of rock was at her back. Before she could gather a new surge of energy, his mouth was against the bridge of her nose.

'Now, damoiselle, you've already discovered how good it feels when you let *me* take control, haven't you? Eh?'

'That was unfair. . .I'd had too much wine.'

'Not unfair. . .no. . .a good way to break the ice, but not for every time. This time, a mouthful of mead is all you get. Come,' he whispered, 'show me the impulsive woman I had in my arms last time. Show me again.'

She felt at his face with fingers and lips because she could not see him and when she reached his mouth, her hand slid around his neck into his thick hair, drawing him to her. 'Why?' she murmured. 'Why couldn't you leave me be? I don't want to go back with you. I don't want to be betrothed.'

'Too late. . .' he played with her lips '. . .too late. Your father and I have settled it. It's agreed. You're mine.'

'Then go and marry my father!'

'It's not your father I want in my bed, but you. I want you by my side, to be mistress of my household. I want you to bear my sons. You're mine, Marietta, mine.'

Punctuated by kisses, their whispered conversation was both savage and rebellious, spurring Marietta on to test his resolve and provoke him to fierce declarations of possession. His blatant determination to make her his roused her as nothing else could have done. No soft words or sweet sighs, few compliments except to say that she had fire, and beauty, and a remoteness that sent men wild.

But, he said, she'd better recognise her master now for he would have her, willing or no. And so they fought a verbal duel while surrendering to each other's arms and lips, closed in by the darkness and undisturbed by the proximity of any but the horses. Here, they could make as much noise as they liked.

No honeyed endearments passed their lips only 'my lord' and 'my lady' or 'lass' and 'brute', for he recognised that *that* set her apart from her half-sister more clearly than the soft pleadings Emeline would no doubt have preferred. New to lovemaking she may have been, but Marietta was eager and warm, and when 'my lord' pushed the bliaud over her shoulders to seek the softness of her skin, she did not complain of the cold but pulled his chainse out of his braies so that she could warm her hands on his back.

'Hell, woman, you learn fast how to keep a man awake. I've a mind to keep you awake a bit longer.'

'You can tell my father you've changed your mind because the woman keeps you awake with cold hands, and I'll tell him you pester me.'

'In that case, my lady, I'm going to pester you some more and make sure you get the story straight, because tomorrow *you*'re going to tell him that you're mine. Understand? Now, what's all this. . .?' His hand passed over the leather chausses she wore beneath her bliaud to protect her legs when she rode.

'My chausses. . .for riding in. And I'm not going to—'

'Take them off!'

'What?'

'Take them off. I want what's inside there.'

'No, you can't. . .please. . .' She pushed his hand away. 'I cannot allow it. . .please, don't ask me. . .'

'I'm not asking you. Listen to me. I know you're playing for time when you say you won't accept me, but you know that I mean to have you and that the consummation makes our betrothal legally binding.'

'*Afterwards*, my lord. Not before. Afterwards.'

'We'll do it the other way round, my lady. I'm not taking the risk. This is to bind you to me.' The fierce words were spoken gently into her ear, caressing her cheek with his lips. 'I'll be careful. . .I know it's new to you. . .we'll go slowly, I promise. . .don't fear me.'

She *was* fearful, and excited, and curious, and she knew that, in spite of her words of rejection, she would have him and he would have her. So she allowed him to draw the leather chausses off her legs and then she helped him off with his, and one by one their garments were placed behind her head as a warm pillow until they lay with only a cloak to cover them.

He kept his promise to go slowly, and skilfully his hands enticed her body to soften and bend to his touch while she came alive with a growing fire and moaned at him to do it, whatever it was he was bent on doing. She had expected that it might hurt, the first time, but he was tenderly careful and the expectation of pain was forgotten beneath his kisses and words.

He moved upon her, claiming her at last as he'd wanted to do since the day he had lifted her into his arms. For him, it was victory, sweet conquest, the beginning of his new life. For her, it was the tenderest submission and the end of her maidenhood. The fierce words were left behind now; this was too rare a moment to play down with ambiguities so easily misunderstood at the moment of receiving. Such a gift must be treasured at the first giving.

Marietta revelled in his loving words as much as in his fierce ones, savouring the strong urges of his body, knowing that her yearnings and conflicts had met and come to terms. She had never wanted loving from any man except this one; her tears were of joy, not of pain.

'Tears, sweetheart? Not tears? Did I. . .?'

'No, Alain, no, you didn't hurt. I'm not crying. . .'

'It will be better next time, I promise.'

She smiled and smoothed his cheek, wondering at

the size of him compared to herself, his ears, his handsome head, the thickness of his great arms. 'My tears are for what I've gained, I think, not for what I've lost. I didn't know I could feel such elation...but now...'

'Now? Now you think I'll expect you to change? To be submissive? Is that it?'

'Yes.' The word was no more than a breath on his throat.

She felt his smile and the heave of his chest beneath her hand.

'It may help to stop you bolting, sweetheart, but I don't have any high hopes that you'll suddenly become meek and mild. Stay as you are, my beauty. I want you to stay just as you are. We'll fight and make love in a hundred different ways and we'll stay together and make fierce sons and wild daughters, shall we?'

That was enough to make her laugh, wondering how she would react to the idea that any daughter—or son—of hers would make love for the first time in a mist-bound cave before the day of their betrothal.

'You like that idea, do you? Good. Then sleep in my arms, woman, and rest now. You've had quite a day, even for one such as you. And I need to regain my wind, ready for the next bout.' He smiled in the darkness.

Marietta lifted her head. 'What next bout?'

His arm tightened about her and he pulled her hips closer in to his body, tucking the cloak around her shoulders. 'I've got you to myself for the whole of the night, and I'm not going to waste it all in sleep,' he said.

CHAPTER FIVE

SOUNDS of young men's laughter, shouts, and the neighing of a horse broke into the more restful thud and clink of gardeners' spades in the soil, causing Marietta to turn to Old Adam with a puzzled expression. He was one of the few people whose names she was sure of in this great place.

'Tiltyard, m'lady,' he said, nodding towards the end of the garden and shoving his spade deep into the ground to rest on its handle. 'It's young squires over in't tiltyard practising wi'their lances. Have you not been to see, yet?'

'No, Adam. Not yet.' In just two days, she'd had no time to see much of Thorsgeld Castle for there'd been so many other things to claim her attention. A day seeing to the garden held the promise of some peace and a space in which to think, though this was not quite what she'd been expecting when Lord Alain had told her that there was a pleasance. It resembled a wilderness more than a lady's bower. 'Has no one tended this ground in the last two years, Adam?' she asked.

'Nay, m'lady. Nobody tended it much before then, either. T'other Lady Thorsgeld warn't that interested in gardens. She 'awked and she 'unted but she didn't do much in 'ere.' He carried on with his digging, heaving the sods to one side and loosening the weeds so that the two lads could pull them out.

'What about the herbs, then? Didn't she grow simples anywhere?'

Adam stood up again and shook his white head. His skin was like brown, crinkled leather, his grin punctuated by four yellow teeth. 'Nay,' he said again. 'She

94

had nothing to do with all that. She let cook grow pot-herbs round by the kitchen. Come on, I'll show thee.' Deciding that it was easier to show her than to explain, Adam led Marietta up an overgrown path and through the wicket-gate that hung to the broken fence by one hinge.

She had seen the top of the dovecote already but now she saw the rest of it, piled high with droppings and old feathers in the angle of the castle wall. Ahead of them were the stew-ponds where fish were kept for the table. They were dirty and littered with last year's dead leaves and weed. All of these plots lay between the western wall of the castle and the high stone wall that she had seen from her father's land across the valley.

Through the next hedge, wild and terribly over-grown, they rounded the corner of the castle wall where, on its north side, a long narrow strip of garden was given over to culinary herbs, for along here were the kitchens. It was better tended, but here were no simples for medicines, nothing for the relief of an ache or to salve a wound.

Old Adam pointed. 'Along 'ere, this is the only bit that's kept straight. An' that over there—' he pointed to the high wall that ran parallel to the castle '—that's the tiltyard where young Master Bruno is learning 'is tricks. Shall we 'ave a look?' he ventured.

A gateway led into the tiltyard from the field where the shooting butts were ranged, a large open space of dry earth where years of hooves and feet had worn tracks beneath the quintain and where a dozen or so young men practised their horsemanship by riding bareback with one hand on the reins. The horses were very large and not inclined to co-operate and one lad with blood streaming from his face was being yelled at by the mounted knight to get back on his bloody horse and be quick about it. Marietta backed away from the gateway, anxious not to interrupt, but Bruno had spotted her from one corner where he was practising with sword and shield and sidled away while the knight's back was turned.

'Marrie! Wait!' he hissed, slipping through the gate after her.

'Bruno! Don't, you'll get into trouble Go back, love.'

'It's all right. We haven't had a chance to talk since you came. Are you all right, love?'

His face was running with sweat, his tunic black-patched and sticking to his body. There was a new bruise on his cheek, but his eyes were gleaming with enjoyment. She noticed that the sword he held was almost as long as he. 'Yes, I'm looking at the gardens. Adam's started to dig it over but it's in a dreadful state, like a lot of other things around here.'

'It needs your hand on it, Marrie. He's been without a lady for two years now and it shows, doesn't it? Little things, eh?' Even in a male domain, the hand of a woman was appreciated. 'Is he being kind to you, Marrie?'

'Oh yes. . .yes, he is, love. But I haven't seen much of him, except after supper. I expect he's busy at this time of the year.'

She had indeed seen much of him at night, for their few hours together in the cave almost a month ago had been in total darkness and he had been as eager to see her naked as she had been to see him. He had been kind, though not perhaps in a way that many new brides would have found to their taste.

She smiled, thinking of their turbulent lovemaking when her feigned reluctance had been once more overcome by his persistence, a game in which rules were made and broken simultaneously. He *had* been kind, recognising her strong will and matching it without arousing her resentment, making his firm hand feel more like protection than tyranny. He had not allowed her to regret her capitulation. Yes, in that he had been kind.

'Well, I'm glad he's kind to somebody.' Bruno laughed. 'It's more than he is to us, I can tell you. He's fearsome if you step out of line.'

'Have you been in trouble, love?'

'Oh not specially. Course, they all want to have a go at me, now they know you're my sister, just to see if I can take it without squealing.'

The concern in her voice showed. 'And can you?'

'Can I? I love it!' He laughed merrily. 'I can beat the lot of 'em. The more I get chance to prove it, the more they'll respect me. I'll make you proud of me, Marrie. You'll see.'

'I'll watch for you, love. Take care, do. Go now, before they come looking. Hurry. . .!'

With a quick grin, he blew her a kiss and was gone.

From the field where the shooting butts stood, Marietta could look up at the high walls of Thorsgeld Castle and be as impressed all over again as she had at her first sight of it. It was an immense square stone building of four towers, built around a courtyard; not a castle built primarily to defend the king's land but more of a fortified manor house on a scale large enough to withstand a raid from the Scots, or a siege. Set on the very edge of a wooded cliff, the views from the western upper rooms were superb.

Managing a place like this was going to take all the skills she'd ever learned, and then some more. For one thing, this was a far more male-dominated household than she'd been used to; apart from the dairy and laundry maids and her own personal women, all the other occupants were men and boys. Married men at the castle kept their wives at home in the town of Thorsgeld, where conditions were more suited to family life.

Since the quiet wedding two days ago, she had kept

well out of the way, pretending to be too busy to go anywhere with him, holding herself back and nourishing her resentment at the coercion they'd all applied. It was sheer pig-headedness, as Lord Alain had warned her, and served only to exacerbate her feelings of isolation and strangeness.

Secretly, she longed for the night and the strength of his arms where she could find solace in this great fortress where the walls rose to five storeys above her. Secretly, she longed for his arms at any time, day or night.

The sun streamed onto that side of the castle, catching the fly-covered surface of the stew-pond and making it glisten like satin. Marietta looked again at the filthy dovecote; this place could be made so very pretty, but it would need an army. She leaned into an angle of the warm wall and closed her eyes, holding her face to the sun, absorbing its kindness, undisturbed by the sound of the rickety gate being moved aside. Old Adam with his wheelbarrow, she thought.

'Time's up!'

She opened her eyes with a start, unused to having her thoughts materialise so promptly.

Lord Alain stood before her with hands on hips, his eyes watchful and serious. 'Time's up, sweetheart. Come on, now. You've been too busy to keep me company for long enough. You've made your point and I've understood. Now you can be seen with me without losing face, proud lass.' His quiet words unnerved her far more than bawling at her would have done, speaking her thoughts so accurately that she wondered if she'd voiced them out loud.

There was no need for her to deny or accept his assessment of the situation, for his arms were held out to her and she walked into them and stood quietly, feeling his hands smooth over her back from shoulder to buttock, his mouth on her forehead.

'That pride of yours is going to cause a nasty fall one of these days, my lass,' he whispered. 'When are you going to let it go? Is it only in bed you lose it. . .in the dark. . .where it can't find a hold? Am I going to have to knead it out of you in the daytime, too? Eh?'

Her reaction to his graphic words was immediate, coinciding exactly with his move to hold her into the wall and kiss her. She raised her arms and linked them around his neck, greedily taking his lips and the close male warmth of his skin on her face. Here, she could close her eyes to the unwanted challenge of overgrown surroundings and imagine that she was elsewhere, with only sensations and desires to attend to.

'Come on, then,' he said, looking down at her. 'Shall we share the rest of the day with each other?'

'Yes,' she replied.

'Good. So, is there something you want to show me?'

Now was her chance. She could not let it go. Taking his offered hand she led him towards the stew-pond, a very large one on three levels in a desolate area of long grass and weeds. 'Look,' she said, 'this could provide quantities of fish for your tables—'

'*Our* tables,' he corrected her.

'Our tables. But the channels and pipes are silted up and it needs men to repair and restock it. In fact . . .' she pulled his hand round to turn him '. . . the whole place needs an army of men. It needs cutting and re-seeding, the walls whitewashed, the hedge and gate repaired and the dovecote. . .look at that!' She pointed to the rotten wooden structure. 'That needs replacing. We need a stone dovecote so that the men can get at the manure, and the eggs, and the pigeons.'

'I only use them to feed the falcons,' he said.

'Well, we should be eating them,' she told him. 'This is a terrible waste; it could be such a lovely place. I could grow ferns round there and have water flowing in channels. I could make a paradise, like the ones they have in monasteries.'

'Queen Phillipa has a paradise in Winchester, I believe.'

'But I need men, my lord. It will take weeks of work.' She led him through the fallen wicket-gate into what should have been a lady's private garden, a pleasance, but which now showed only the recent efforts of Old Adam and two lads. 'Look at this place, there should be herb-gardens here where I can grow my simples, and an arbour, perhaps. Do you think so?'

It was an L-shaped plot, taking in the corner of the southwest tower and now bathed in sunshine, sheltered by the high walls but with a view through the battlements out across the valley. A paradise indeed, but sadly neglected.

Lord Alain was almost glad that it was in this state for it would give her a new objective and soften the sting of her hasty removal from Monksgrange. Keeping hold of her hand, he entered fully into her enthusiasm.

'Over there—' he pointed to the wall '—that's where an arbour should go, so that you can sit on a raised bench inside, out of the heat, and look through the leaves and the crenels of the wall over towards Monksgrange. Do you see that tiny black spot on the fell there? Do you see it?'

'Yes,' she yelped. 'Yes, I can see the cave. That's it, isn't it?'

'Yes, lass . . .' he lowered her down, allowing his hands to linger purposely over her breasts. '. . . that's where we spent our first night together. There, in that cave. In the mist. One month ago.' He held her, laughing at her blushes. 'How many times did I have you before I took you back to your father? Enough to make you change your mind?'

'That was a totally unscrupulous deed, my lord!'

Marietta feigned anger and pushed at his chest, quite ineffectually.

'Hah! Unscrupulous, my foot!' he laughed. 'You went into the cave, shooed your stupid horse away and waited for me. You know you did. You knew I'd come looking for you. . .you knew what I'd do. . .!'

'Oh, you ungodly oaf! How *can* you think that? I was a maiden. . .an innocent maiden, and you seduced me intentionally.'

'Aye, that I did, wench. Rest easy. . .don't be angry. It was the perfect chance. . .I had to make sure of you.' Hungrily, he sought her lips again, oblivious to Old Adam who came and went with silent tread. 'Have you forgiven me for taking advantage of you?' he whispered.

Marietta prolonged the act of absolution. 'It will cost you a garden, my lord, at least.'

'A garden, two, three, a dozen gardens, sweetheart,' he promised. 'I'll set men to it tomorrow morning, as many as you need. We'll have new hedges, little fences, herb-plots, an arbour, whatever you wish shall be done. And we'll have a new dovecote made and paths laid, and clean well-stocked fish-ponds. And then, you'll forgive me, will you?'

She smiled at his boyish eagerness. 'Yes, my lord. Then I will forgive you.'

Hand in hand, they walked on through the orchard, discussing how that, too, could be tidied and the bee-skeps attended to, then back through the gardens, seeing it all in their imaginations as a place of sanctuary, pretty with roses, honeysuckle and ivy, trim with box-hedges and lavender clumps, scented with blossom and heavy with bees and butterflies.

Marietta had seen no further than this; what lay on the rest of the southern side she had yet to discover. She had not realised that the stables on the ground floor of the castle were only for their immediate purposes, neither had she fully understood that when Bruno had told her that Lord Alain bred horses, he meant it on a scale like this.

Through heavy and high wooden gates, a huge courtyard opened up opposite the orchard, with a long stone-built stable block along one side. Storehouses, a well, water troughs and a mews ranged around the high wall and elegant heads of expensive palfreys and destriers arched over stable-doors, whinnying their greetings as Lord Alain entered. Immediately, a small wiry man came to meet them, bowing courteously.

'Greetings, Seth.' Lord Alain explained, 'Seth is my Horse Master, and he agrees with me that that grey mare of yours is as daft as a brush and should be used for breeding. So, if you can bear to part with her, we've found something more suitable.'

Seth grinned at her. He could not be old, she thought, for his body was lean and muscles rippled over his bare arms, his face well-used looking, like a walnut, almost. 'I think you'll like this'un better, my lady. Well-mannered, she is. A beauty.' He called to a groom crossing the yard. 'Bring the grey out, Ned.'

It would have been an understatement to say that Marietta was surprised at this; it was a part of Lord Alain's business affairs of which he'd said nothing to her.

He saw her amazement. 'These are only a few,' he said, indicating the row of curious heads and the occasional crash of a hoof against a door. 'Mostly stallions we're using. There are ten mares and foals in the paddock over there, and another ten further on...' he nodded towards a field beyond the orchard '...then some more on the other side.'

'I had no idea. Do you breed *and* sell them, my lord?'

'Yes, men will always want destriers and there's nobody around these parts who breeds them, except me. Palfreys, too, for ladies. We have a stud of about twenty mares and four stallions and then we have young stallions that we train as war-horses. Ah, here's your new mare, Marietta. Come and meet her.'

The young groom led the mare out, watching her legs move at his side in a quick tap-tap, the lovely dark muzzle almost touching her knees as they high-stepped towards the group. She was, as Seth had said, a beauty, larger than Dulzelina, pure white except for her amazingly luxuriant dark mane and tail that rippled in pronounced waves as though they'd been crimped.

Marietta's long "Ooh!" was as much as she could say at that moment, quite overcome by the mare's exceptional beauty and by the revelation that her new husband was not the leisured aristocrat she had thought him to be but a man of business, a breeder of war-horses, fabulously costly animals, specially trained for knights in battle. Now she understood his reputation as an expert at jousting; he must have won a fair number of stallions from his opponents.

'She's a Spanish horse,' Lord Alain told her, stroking the mare's soft velvet muzzle and collecting her forelock in his hand. It came well over her dark eyes and was as silky as a woman's hair. 'From Andalucia. You like her?'

'She's superb,' Marietta breathed, 'simply superb. Is she fast, my lord?'

'No, Spanish horses are not known for their speed but for their high showy action and their great strength and good manners. She's quite a fiery piece, but good mannered, and obedient.' He glanced at her wickedly, his eyes dancing with hidden meaning. 'And she has the most amazing canter. Did you ever ride a rocking horse, Marietta?'

'Yes, I had one when I was tiny, until Bruno broke it.'

'Well, riding this at a canter is like that, only faster.
You'll see; we'll take her out tomorrow, shall we?'

'Yes, oh yes, can we. . .tomorrow?' She fondled the
muzzle and ran a hand over the neck and ears. 'Thank
you, my lord. She's the most beautiful thing. How old?
What's her name?'

'Five years old. She's had one foal, a filly. And we
have a stable name for her, but she's yours now,
sweetheart. You can name her yourself.'

Impishly, Marietta slipped a hand into his. 'What
about Mist?' she said, peeping up at him.

He took her hand and kissed the knuckles, sharing
her mischief. 'I think, m'lady, that Mist would be a
perfect name, in the circumstances.'

They watched the mare trot around the courtyard,
lifting her knees daintily and arching her beautiful
neck, the long mane and tail flowing like silken veils.
In their boxes, the stallions pricked up their ears and
whinnied to her, flaring their nostrils, asking for their
fair share of the attention, and Marietta was introduced
to them, one by one.

It was then that many of Lord Alain's previous
remarks began to fall into place, his teasing about her
bolting, her refusal to jump to anyone's command, her
riding for a fall. As a breeder of horses, he was bound
to think along those lines, she supposed, watching the
way he handled the great creatures so assuredly, and
she was unable to suppress a shiver of excitement at
the thought of the night to come when, he'd whispered
to her, she'd be able to thank him more profoundly.

Marietta's own private solar was in the southwest
tower, overlooking the very garden she intended to
restore. It was a large whitewashed room with a stone
fireplace and high timber ceiling and windows on two
sides. Tapestries lined the walls, filling the room with
colourful people and galloping horses, stags, hounds,

even rabbits, a scene depicting, by all accounts, the previous Lady Thorsgeld's favourite pastime, hunting. She asked Lord Alain about it after supper, but he was not eager to discuss his first wife.

'Yes,' he said, drawing Marietta down beside him on the deep cushioned window-seat, 'there's a deer-park that stretches northwards from here; some very good hunting country. Does Sir Henry hunt much?'

'He loves it,' she replied, putting her feet up on the cushions and leaning back against his chest, 'but we're not too familiar with this area yet.'

'What about Beckington Manor, then, sweetheart? Your new property—it borders on my demesne between here and Monksgrange. Have you never seen it? You ought to, you know.'

'No, I've never even thought about it until recently. I think Father was quite content to have the rents from it each Michaelmas and leave it at that. Apart from being determined not to let Sir Nicholas get hold of it.'

'Sir Nicholas Bannon? How could he get hold of it? I thought it passed down the female line.'

'It does, but Father said that, if he got hold of it, there'd be nothing left of it in two years.'

'Well,' he kissed her neck, 'that's very interesting, but I fail to see how he could get near it, unless he married one of you. And he's too late to do that, isn't he, lass?' His arm was firmly across her ribs.

'Silly. Uncles and nieces don't marry.'

'He was coming on very strong with you in the passageway that evening, though, wasn't he? Had he tried it on with you before?'

'No,' Marietta turned her head to him, piling on the scorn, 'of course not with *me*. It's always been Emeline he had an eye for.'

'You mean, Emeline and he are. . .?'

'No! Heaven's above, no. Not that. But she's always done whatever he told her, ever since she was a child.'

'Mmm. . .!' The memory was still clear in his mind. He had been at Monksgrange on the morning after the Wardles' arrival, hoping to meet Marietta again as the solar door had opened. Instead of that, Sir Nicholas had escorted Emeline. Saints, how the lass had simpered! And that dress! Had Sir Nicholas had something to do with that, perhaps? Sir Henry had apparently been ill at ease and puzzled by the girl's silliness. Still, no matter, it had been this one he'd wanted to see. But how much did the manor of Beckington mean to Lady Alice's brother? he wondered.

Had he pressurised Lady Alice into pushing Emeline to fill the first Lady Thorsgeld's shoes? God forbid! 'Shall we go and have a look at your property tomorrow, Marietta? Would you like that?' he whispered into her neck.

She loved the way his forelock tickled her nose. 'Tomorrow,' she reminded him, 'you are going to organise my team of gardeners and take my new Mist out. Remember?'

'Tomorrow, I shall send for my steward and you shall tell him exactly what it is you want, draw plans for him, take him down to the plots and say what must be done. And he will obey every order, I promise. Then, sweetheart,' he began to remove the veil from beneath her coils of hair, 'then we shall visit your new manor on your new mare, for which you are about to thank me in great detail, are you not?' He unbraided one plait, shook out the hair over her shoulder and began on the other one. 'Yes?' he said.

'Yes,' she whispered.

It was wellnigh impossible for her to maintain her former ill will in the face of such opposition; even the glorious sunshine dissolved any remnants that might have lurked at the back of her mind, washed away on the memory of last night's loving in the guise of showing thanks.

It was impossible to say, she mused, who was the giver and who the receiver, for the exchange had been remarkably equal; about that, she was unable to pretend. He had introduced her to a new way of expressing herself and it was like the beginning of a new adventure with unknown excitements waiting to be revealed, with herself as participant and storyteller combined.

Her new mare was all that he'd said it would be, a far cry from Dulzelina's unpredictability and the most comfortable ride she'd ever experienced, the trot smooth and exhilarating, the canter somewhere between a prance and a rocking motion, wonderfully showy and a sure focus of everyone's attention.

But it was not only the beautiful white mare with the dark mane and tail that they watched. Marietta, eager to do justice to the occasion, had dressed with care in a yellowy-cream cote-hardie and deep gold surcoat edged with lynx fur, a full-skirted outfit that complemented the horse's colour perfectly. Her long veil streamed behind her, attached to the back of her head beneath a double row of horizontal plaits and leaving her smooth crown adorned only by her plain gold circlet.

She was not aware that it was she who turned the men's heads more than the horse, or that her beauty alone was the cause of their undisguised stares. Trust their lord to find such a one, they commented, he had an eye for the loveliest creatures, though he'd had them all fooled for a week or two.

Well, if she'd been purposely eluding him, she'd have stood no chance against his persistence, for some of them had been waiting at Monksgrange when he brought her down from the hill that morning. There'd been no doubt about which one he was after after that.

'Where is this place, my lord?' Marietta called, keeping her mare alongside the bay stallion. 'Is it far?'

'Beckington? No, midway between Monksgrange and Thorsgeld. But you don't see it from the track, it's way behind that outcrop of limestone, between my deer-park and the river. See...?' He pointed as they cantered down towards the white limestone boulders where the soil was thin. The narrow valley between crag and forest held the distinct marks of a track, and sheep and lambs scattered at the sound of their hoofbeats.

'Plenty of signs of coming and going,' he remarked. 'Looks as though your father's bailiff kept a close eye on things.'

'Not the Upperfell bailiff,' Marietta replied. 'Too far for more than once a year, I know that for certain. Perhaps the new one at Monksgrange has paid them a bit more attention since my father took him on.'

'Well, somebody certainly has.' He pointed to the imprint of hooves in the hardened mud. 'Who are the tenants?'

They slowed to a walk as the track narrowed between hillocks. 'An old couple, John and Betty Fuller. They've been there since before Lady Alice married my father. I think she would rather it had passed to one of her own daughters than me.'

He made no answer to that. It would have made no difference to his decision who it had passed to, though he knew Marietta still had a hard time convincing herself that flighty Emeline was not every man's desire. 'Ah, here we are. Look through the trees. Can you see?'

It was well hidden against the crags in a grove of beeches and oaks, an elegant three-story house in which the undercroft was used for storage, and stone steps rose diagonally across the outer wall to the first floor. As they drew nearer, however, they noted how the moss and house-leeks on the roof barely hid broken tiles, how the place was in dire need of attention and how nobody had even noticed their approach.

Lord Alain's bailiff rode ahead of them and round the back of the building towards outhouses and a stable-yard, calling for the occupants, and while he scoured the tumbledown site for a sign of life, Marietta was lifted down and led up the steps to the battered old door.

It was not what either of them had expected, not the neat solar with table and stools and tapestried walls of most manor houses, with rushes on the floor and the welcome of homely faces, of hounds, of cooking smells. Smells there were, but of the kind to wrinkle the nose, and faces, too, but wizened, staring-eyed and mortally afraid.

Two old people cowered away from the door as far as it was possible to cringe, the old man holding his hands across his wife as though protecting her, shaking his head at the speechless group who entered his room, then frowning with uncertainty at the sight of Marietta with them.

Marietta went forward, holding out a hand in friendship. 'John?' she said. 'John Fuller? Betty? Is that Betty there behind you?'

The old man lowered his hands and turned briefly to look behind him, as though warning her not to move until he was sure. 'Aye,' he croaked. 'John Fuller, m'lady.'

'You won't remember me, Marietta Wardle. Sir Henry's daughter.'

His eyes widened and the woman made a move, ready to emerge, but she was held back. 'Wardle? Sir Henry? Are ye sure?'

It was the most absurd question, Marietta thought, but in the circumstances it had the required effect, for the smile it provoked did more than any words to assure him of their safety.

'Come,' she said, laying a hand on his shaking arm. 'Come and meet my husband, Lord Alain of Thorsgeld. He's a neighbour of yours, you know. Come. You, too, Betty.'

Now convinced that they were in no danger, they came forward to make a bow and a courtesy; in the light from the unglazed window, the guests were able to see that they were indeed old and bent with the rheum, gnarled and hollow-eyed and only just recovering from a terrible fright. Their clothes were little more than rags and covered with old stains, and John's hair was unkempt and spidery-thin. Betty wore a wimple, but neither that nor her apron had been laundered recently. A commotion from outside caused them both to stagger across the room towards the door where a young girl was being thrust forward by the bailiff's strong hands.

'In the dairy round the back, my lord. She's a half-wit. And they've just lost their pail o' milk cos she's just thrown it at me. Good job it missed,' he finished, laconically.

'Oh, no! Not the milk. . .' Old Betty ran to the stupefied girl and dragged her into the room. 'Now what? Come, lass. They won't harm you. Come on.' She drew her daughter away from the men and into the room.

The girl, pretty but very bedraggled, was probably about fourteen and clearly as afraid as her parents. Marietta could not imagine what could have caused this reaction in them; surely her father was not aware of this state of affairs.

The same thing must have been on Lord Alain's mind. 'How long since the bailiff was here, old man?' he said.

Old Betty piped up, 'He was here—' but her husband grabbed her arm to shut her up and answered with a question of his own.

'Beg pardon, m'lord, d'ye mean Sir Henry's bailiff?'

'Of course I do, man. What other bailiff would visit? When was he last here?'

'Michaelmas, m'lord. For the rents.'

'He didn't come on Lady Day?' the bailiff asked; that would have been only twice a year, September and March, the least the man could have done.

'No, sir. Onny once.'

Lord Alain walked around the room, frowning and moving the squeaking shutters, noting the lack of food and furniture. 'Then what is it that terrifies you so, John? Have you suffered from thieves?'

Again, they noted the quick glance at his wife, a quelling look before he answered, a trifle too eagerly, 'Ah, yes, m'lord, yes, thieves. They took just about all our cattle. Left us hardly any food.'

'And horses? Took your horses, too, did they?'

'Ah, we didn't have no 'orses, m'lord. Me an' Betty an' the lass have two donkeys and two oxen and a cow. But no 'orses.'

Lord Alain and his bailiff shared a significant glance. 'Stay here, Marietta, if you will,' Alain said, 'while I go outside and take a look round. Explain to them what's happened.'

The old man looked anxiously from Lord Alain to the bailiff and back again. 'Nay, m'lord, there's nothing out there. Only empty sheds. . .'

But the bailiff steered him back into the room and followed his master outside. Marietta dusted off a rickety stool and sat.

'Come, Betty. Bring John and your daughter over here, I have some news for you.'

In the dim solar that stank of refuse-soiled rushes and mice droppings, Marietta told them how the estate had now become her property and how, from now on, Lord Alain's bailiff would be keeping an eye on them. She had not been prepared for the relief by the old people who were hardly able to speak for tears, and while they struggled to contain themselves before their new mistress, the young girl looked steadfastly at Marietta without blinking.

'Are you like *'er*?' she whispered. Her tone was flat and unemotional.

'Her?' Marietta queried, gently. 'Who?'

'Lady. . .Thorsgeld. '

'I am Lady. . .ah! You mean the last one. Er, I don't know. I never saw her.' Marietta glanced towards the door. 'Did you know her?'

Once again, the budding conversation was cut off by John. 'No, m'lady. It's first time we've seen Lord Thorsgeld. We've been neighbours long enough, but we've never met till now. 'E's a fine-lookin' chap, though, in't he, Betty? A right grand-lookin' chap. Breeds some grand 'orses. . .'

'How do you know that?' Marietta asked, sharply. If he had as little to do with Lord Alain as he made out, how had he seen the horses?

'Oh. . . I 'eard.' John clapped a hand on his bony knee. 'Everybody around here's seen 'is 'orses. They all say what grand ones they are.'

Marietta was convinced that this was not what John Fuller meant, but there was no pause before the girl spoke again as though she had not been interrupted. 'Yes. I knew 'er, I did. I knew 'er.'

Betty stood up, wincing with pain. 'Shut up, Milly, do.' She turned to her guest. 'She didn't know her. Never seen her. It's good news that this place is yours now, m'lady. Good news. There's a lot wants doin' that we can't afford to do. Our workers all went, you know. Didn't your father tell you? Oh, aye. . .' she went on, taking Marietta's blank expression as a sign of ignorance '. . . John couldn't get them to work on the demesne so we've just had to let it go. That's why things are in such a mess.'

'But why were you so afraid when we came?'

'Robbers!' John said, sharply, before his wife could answer.

'Aye, robbers,' Betty repeated. 'Took everything. Beat us up once.'

'Do you have a garden?' Marietta enquired, desperate to get out of the stinking room. The girl's eyes had not left her face for one second.

'A small one, m'lady. Nothing grand. Nay, you don't want to see it, do you? It's only a little one. Not for a lady to see.'

'I love gardens, Betty. I have one, too. Will you show me?'

Surrounded by high nettles, willow-herb and cow-parsley, the garden was only discernible by the level of its plants being lower than those of all the others, except for a few heads of cabbages which might have been mistaken for small trees. To one side, where the sunlight peeped through a gap in the trees, Marietta recognised the waving plumes of fennel and lovage, and the mauve pom-poms of chives. 'Herbs,' she said.

'Aye, those are pot-herbs, and my simples are over there.' Betty pointed to one side. No one would have known; they ran into each other. Marietta tried to recognise them. 'Feverfew, vervain, hyssop. . .'

'I know them. . .' Milly spoke quietly behind her.

'Shut up, Milly. No, she doesn't, m'lady. It's me what does the simples, not 'er She knows nothing.'

'Then I think we shall have to put our heads together, Betty. I'm only just putting my plot to rights and I shall be looking for seeds and cuttings. Can I come to you for help?'

'Aye, that you can. Take anything you please. There's balm over there, look.' She pointed to a pale green thriving plant.

'That's mint, Mother,' Milly said in the same flat voice.

Marietta smiled. 'Difficult to tell apart, aren't they? Even when they flower.' She tried to be diplomatic but privately wondered how much Milly knew that her mother insisted that she didn't. Or how many times Betty had drunk the wrong infusion or administered the wrong salve if she was so easily confused. 'I'll do what I can to make life a bit easier for you, Betty,' she said. 'I'd no idea my father had neglected Beckington so. My mother should have made an effort to look after you, but we've lived so far away, you know. Monksgrange is the furthest we've ever been down the dale.'

'Monks. . .? What. . .?' Betty's mouth made a hollow cavern of astonishment, for her lips had long since disappeared. 'Monksgrange?' she repeated.

'Yes, did I forget to mention that? My father bought it from the priory at Bolton and he'll be there until September, at least.'

Suddenly, Betty's hand was clasped tightly across her mouth and, as she caught the sound of her husband joining them, blurted out, ' John. . . John, Sir 'Enry's bought Monksgrange, John, just think, we'll be. . .!'

'Stop your shouting, woman!' he frowned at her impatiently. 'She gets so worked up,' he explained. 'It's because we don't see anybody.'

Growing more and more perplexed by these strange people, Marietta was glad to see Lord Alain and the others come round from the back of the building to meet them. It had taken only a glance to see that the building needed much attention and that John and Betty were far too old and incapable of managing such a place alone.

She could not get away fast enough. 'We *must* try to do something about it,' she said, looking back barely out of their hearing. 'I'd no idea it was in such a state. Could we send them some supplies, do you think?'

'Aye, lass. I think we'll have to keep an eye on them

or the next puff of wind might blow them away. A good thing we went, I think.'

'What did you see at the back? Anything?'

'A lot of milk all over the floor, but no supplies to speak of. Something else interesting, though. Horse-dung.'

'Horse-dung? That's interesting?'

'For someone who says he has no horses, very.'

CHAPTER SIX

MARIETTA could not help but wonder, every now and then, how Lord Alain would have managed if he *had* married Emeline, after all. There were, of course, dozens of well-trained men-servants for every department, efficient men under the sharp eye of the chamberlain, the second steward and the marshal, the butler, the cook and the constable. But, as Bruno had been quick to notice, it needed a woman's touch.

During the week that followed, Marietta was kept busy from morn till night finding out how things worked and exactly who was responsible for what. If she found it hard going, Emeline would have found it impossible.

The castle was built to be self-sufficient. Ranged around an inner courtyard were stores, granary and malting-house, bake and brew-houses, a horse-mill for grinding corn, a forge and armoury and rooms for soldiers. It took Marietta many miles of extra walking, upwards and downwards, to find her way round the four sides, for there were five levels.

The first floor held the great hall, the kitchens and guest rooms, the second floor was well above the noise and held the large chapel and the chaplain's rooms, the bailiff's chamber, retainers' hall and various solars for the lord, his lady and their servants. Spiral staircases were let into the thickness of the wall, and passageways were maddeningly deceptive, leading to garderobes or to anterooms or to somewhere Marietta didn't want to be at all. The place was trickier than a maze.

The household of men, far from resenting her interference in their domain, actually vied with each other to show her what they did, and where, and with whom.

On each day, Marietta made a point of inviting one of the household officials to sit with her and to talk about himself so that she could get to know them better.

In this way, by careful observation and by listening, she discovered as much about the former Lady Thorsgeld and what she had *not* done than by asking what she had. Strangely enough, it appeared that she had taken as little interest in the management of things indoors as she had out of doors, making Marietta wonder how she had occupied her days when she had not been hunting or hawking.

With the restorations of the gardens well under way, she began to see how it would look when stocked with plants. Already the plots had been dug over and manured, paths laid with stone slabs, edges and raised areas built up, gates and walls restored and turf laid flat and lusciously green.

Old Adam now had an army of men at his command, working them from early until late while the good weather held. Marietta spent as much time as she could spare, making lists of plants she needed and talking to the cook and the steward about which fish to buy to stock the clean stew-ponds.

While she made headway with this venture, she was every bit as concerned to renovate Beckington Manor, too, for the pathetic plight of John and Betty Fuller was constantly on her mind, and the strange girl who seemed to want to say more than either of her parents would allow. Marietta broached the subject the day after their visit to be told that it would be looked into, shortly. But two days later, when she asked if shortly had arrived, Lord Alain frowned with impatience.

'Hold hard, girl. You're doing the gardens at the moment, and you have your hands full with organising things in here. Enough for the time being, I think. I can't spare more men to work at Beckington.'

'They could leave the garden then, couldn't they? I

can't bear the thought of those three living half-scared out of their wits by thieves, and in that squalor.'

'No, the garden will be done first. They've lived like that for years, sweetheart, they'll not come to any harm over another few weeks.' He saw her disappointment.

'Weeks? Alain, when we visited them, you said. . .'

'Enough! Beckington will take its turn. Now, tell me if we're ready to invite guests to stay, m'lady, if you please.'

Marietta turned away without replying. If she had her hands as full as all that, they were too full to receive guests.

He took her arm and led her towards the window where the light fell full on her face. 'Marietta,' he said, 'guests will keep you company while I'm away.'

That did the trick. Her expression changed from one of vexation to one of surprise. 'You're going away? Why?'

Lord Alain smiled and laid his arms loosely across her shoulders, amused by her reaction. 'Now that's an improvement, my girl. Only a month ago you'd have said good. Now you're saying why.' He lured a smile into her eyes. 'That's better. You care, don't you?'

'No.' She tried to pull the smile back into line but it wobbled. 'I don't care, my lord. But why do you go so soon?'

Laughing at her perversity, he slid a finger around her chin, lingering over its smoothness. 'Business, sweetheart. I go to York for a few days next week, that's all. Why not send an invitation to Monksgrange and have your family stay here to keep you company? Would you like that?'

'Yes, my lord, I would like that. Do you mean all of them?'

'As many of them as you like, love. There's room enough.' It was true; the whole of Monksgrange could be swallowed up in Thorsgeld in one gulp.

'Could I not go to York with you? I've never been.'

'Another time. Will your garden be finished by the time I return? We have something to celebrate when it's complete, remember.'

She took the hand that caressed her chin and rubbed her cheek along the knuckles and, moving them under her lips, bit softly into them, drawing a huff of laughter from him. 'No,' she said. 'I do not remember,' she murmured.

His hands slipped beneath her arms like two crutches as he kissed her. 'No matter,' he whispered. 'I shall take pleasure in reminding you.'

Aye, she thought, watching the heavy studded door close behind him, you could make a woman do most things if you willed it, I dare say. With her, he was not always gentle but then, neither was she with him. He was, however, intent on obedience.

Trying to push the sad spectacle of John and Betty Fuller out of her more immediate thoughts, she sent a message to Monksgrange that day, charging Bruno to return with all speed so that she could begin preparations.

He was back before dark. 'Father's too busy and Lady Alice doesn't want to leave him, but Emeline and Iveta want to come. How does that suit you?' Bruno gave his sister a hug, a familiar gesture he would not have chanced if Lord Alain had been there. He was ruddy and breathless from the ride.

'Only Emeline and Iveta? Not Father, too?'

Bruno understood her fears. 'It's all right, love, she'll have got over her anger by the time she gets here. She looked excited enough by the idea, already. Surely you don't think she'll bear a grudge any longer, do you?'

'She wouldn't speak to me.' Marietta swirled one finger into a mass of rosary beads lying on her prayer book, listening to their soft rattle. 'That's why I didn't want to have a big celebration at the betrothal or the

wedding. It would have looked like rubbing salt into
her wounds, wouldn't it?'

Bruno took her hand and swung it out wide. 'Marrie,'
he said, 'you can't organise everything you do, or don't
do, around what Emeline will think, you know. I should
think you have your work cut out simply pleasing Lord
Alain, don't you? And he's more important than family
now, isn't he?'

She nodded.

'Well, then, just welcome her as though nothing had
happened. Once she sees those lads out there falling
over themselves to get her attention, she'll be in
heaven. You'll see.'

His breezy good nature lifted her introspection
towards the possibility that she might indeed be doing
Emeline a favour and that the absence of her father
and mother might, for once, be a good thing. Bruno
was right, of course; he knew how Emeline would
exchange her disappointment for the adulation of so
many young men all eager to impress. She would not
bear a grudge.

As though to put right all the wrongs of the past weeks,
imagined or real, Marietta set about making her half-
sisters' visit one that would highlight the advantages of
being free rather than married in a man's stronghold in
the few days available to her before Lord Alain's
departure for York.

She had the largest guest room cleaned and the bed
re-hung with another brighter set of curtains, matching
bed-cover and cushions, fresh rushes laid everywhere,
sweet-scented logs for the evening fire, bowls of herbs
to perfume the air and best beeswax candles in the
sconces. Extra maids were briefed, for she knew how
Emeline loved to be tended, and two great mirrors
were brought in to stand on the floor by the windows.

'Take them hawking one day,' Lord Alain suggested.

'You can take any of the falcons except mine. But don't let Emeline on your new palfrey; she's nowhere near as good a horsewoman as you. Let Seth find a horse each for them.' He hitched his purse-belt down over his hips and stood with fingers splayed over the leather—his most usual pose.

He was about to go, and Marietta wanted to delay him, to challenge him, anything to stop him walking away from her calmly, thinking of what was ahead instead of what he left behind. In her innocence, she said the wrong thing. 'I'll be able to go to Beckington while you're away and get some plants for my garden.'

It was not to be the light-hearted delay she had intended. 'You will not visit Beckington without me, Marietta. Is that understood?' he answered, unsmiling. 'Wait till I return.'

'It is my property, my lord. Surely I'm allowed to—'

'You want me to put you under house arrest, do you?'

'No.' This was particularly high-handed talk, she thought.

'Then obey me, woman. Beckington is out of bounds.'

His tone riled her, adding to her annoyance that what had been meant as a delaying tease had now become an issue in a clash of wills.

'Then why did you assure me that something would be done about it? If it's left any longer, it will be too late to salvage any of the crops. And they're half-starved already. Why am I not allowed to help them? My own tenants? Is there some reason why you want the place to fall apart from neglect?'

'Marietta! That's enough! I don't have time to argue about this. . .the men are waiting. You'll do as you are told. Come, bid me farewell.' He held out his arms.

Bid him farewell? Like hell she would. 'Yes, my lord. I'll bid you farewell, gladly.' Grabbing at the window-seat cushion behind her, she spun and hurled it side-ways at his chest, meaning to knock him over.

With barely a glance, he caught it in mid-air and tossed it back to the window-seat, advancing on her before she could regain her balance. She was still deciding which way to dodge when he picked her up in his arms, held her high off the floor and threw her onto the bed. She landed with a thud into the covers, totally disoriented and thoroughly angered.

'Now, my girl, if you want to make something of it, you'll have to wait until I return. And *when* I return, I'll give you a lesson in good manners.'

He paused only long enough to pull the points of his sleeves back over his hands, then strode to the door and was gone. He did not hear the thud of the pillow, for by that time he was halfway down the passageway, his mind already on the journey ahead.

She had, she supposed, brought it upon herself. If she had used more wit, she would not have mentioned the place in jest, knowing his earlier thoughts. On the other hand, there had been no need for him to ride his high horse so seriously that he could ride away from their first parting without even an attempt to humour her, making her first night alone in the big bed oppressively forlorn. Emeline and Iveta's company would be a welcome diversion.

Bruno had been right, it was much better to ignore the former acrimony and to greet Emeline with a kiss and a smile of welcome. It was not as difficult as she'd feared when they had taken such care to impress, when Iveta's excited chatter, her exclamations of admiration for Mist and her joy at seeing Marietta again were so very genuine. And if Emeline's greeting was more subdued, Marietta understood that that was her way and that her smile and obvious pleasure were no less authentic.

Emeline had indeed made every effort to impress without any persuasion from her mother, for in the weeks since the family's arrival at Monksgrange, she appeared to have developed during one of nature's inexplicable surges, which abandons the slow and unobtrusive progress into adulthood in favour of the sudden and far more dramatic blossoming that takes even the closest relative by surprise. Overnight, the bud had opened. Here, at last, was the woman.

They rode, three abreast, Marietta between them.

'You're looking well, Emmie,' she said, eyeing the rich jade-green velvet surcoat edged with fox-fur. This time, the wider front panel was less revealing but the curve of her breasts under the blue cote-hardie was every bit as fascinating as the more explicit version had been.

'Thank you,' Emeline said in reply.

There was no reciprocal comment on her part, but then, Marietta thought, there never had been. It was not a part of Emeline's repertoire to show an interest in others, however superficial.

'Is our lady mother well? And Father?'

'Yes. They send their love and blessings to you. Would there really have been enough room for them, too, Marietta? Is Thorsgeld big enough for so many?'

Marietta laughed. It had been difficult for *her* to appreciate how many rooms there were after having shared space all her life. Now Emeline and Iveta were due for a shock. 'Yes, enough and to spare. I'll show you.'

'You have a new palfrey, too. It's very beautiful.'

'Lord Alain breeds horses. Did you know that?'

The blue eyes opened with acquisitiveness. 'Do you think he'd give me one if I asked nicely? When does he return?'

'At the end of the week.' Marietta kept her tone

light, though secretly she was amused at the speed of Emeline's covetousness.

Having survived the ordeal of learning her way round the vast network of rooms in the castle, Marietta enjoyed leading the two sisters through the labyrinth, peeping into the work shops and stores that surrounded the courtyard and then upwards into the living quarters. If Marietta had feared she might lose her way, she need not have feared, for the pack of admirers seemed to grow as they progressed from one part into another. She shook them off at the door of the room she had prepared for her guests, immediately above her own, laughingly shooing them away.

'Do you have them following you everywhere?' Iveta said, whirling round with a surfeit of energy. 'I like the boy called Ian. He's Scottish.'

'Not quite as many as that, love. Some of them came to Monksgrange with Lord Alain...' she faltered, looking for a quick way out of the reference to those times. She let it go.

Emeline made no comment, but wandered round the large room, touching, smoothing, fingering. The maids unpacked the eight panniers, as silently curious about their lady's sisters as about the contents of their baggage. 'Don't stand and gawp, you two,' Emeline chided them, 'you haven't seen a ghost. Get on with it! I want those baskets out of here, quickly!'

Averting their eyes as they had been bidden, the maids hauled out gown after gown, stowing them into the clothes-chests and arranging Emeline's brushes and combs, her jewellery casket, her lotions and potions, her accessories, wondering how it could be that anyone could so resemble the first Lady Thorsgeld in every way, even down to her waspish command, that they'd been convinced, for a moment or two, she'd come back to haunt them. 'God forbid,' one of them had muttered.

'Amen to that,' the other one had replied, before she

was summoned to dress Emeline's hair. 'I don't know what the master's going to say about this one when he gets back. He'll think he's dreaming.'

'Nightmare, more like.'

'How long's she staying?'

'Not long, if I've anything to do with it.'

Emeline put a stop to the whispered interchange. 'I'm waiting!' she snapped.

Noting the maids' glances, Marietta called to Iveta. 'Come, Iveta, we'll leave Emeline in peace until later. I have something to show you.'

She didn't, but Iveta was happy enough to escape, skipping and dragging Marietta forcibly until she had to skip, too.

'She's been like a bear with a sore head until Bruno came with your invitation,' Iveta told her, merrily. 'Are you really Lady Thoregeld now, Marrie? Are these people all your servants? It's been so strange without you.'

Neither the questions nor the observations needed answers.

Following Lord Alain's suggestion, Marietta arranged a hawking party for the next day, confident that in the company of so many attentive men Emeline would enjoy herself whether she caught anything or not. She did, but not until she had argued with Seth about which palfrey she was allowed to ride, insisting that Lord Alain would wish her to use her sister's new one, and it was not until Marietta intervened that she would accept another mount. In the circumstances, Marietta herself chose another mount to ride rather than flaunt Mist before her sister all afternoon, yet all the while cursing herself for ignoring Bruno's advice.

Marietta, with a group of Lord Alain's closest companions, was content to let Emeline show off her paces to the adulation of the younger set. She was struck, even more forcibly, how the pretty simpering blonde beauty had grown so quickly into the role of cajoling woman, flirting openly like a butterfly trying out its new wings, posing gracefully with arm upraised long after the merlin had flown from her wrist, pouting and cooing at it when it returned, glancing and laughing as she stroked its breast with one finger, knowing how they watched, entranced.

Relieved that all bitterness and rancour had now been put behind them, Marietta let Emeline revel in the sport while she and the men showed Iveta how to send her merlin up to stoop at a skylark. When it came time to go, they followed Emeline's group at a more leisurely pace, tossing coins into the cadgeman's cap to thank him for carrying the falcons.

Later, at supper, when Emeline had changed into a gown of deep madder red and had her hair dressed in a most elaborate coil of plaits around her ears, she graced the high table between the chaplain and Lord Alain's most senior member of the household, the treasurer, Sir Hugh Midgeley, two kindly and intelligent men who were firm favourites with Marietta. She had thought that this would put Emeline at her ease, but the effort misfired.

'For heaven's sake,' Emeline hissed, 'don't put me next to those old dotards again. I couldn't understand a word they said.'

'Oh, I like them. They've both been kind to me since—'

'Yes, well, they're the kind of old men you like, Marietta. Put me next to that dark-haired man called John next time, and some of the others who laugh a lot.'

'They don't sit at the high table, Emmie. There isn't room.'

'Then make room. You're Lady Thorsgeld. And

please don't let them hear you calling me Emmie.
Mother says it's childish.'

Marietta's fingers itched to box the girl's silly ears
but she held her peace. This was, after all, only the first
day of her visit and there was plenty of time for her to
settle down. Marietta changed the subject.

'We shall leave the men in the hall while we go up to
my solar, Emmie.' She took Iveta by the hand. 'Some
of the men will join us in a little while. Shall we go?'

Emeline pouted, catching the eye of one young man
who hovered, picking his teeth and watching. 'No, I'll
stay here. You go.'

'Emmie...Emeline, you can't stay here on your
own.'

I won't *be* on my own. Anyway, my maids are here,
somewhere.' She turned to look over her shoulder at
the young man who then pushed himself off the wall
and sauntered towards them, ready to escort Emeline
away.

She's not yet fifteen, for heaven's sake, Marietta said
to herself; either I have to stay with her down here or
she has to go with me. She decided to compromise.

'Very well, we'll stay a bit longer, if you wish, and
then we'll go upstairs. That way we'll both be happy,
won't we?'

'You, too? I don't need you to stay, Marietta...'

Marietta had had enough. Speaking to the young
man who had by now intruded upon their argument,
she told him, 'Be good enough to leave us alone while
we talk.' She watched, stony-faced as he bowed and
walked off.

'You've no business to do that...!' Emeline coloured
up in anger, fearing that the young swain would now
abandon his vigil.

'You're quite wrong, Emeline! I *am* Lady Thorsgeld,
remember? You reminded me of that yourself.'

Her voice was firm, though this was the first time

she'd ever had to use her authority to enforce her wishes, and the method held no appeal for her.

'Life here at the castle is not exactly the same as it is at home. We are the only women, and we do not stay in the hall for long after the meal unless Lord Alain requests us to. And since he's not here, I prefer to leave the men to have their own fun without me watching. I told you, there'll be some of the men to join us upstairs in a little while.'

'Your friends, not mine!' Emeline sulked.

'Yes, my friends,' Marietta agreed. 'What else would you expect, enemies? And you can invite two of your friends to accompany you, since you are my guest. You, too, Iveta, you invite your friend Ian, will you? Now, we'll have another few moments in here and then we leave. And you will come too, Emeline.'

It was an uncomfortable few moments. Predictably, Emeline's ill-natured chatter was directed towards Marietta like crossbow fire but, pretending not to notice, Marietta made a point of inviting Sir Hugh and the chaplain, Father Dylan, to her solar, as well as the other senior officials, as she would have done for any guest, though now she had no high hopes of Emeline remembering the duties due on her part.

As she had expected, the men could see which way the wind was blowing and were conciliatory.

'Don't be concerned, my lady,' they told her, 'we'll remind the lads of their courtesy to the young ladies. Wait until you've gone up, then we'll make sure they understand. They know what will happen if they put a foot wrong.'

She was consoled. Still, the first evening was not a resounding success, for Emeline made her impatience known in a way far removed from the compliance she had shown while Lady Alice and Sir Henry had looked on. It was as though, freed from their constraint and suddenly aware of her new glamorous image, she was compelled by some inner urge which she could not control to try out every device, instinctive and learned, on the eager and ready-made audience.

And on the less-favoured audience, who were by no means as eager to receive her attention, she was merciless in her demands, scolding and ordering as though taking on the role of mistress of the household. Her argument with the head groom on the previous day was nothing compared to the ones that followed.

Carrying bucket after bucket of hot water up two flights of winding stairs, a team of pages was brought almost to the point of rebellion when she protested that the water was only warm, not hot, and sent it back.

Marietta intervened yet again, her heart sinking with dread at the sure knowledge of another day's wrangling.

'Emeline, you never have a bath every morning at home. Why have you decided you need so many here?'

'Because I *fancy* having a bath every morning. There are plenty of ser—'

'There are plenty or servants to do the essential work of the castle. No guest is entitled to commandeer the services of so many people, just to carry bathwater. Those lads are having to neglect their other duties for your pleasure. How *can* you be so thoughtless?'

'Don't you have a bath every morning?'

'No, I have one when I feel like it.'

'Well, I feel like it every morning.'

'Then you can do without, Emeline, or you can come down to my solar and have my bathwater before I use it. I'm not having the servants toil up here every day. One slipped this morning and fell on top of the one below. Two arms and a collar bone broken, just for your thoughtlessness.'

Iveta followed Marietta along the dim passageway.

'Marrie, can I come and share your room? I can't stand being with her again; she's unbearable. She embarrasses me, going on so and scolding at the maids. She made one do her hair three times yesterday and the poor thing was in tears. Please don't make me share with her.'

So Marietta moved Iveta's things into a small chamber at one side of her maids' room overlooking the inner courtyard where she could see all who came and went, and Marietta assigned one of her own maids to care for Iveta's needs.

Had it not been for Iveta, the week of Lord Alain's absence would have collapsed into total disaster, each day throwing up some new conflict based on nothing more serious than Emeline's imperious attempts to divert the servants' duties towards herself, to belittle Marietta's position as often and as loudly as she could and to find every means to be contrary in order, it seemed, to amuse and captivate her throng of young admirers.

The Master-at-Arms asked her at one point if she would leave the tiltyard, after sitting amongst the squires' armour and actually hiding the helmet belonging to one of her young friends. Emeline stormed round the side of the castle and into the garden where a team of gardeners were working, placing her hand on the wet white paint of the little wooden gate from the stew-pond area. The furore that followed was expected but no less uncomfortable for all that, especially so for Marietta to whom the garden was a haven, a place of peace and pleasure.

Now, at the end of her patience with Emeline's perversity, she pacified Old Adam, who had tried to defend the lad with the paintbrush against Emeline's attack on his ears, and then took the girl's arm in an iron grip and marched her back up the path to the relative seclusion of the stew-pond.

At first, Emeline was too surprised to resist, standing with a white-striped hand splayed out like a scarecrow as Marietta manoeuvred her back into the recess of the castle wall. By the time she had overcome her surprise, Marietta had launched into an attack fierce enough to keep her speechless.

'Now listen to this, you stupid child, I've had enough of you, do you hear? Enough!' She spat the words at her like pellets, stinging her into stillness.

'In four days you've turned this place upside down, and now you can either behave like the lady you claim to be or you can go back home this very morning. I can summon men like *that*...' she snapped her fingers in Emeline's face '... to escort you back to Monksgrange whether you will or no, and I can make damn sure you never *ever* get another invitation to stay here again. Do you understand *that*?'

She didn't wait for a reply. The forget-me-not blue eyes widened in total comprehension.

'You've antagonised everyone I've tried so hard to win over since I came here, and it's not been as easy for me as you seem to believe. And then you come along and undo it all with your counter-orders and your rudeness, you silly little chit. How *dare* you? And your behaviour with the squires and the young men... they're not here to amuse you, Emeline, they have duties to perform. Neither can they fulfil obligations to a guest if it conflicts with their orders. *You* should know that.

'A guest may not make demands on any servant without the permission of the host...and that's *me* until Lord Alain returns. God in heaven knows what these people think of you, screeching like a fish-wife and lashing out at the gardeners. If you'd looked what you were doing, you wouldn't have touched the gate. Any fool could have seen the lad on the other side of it.'

She glanced up the path towards the shooting butts. 'Where've you come from, anyway?'

'Up there,' Emeline nodded. 'The tiltyard.'

'While the men were *practising*?'

'Yes.' Emeline's lids covered the blue stare of innocence

'God in heaven! Have you no sense, child? Are you so taken up with yourself that you try to distract them when they're in training? They're not playing games, Emeline. Was the Master-at-Arms there?'

'Yes . . .'

'And?'

'He asked me to leave.'

Marietta groaned and heaved a sigh of exasperation.

'For pity's sake! Another one! I'm going to have to go round the whole damn castle apologising for your behaviour. Go and pack your bags. You've done enough damage for four days. I've had as much as I can take.'

She would have turned away but Emeline caught at her arm and held on.

'No, please. . . Marrie, don't send me back. I didn't know—'

'Didn't *know*? Didn't know what? No lady throws her weight around like you've been doing. Is that what you didn't know? Well, now you *do* know and you can go home. I don't want you disturbing the peace of my garden. . .this is my special place and I don't want you in it!' A warning voice told her not to tell, but it was too late. The words could not be recalled.

'Marrie, please don't send me home again. I'm sorry. Truly. If I promise to try very hard. . . I will do everything you want me to do without an argument.' Emeline peeped up at the angry face and saw that she had Marietta's attention. 'And we'll be friends again as we used to be and. . .you'll see. . .my manners will be perfect. Let me stay for a few more days, please. I'm having such fun without Mother breathing down my neck.'

Marietta let out a breath in a gust of indecision. She

wished that Alain was with her to take away this
dilemma; he would know what to do. He would be
back some time tomorrow. Let her stay till then.

'Is that what it's all about?' she said. 'Lady Alice
constraining you?'

'Yes, Marrie...that's it.' Emeline saw her chances
rising. 'Mother and Uncle Nicholas between them. It's
the first time I've been away alone. *He* wanted to come
too, but Father would not allow it. I didn't know I
wasn't supposed to go into the tiltyard... I won't do it
again.'

Or make a fuss in my garden. Or take my horse. Or
order my servants, or dictate who sits at my table... I
could go on, Marietta thought.

'If you can make an effort to behave as a lady should,
Emeline, you can stay. I want to be friends, heaven
knows I do, but you must see that I have to live here
when you've gone home, and I won't have the place
upset by your silliness.'

She would like to have added that Emeline had
caused enough problems before they were married, but
knew how that would boost the girl's ego higher than it
was already.

'You'll let me stay?'

'You can stay.'

Emeline threw her arms around Marietta's shoulders
impulsively, something she'd never done before.

'Thank you. Is it tomorrow that Lord Alain returns?'

Without knowing why she should lie instead of telling
Emeline the truth, Marietta answered, 'I'm not sure. A
few days, I think.'

CHAPTER SEVEN

FOR the time being, at least, the two sisters shared a
type of peace which both of them recognised as a time
of trial.

Marietta was torn between needing her husband's
support more than ever she had believed she would
and being unsure of his attitude towards her after their
unhappy parting. Not only was that an area of unsure-
ness, but Emeline's presence was bound to force
Marietta herself into a penitent mode, for anything less
than obvious joy at his return would be construed as
uneasiness more to do with Emeline than with their
misunderstanding about Beckington.

Marietta took her troubles to Father Dylan. To be
more exact, she brought Father Dylan out to the garden
on the pretext of showing him the progress so far. The
golden-orange sun balanced precariously on the edge
of the parapet as they sat on a rustic bench against the
warm castle wall, and as it edged its way downwards
and onto the opposite hillside, she told him the whole
story of Emeline, herself and Lord Alain of Thorsgeld.

Father Dylan was an Augustinian monk on loan for
a period of five years from Bolton Priory. He was not
an old man, but wise for his years, well travelled and
worldly and a considerable scholar, far from the doom
and hellfire that typified many chaplains, including her
father's. His face reflected his love of life and stimulating conversation but he knew how to listen, too. It was
this quality, and his understanding, that made Marietta
confide in him.

He heard her story in silence, occasionally nodding.

'Well, then, in a situation like this,' he said, 'it always

helps to pull out the parts that don't allow you a choice and examine those first. The duties. And since you have a duty to your husband more than a duty towards your sister, *he* must be put first, don't you agree?'

'Yes, Father. I can't disagree with that. But I don't know how he will greet me, after his last words to me.'

'Marietta...' he turned his tonsured head towards her, not knowing how his shining pate reflected the orange sun '...he's been away for the best part of a week. No man in his right senses holds onto such a mild threat of chastisement for so long away from home, especially when he has a new wife he fought so hard to bring under his roof.'

He smiled at her as though enjoying their feud.

'I think...no, I'm sure you will discover that as soon as he sees you go out to meet him on the road, he will think no more about your little tiff, only about how glad he is to see you. Put on your loveliest gown and your best smile, deck the hall as though he was expected, have the gleemen ready, prepare his favourite food and do all you can to show how you welcome him. You won't even need to refer to your last words together. He'll see for himself, won't he?'

It was what she had hoped he would say.

'And at the same time,' he continued, 'the other question will resolve itself in the first one, because when he sees you and your loving welcome, he won't even know that your sister exists. It was you he wanted, don't forget. Not Emeline.'

'According to my father, she looks something like his first wife.'

'Is that so? I was not here then, so I have no way of knowing.'

It was only a little less than the truth, for he *had* a way of knowing; he had heard talk, but gossip was not something he passed on.

'In any case, people change, and that was obviously

not something that attracted Lord Alain a second time. So put it out of your mind, m'lady. Take your cue from him. You can't allow your marriage to be influenced by another woman, whether she exists now or did so in the past. And as for what your sister has been up to in his absence, well, he'll find out for himself soon enough. If I know anything, they'll all be at pains to tell him as soon as he gets his nose through the gates.'

'And what about the ruffled feathers, Father? Should I apologise for my sister?'

'On balance I think not, m'lady. Far better if you were simply to visit the birds who have had their feathers ruffled just to show them how much you care, ask about the broken arms, discuss the horses, admire the paintwork. . .you know. Only the guest can apologise; you cannot do that for her. She'll not come to confession tomorrow, I suppose?'

Marietta smiled. 'Father Dylan will have a couple of hours to spare, will he?' Then, realising that her peevishness still showed, asked his forgiveness.

'There's nothing to forgive, lady. A dilemma is neither good nor evil and to ask for guidance shows humility. All will be well. You'll see.'

The early morning had always been Marietta's favourite time of day, so it was no hardship to be up at first light with an exciting urgency tingling through her body. But now, at the back of her mind, there lurked the dark suspicion that once Emeline became aware that Lord Alain was due home today, she would do her level best to put a fly in the ointment. And that, Marietta swore, was something she'd not let happen.

With this in mind, she dressed with infinite care in a fitted cote-hardie of rich golden apricot with a neckline that exposed much of her lovely neck and shoulders, hugged her waist neatly and flared out to wide folds at the hem, its long pocket-slits trimmed with squirrel fur.

The sleeves were so long that they touched the floor unless she tied loose knots in them, the edges deeply dagged to show linings of cream silk which matched her under-tunic. She wore no surcoat.

Her hair was plaited and coiled into two gold-mesh cases which hung from her gold circlet, framing her face and sparkling in the early sunlight with pearls and topaz. Apart from her ring, it was her only jewellery.

'Oh, m'lady,' Anne whispered, standing back and nudging Ellie with her elbow, 'I've never seen anything so lovely in my life. Honest.'

'She's right,' Ellie agreed, tucking a stray lock of hair behind her ear and grinning, 'and what's more, I know somebody who won't get a look in. Anyway, her maids aren't as good as us, are they, m'lady?'

'Nobody's maids are as good as you, cheeky-puss,' Marietta smiled. 'Now hurry up and tidy this place and then make preparations for the bath. My lord will be hot and dusty after his travels. Plenty of towels on the floor, Anne. You know what a splash he makes.'

Anne pretended to scold. 'Aye, well, don't let him pull you in on top of him this time, m'lady, or we'll have to dress you all over again.'

A blush rose to Marietta's cheeks at the memory. He had scooped an arm around her waist and had pulled her backwards onto his submerged lap, ignoring her cries of protest and kissing her into silence. Then he had sponged all the parts he could reach, just as she had been doing the moment before and, though it had soaked her dress, it had been a hilarious and novel experience for her. Nor had it ended there but on the floor, on a pile of towels.

After mass, she broke her fast, conferring with the household officials as she ate, checking on details. A messenger arrived to say that Lord Alain would not arrive until mid-afternoon; dinner would have to be delayed until supper-time.

The later-than-expected arrival, while giving them more time to prepare, also gave Emeline more time to discover what was happening, prompting Marietta to elaborate on her plans to ride out and meet him further along the highway to York, taking with her as many men as were available and leaving with such speed that Emeline would be nowhere near ready in time to join her.

The departure could not have been kept secret from Iveta whose room overlooked the courtyard, but she was as glad as anyone to leave her sister in the dark and ride off with Marietta and her new friend Ian, and it was past noon when the two young people gave a shout and pointed to a cloud of dust over in the distance.

Rounding a bend of the forest-covered hillside, the dust-cloud was too large even for a team of oxen, and the occasional flash of silver indicated nobility rather than peasants. It must be them; they were sure of it.

Ahead of the others, Marietta cantered across the turf towards the lone rider who had singled himself out from the rest, unmistakably her proud lord whose arms were held out wide towards her and whose laughing face showed pride as well as astonishment. The sight of her golden figure on the creamy-white horse convinced him as nothing else could have done that her days of bolting were over.

'Come on, my lass!' he called to her, 'come on, then. That's more like a greeting! Hah!' His great arms almost pulled her from the saddle as he kissed her while their mounts wheeled, head to tail. 'You've come all this way. . .just to meet me, sweetheart? What a girl! Let me look at you. . .hah. . .tears, lass?' He laughed, pulling her chin to him. 'What a welcome.'

'Welcome, my lord,' she said, laughing back at him

between tears. 'I couldn't wait when I heard you were on the way. I had to come out. . .to find you. . .to bring you back.'

'You've missed me, then?'

'Yes, I've missed you. Look, here's Iveta to greet you.'

'Well, well! So your sisters came?'

'Yes. Emmie wasn't up in time to leave with us.'

There was something in the way she spoke that made him stifle the quick retort with a more searching look, and the way she glanced quickly up at him as they rode verified his impression that all was not as well as he'd hoped it would be. Was the silly child still sulking, then?

'Good,' he said, taking her hand, 'then I've got you all to myself for a bit, haven't I?'

'Almost,' she said, nodding towards the retinue of at least twenty men ahead and as many behind them. 'Almost.'

The rich aroma of cooking from the great kitchen wafted well beyond the castle gates. Lord Alain lifted his head and breathed in deeply. 'If that's not venison, I'll eat my saddle,' he said.

'Hush,' Marietta told him. 'You must be surprised. Promise me you'll be surprised.'

Twinkling, he nodded. 'I'll be surprised, I swear it.'

As it transpired, he had no need to swear, for the surprise that awaited him in the courtyard was more in the nature of a shock, one so tangible that Marietta could feel his reaction even at her distance from him.

Emeline, taking advantage of the extra time, and no travel to weary her, had sought her most beautiful gown of gold silk shot with mauve threads under a violet silk surcoat edged with gold braid. Her hair, like Marietta's, was in cauls of gold mesh studded with amethysts. She was busily issuing commands to pages and ushers, to grooms and porters as Lord Alain's party clattered through the echoing gatehouse, and she turned in feigned surprise at his entrance, holding his eyes.

'God's truth!' he murmured.

Marietta watched him pale, blink, and then recover himself as Emeline ran forward to make a graceful courtesy.

'Welcome, my lord—' her voice was breathless, excited '—we're all prepared. Your favourite venison, with frumenty and pepper sauce. . .'

'Emeline. . .no, don't tell him, it's to be. . .' Marietta waved a hand at her to stop the leak.

But Emeline ignored her, fluttering around as Lord Alain dismounted and went to Marietta's side, holding up his arms to lift her down. 'And we've decked the hall so prettily, and a new troupe of jugglers, and there are gleemen, too. . .'

Clapping both of her palms over her husband's ears, Marietta made him look at her, showing him the fury in her eyes, shaking her head at him, almost in tears. 'Don't listen, please. . .she's telling you all my surprises.'

Immediately he understood and took her hands away, holding them before him and bending to her ear. 'I have not heard one word she's said, sweetheart. Come, let her prattle on; you shall show me everything.' Plunged into the middle of sisterly rivalry and stunned by Emeline's sudden transformation into womanhood, Lord Alain greeted her courteously with a kiss to both cheeks, firmly refusing to respond to any more of her attempts to spoil Marietta's preparations.

On two counts, however, the damage had been done; one was shown by Lord Alain's look of incredulity as soon as he'd seen Emeline, his murmured exclamation, the second was that the edge had been taken off Marietta's personal welcome in which she had tried to say, without words, that she was sorry for her poor farewell. While the latter incident had been planned to cause damage to Marietta, the former was far more devastating in its effect, the reaction being unplanned, totally spontaneous. Not even Emeline could have foreseen that.

Still very new to the notion that it was she he wanted, rather than Emeline, Marietta was neither brash nor secure enough to be unmoved by his impromptu reaction there in the courtyard, and while Emeline's behaviour during Lord Alain's absence had been seriously unmannerly, this appeared to be a foretaste of real power of a kind that Marietta could do little to curtail without sending her home straight away.

That was the answer! She would send her packing as she should have done yesterday. What a fool she'd been to take her assurance of good behaviour. What a blind fool!

'Nay, lass! Don't overreact so.' Lord Alain laughed at her from deep in the steaming bath. His chin rested on the surface of the water and reflected pink between the rose petals. Occasionally, he would disappear altogether, leaving only a shimmering mass of black hair like pond-weed, then come up with it streaked over his face and dripping into his eyes. He pushed it away and held up an arm for Bruno to wash.

'It's no great matter,' he said. 'I haven't seen anything, so it *will* be a surprise. There's no need to send her home for that, surely?'

'It's not only for that,' Marietta said, handing him a towel. 'You don't know the half of it.'

'Well, I expect I shall soon enough. She's only a child, still. It's all innocent stuff, Marietta.'

Foolishly, Bruno could not resist joining in as he reached for another bucket of hot water. 'You don't know my sister, my lord,' he said.

Before he could move away, a sponge heavy with

water landed on the side of his head, making him lurch with the bucket and splash his tunic, and without heeding the consequences, Bruno poured the water onto his lord's head, sending much of it splashing over the sides.

With a roar of outrage, Lord Alain leapt out of the tub in a torrent of water and steam and, in spite of Bruno's quick dive to one side, grabbed him with an arm around the neck and a hand on his wrist and hustled the squirming lad towards the bath. 'Here then. . .if you're so keen that I should be clean, you can get in now. . .get some of that dust off. Ready?' He thrust Bruno forward.

'No, my lord!' Bruno yelled, his lad's squawk mingling uncomfortably with his man's growl. 'No. . .let me get my clothes off first. . .I beg you!' His laughter fought with his panic, for he stood no chance against Lord Alain's greater strength. 'Please, let me undress first, my lord. . .'

Lord Alain, stark naked and glistening with water, released him. 'Right. . .while I count to ten. . .one, two, three. . .'

Bruno had never undressed quite so fast in all his life, falling almost headlong into the tub before the sound of ten had faded, coinciding precisely with the splash and the yelp of relief.

By this time, Marietta and her maids were both appalled by the mess the men had made on the towels and rushes, but helpless with laughter at the rough and tumble and creased up as much by Bruno's expression of jubilation as by his master's quick retaliation. Even through all that, Marietta was spellbound by the magnificent naked body, gleaming and wet, every hard muscle picked out under the shine like polished marble.

Her brother's nakedness was familiar to her, filling-out and newly firm, but her husband was tall and hardened to the temper of steel and her longing for him obliterated her niggling doubts about Emeline and his thoughts concerning her. If he'd had some kind of shock, well then, he had apparently forgotten about it in his delight to be home. Why should she insist on recalling it, spoiling her first few hours with him?

She dried him herself. 'Be kind to Bruno,' she whispered.

'Kind?' He glanced at the lad in the steaming bath. 'How many squires get to be bathed in their lord's bathwater, I'd like to know?'

Disarmingly, Bruno smiled at them and popped a rose petal into his mouth.

Later, when they were alone at last for a few moments before supper, he pulled her into his arms. 'The sooner I can kiss you without this contraption on your head, the better I shall feel.'

'Don't you like it?'

'You look amazing,' he murmured, 'a dream. When I saw you come cantering towards me across the field, I nearly burst with pride. Golden and glowing like a ripe peach... I want to sink my teeth into you...shall I?' He bent his head to her throat.

'Later, my lord. I'll take this contraption off for you.'

'Is that all?'

She giggled. 'No, I'll take everything else off too, if you wish.'

'I do wish...' His mouth moved up and they clung together, rapt in the touch and taste of each other's lips, making up for lost days of wanting. Reluctantly, they pulled apart, not wishing to keep supper waiting.

'I brought something back for you, sweetheart, to celebrate our first parting. Look...' he presented her with a package, linen-wrapped and tied with red ribbons. Inside were two jewel-studded velvet and leather dog-collars, obviously for a very small dog.

Marietta looked at him with a question on her eyes. 'Dog-collars? They're exquisite, my lord, but...'

'Where is the dog? Good grief—' he pretended concern '—don't say it's escaped. I'm sure I wrapped it properly.'

'Stop teasing!' she laughed. 'Is there one?'

'Well, let's go down and see if anyone knows anything of it, shall we?'

Someone did, of course; it was Bruno who held the little white creature in his arms, a delicate greyhound pup with great deep blue eyes. Lord Alain placed it in Marietta's outstretched hands. 'The lady of the manor always has a lap-dog, I believe. And here's yours, sweetheart.'

'Alain. . .it's. . .it's beautiful. Thank you, thank you. Look, Iveta. . .Emeline. . .look!'

But Emeline had turned away to talk to the young man at her elbow and it was Iveta who came forward to nuzzle the tiny thing and help to put its collar on. And while Marietta and the little hound came to know each other, Lord Alain exclaimed obediently at the blossom-decked hall and the trails of ivy on the tables, the favourite food and the welcoming minstrels who sang from the gallery throughout the meal, assuring her that it was the best homecoming he'd ever had.

Even so, as the dinner-cum-supper slowed to a halt and the tumblers came forward to entertain them, Marietta could not help but notice how her husband's eyes strayed occasionally towards Emeline when he thought neither of them was looking and how his thoughts appeared to have taken him far away once or twice when she spoke to him.

As before, all fears fled once they were together again in the haven of each other's arms, nothing existing except the soft smoothness of skin and the warmth of tender words, the touch of hands and lips, the urgency of desire. No one came between them then, nothing pushed them off course while they loved, slept, and loved again, holding the dawn away as lovers always do.

Intent on maintaining an amicable mood, despite her husband's wish that Emeline should stay, Marietta waited for an opportunity to show him the progress being made in the garden and the re-stocking of the stew-pond. She had had the two areas enclosed by new walls and white-painted fences with doors and gates and pathways leading through. He would be impressed, she was sure.

Her expectations that Emeline would stick to him like a leech were realised from the moment their business in the hall had been concluded. Taking no heed of the fact that he preferred to visit his stables with his men, Emeline tagged her arm into his, ignoring Marietta's quiet promptings that he was still on castle business. Like a father with a clinging child, Lord Alain unhooked Emeline's arm with an indulgent laugh and turned her towards Marietta.

'The stables are no place for you, young lady. Go to the garden with your sisters.' He looked over the top of her head to Marietta. 'I'll come to you there, sweetheart. Then you can show me.'

Emeline pouted. 'But Marietta doesn't allow me to go into her garden,' she whined.

'What?' He frowned, sure he had misheard.

'She said she doesn't want me to go into her garden.'

Marietta was astounded by the flagrant attempt to twist the truth.

'Wait a moment. . .' she said, keeping her voice low so that the waiting men should not hear, 'you know full well why I said that.'

'It was because I put my hand on your wet paint.' She held up her fingers to look at them, petulantly glancing up at Lord Alain and seeing his quick look of astonishment at her sister. 'She was so cross,' she told him.

'That's not true, Em. . .!'

'Enough!' Lord Alain said, gruffly, dismissing the budding argument. 'Get off to the garden, both of you, and settle your differences there. Of course you're allowed to go there, Emeline.' His wide back put an end to the conversation.

Marietta was seething, unable to continue the dispute in the servants' hearing and now totally unwilling to accompany the little minx to her garden where she would either have to spoil its atmosphere of tranquility with a showdown or pretend an indifference she did not feel, neither of which would do.

Leaving Emeline to swish away in triumph, she signalled to Iveta, and together they took the little greyhound pup round to the shooting butts, picking up bows and arrows on the way. An hour's archery would, she thought, release some of the aggression before it became any more obvious.

Iveta, who had had little tuition with the bow, suddenly found that she loved it, especially since her friend Ian and his young pals were also practising. Soon, she was in the midst of them being tutored from all sides, and Marietta was left to a lone contest with her hostility in which the straw butt became, once or twice, Emeline. If it *had* been, the lass would surely have been mortally wounded, for Marietta was a fair shot.

The lass in question, however, was at that moment very much alive to the effect her presence was having on the two garden lads who were doing their best to erect a wooden arbour over by the crenellated wall, as Old Adam had instructed. But while she leaned so prettily against the wall to watch them, and when they had to ease round her so carefully in order not to brush up against her or to catch her long skirt with the struts of wood the job threatened to slow to a standstill if she didn't get out of the way.

The two lads eyed her and then each other, fully aware of her game and yet not daring to take advantage.

'Mistress, would you please. . .?' One of them indicated a point away from the entrance. 'We need to climb up there to reach. . .'

She looked down and then up. 'Plenty of room,' she said with a smile.

The younger lad blushed uncomfortably, nonplussed, then looked for help to the other one. 'Could you move, please?' he whispered.

'What if I don't?' she whispered in reply.

The elder one stuck his thumbs into his belt and took a step towards her. 'I'll show yer summat'll move yer, shall I?'

Recognising imminent danger, Emeline yelped, turned and fled out of the trellis entrance then stood, half laughing and flustered to see Lord Alain standing watching the dilemma, his hand still on the latch of the door in the wall. She had no idea how long he'd been there, for by the time she had looked over her shoulder, both lads were about their business.

His expression was serious, and for an embarrassingly long time he made no move, but regarded her as though deep in thought while Emeline had time to spare for her blush to subside. He closed the door very slowly and glanced along the new-made path. 'Where's Marietta?' he said.

She thought how handsome he looked in his tight-fitting chausses and short blue tunic. He had wonderful legs, but the younger boys were more fun. 'I don't know,' she replied, truthfully. 'She wouldn't come to the garden with me. I told you, my lord, she doesn't want me here.'

'Nonsense, Emeline. You know how hot-tempered

she is.' He led her to a bench at the end of a new plot and invited her to sit by him.

'It's not nonsense, my lord. . .' her eyes were downcast '. . .she wants me to return to Monksgrange.'

'She told you that?' After what they'd said before supper, had she then disobeyed him and told the lass to leave?

'She told me before you returned yesterday, my lord.' She sighed, looking away. 'She said she'd make sure I'm never invited back again. And all because I wanted a bath.' Her voice trembled to a whisper.

'What, Emeline? Not let you have a *bath*?' He tried hard to sound shocked.

She nodded. 'Yes, she said I could have her bath water when she'd done with it and not to ask for hot water to be sent up. I think I should go, my lord. I can see it was a mistake to come.'

A tear trembled on her long fair lashes and she nibbled at her lip while watching his hands. When he made no move to comfort her, as she had hoped he might, she stood as if to leave, ostensibly to begin packing.

Gently, he forestalled her. 'There's no need for that, Emeline. This is a difficult time for both of you, I realise that. And I believed that you would appreciate a chance to be alone together, to patch up your differences. Of course, if you insist on going back to Monksgrange, I will do all I can to make your journey comfortable. But I would like you to stay. Will you?'

For what she deemed to be an appropriately long pause, Emeline played with her fingernails and brushed a non-existent tear from her cheek. Then she sniffed prettily and nodded. 'If that's what *you* want, then I will, thank you. But do you think I could have a bath each morning as I'm used to doing at home?'

Lord Alain held back the urge to laugh at her charade. It was well done, he had to admit it, especially as he'd only just discovered that it was two of his young grooms who'd broken their arms after having been drafted in to carry Mistress Emeline's bath water every morning. And just now, he'd met Old Adam who had assured him he'd not go near Lady Marietta's garden if that sister o' hers were in theer, little troublemaker that she wor. An' had Lord Alain 'eard what she'd been up to in't tiltyard?

No, not yet, he would discover that, too, all in good time. But he'd seen for himself what she was up to here with the two young garden lads and that had been enough to assure him that he had a very appropriate role for her to play in the near future. As for making Marietta understand what it was, there was no hope of that at the present.

He knew, as he walked away towards the shooting-butts, that both he and his young wife were in for a rough ride. As for young Emeline, the time had come and gone when he didn't know what was going on under his own nose. Nowadays, he took good care to find out.

There was no sign of Marietta at the butts, only Iveta exercising her new-found skills with a team of young pages. They were behaving impeccably; no tomfoolery with weapons, they'd been told.

'Where is the Lady Marietta?' Lord Alain asked.

Young Ian pointed towards the deer-park. 'She took her pup for a walk, my lord. Only a few moments ago.'

He watched Iveta shoot. 'Find her a shorter bow, Ian. And show her how to push. She's still pulling.'

'Yes, my lord.' Ian grinned, not only because his hero had remembered his name but because he'd been told to instruct. Rare praise indeed.

After the muggy heat of the day, the cool woodland was a welcome change and the general noise of castle life was replaced by the soft sighing of the beeches, ash and oaks. Standing quite still to listen, he was rewarded by the unmistakable yap from deeper in the wood and, making his way towards the sound he called, 'Marietta! Marietta, where are you?'

He smiled at the lack of communication. If he had heard the pup's yap, she must have heard his voice, yet was making no reply. So, that was her game: she was angry with him, with Emeline, with everything, no doubt. And she was hiding. . .somewhere around. . . here. . .if only he. . .yes, she was wearing green, as she so often did. Then it was all over. . .the pup yelped again, wriggled free of her grasp and came bounding towards him, trailing its lead through the grass and twigs and indicating quite clearly where the figure in green held herself rigidly on the far side of a tree, convinced that she would not be spotted.

'Where's your mistress, then? Where is she?' he said, loud enough for her to hear while tying the lead to a fallen branch. He stalked, silently, coming at her from one side to make her run towards a fallen oak so large that no one could have cleared it without a ladder. She swerved away with a yelp, was caught around the waist and brought down backwards on top of him, angry to have been discovered so soon and so easily.

'Leave me. . .alone!' she growled, fighting to free herself from his grasp. 'Leave me. . .leave me *be*!'

'Hold it, my girl! That's enough!'

'That's what you said earlier,' she yelled at him, beating his chest as he pulled her into his arms. 'Well, I've had enough, too! Enough of that little viper! Enough!' She hammered at him until he caught her wrists and held them.

'Hush, sweetheart, you're taking it all too seriously. . . Hush. . .you surely don't think I'm ignorant of what's going on, do you? That I can't see what's happening? Do you?'

Marietta stopped struggling at that, wondering what it was that he understood. 'Well, of *course* I'm taking it seriously you great insensitive oaf!' she snapped, disconcerted to see his face break out into a laugh. 'How can you laugh. . .?'

She twisted away, but he threw her backwards with a thud onto the softly padded forest floor and lay over her so that she could not move.

'Ouch! Let me up! You don't understand. . .' she howled. 'She's determined to make trouble. She's done nothing but throw her weight around since she got here. I've had enough! And she told you I'd forbade her the garden because she touched the white—'

'I've seen Old Adam.'

'What?'

'Ask me to kiss you, and I'll tell you, if you give me half a chance.'

She paused, reading his eyes.

'Go on, ask me.'

'Tell me what. . .?'

'No! Ask me to kiss you,' he insisted.

Her reluctance was not altogether genuine. 'Kiss me,' she whispered.

He could have prolonged the lesson by making her say please, but there was no guarantee that she'd comply, even if she'd been lying in snow. So he kissed her into stillness, until he felt the tensions of her body soften beneath him and her arms steal around his neck, felt her fingers push into his hair and hold him, twisting her head to take in more of him.

For Marietta, this was more effective than archery, for this opponent could fight back, make her win or loss worth something, sap her energy and drain her anger, take her punishment and return it. With a surge of pent-up rage, she tore at him with her teeth, catching his bottom lip and clashing her teeth against his before he was able to pull his head away.

She tried to pull him back again, but by now he had seen her eyes, wild and dark with passion and knew that the time for kissing had passed. Silently, he untied the cords at the neckline of her green bliaud and pulled it down off her shoulders while she fought at him in a frenzy of contradictions, wanting him but determined not to give in, finally forced into immobility by his large hand gripping her chin while his mouth roamed over her breasts.

Moaning, unable to bear the torment of his nibbling lips any longer, she heaved his hand away with both of hers and pushed it aside. But he caught her wrists together and held them, taking her conflicting signals of willingly opened thighs and struggles to be free of his weight as a personal denial of her own desires, not a fight against him.

Still, without a cry for aid or mercy, nor even a word of protest, Marietta both helped and hindered him, beating ineffectually against his great shoulders when he released her at one end to bind her to him at the other. Only then did she release a whispered complaint, 'No, I don't want you! Ah! I don't want. . .'

'Yes, my wild cat. That's it, isn't it? Eh? Isn't it?'

'Alain. . . Alain,' she gasped.

'What, sweetheart?'

'It's not you. . .'

'Ssh! I know. I know what it is.'

'Do you?'

'Yes. Fight me as much as you like. You won't hurt me. Go on. . .take it out on me.'

She would have taken up his offer if she had not already expended her energies beforehand. Now, her antagonism stood no chance against the physical onslaught of his loving; there was no room for them both and he was there, above her, moving, relentless and brutally efficient as though accepting her challenge like a knight at a joust. Too far gone to reciprocate, Marietta wept at her own incompetence, at being unable to conclude what she herself had started.

'Don't cry, sweetheart. Don't reproach yourself. Do you want me to stop?'

'No, no, no. . .go on—' she pushed the tears away, angrily '—go on.' Words came and went, floating past on the hushed breath, the sigh, the moan of pleasure too great to contain. There was no grand and glorious release for Marietta, this time, for that had come earlier in a different form. She had sought only the contest, not the prize, and though vanquished, she was treasured against Alain's great chest as though she had been his equal, which she knew she was not.

Peaceful at last, she whispered in his ear, 'Alain, where's the pup?'

'Tied up, over there. It's all right, she can't see us.' He lifted his head from her shoulder and nuzzled into her neck. 'Has the anger gone, now?'

'Yes, brute. Pity anyone who's drawn against you in a joust.'

He chuckled. 'I love it when you fight. But I don't want to make you angry, sweetheart. Shall we talk some now? I have things to tell you. Do you want to hear? Shall I let you up?'

Sitting against a branch of the fallen oak, they nestled closely like lost children, savouring the peace within themselves. Alain rescued the pup and brought it to her, laughing at the zeal of its pink tongue on his face and its flying leap onto Marietta's lap. She reminded him of his promise. 'Alain, you said you'd seen Old Adam.'

'I've seen Old Adam and I've also heard how two of my grooms came to have broken arms, which I am very angry about because that has a direct bearing on something else that happened last night. You didn't tell me about the accident on the stairway, sweetheart. Why not?' He thought he knew the answer to that already.

'You saw how Emeline stole my thunder as soon as

you arrived home. I was furious then, but I wasn't going to plunge you into a catalogue of her doings straight away and I didn't want to spoil our reunion.'

His arms pulled her even closer against him while he kissed her. 'It was good, wasn't it?' he whispered. 'I knew you'd be good as soon as I saw you, all those weeks ago.'

'Oh, Alain, what nonsense you talk. All grazed like that, and half-dazed?'

'Yes, half-dazed you still fought me off. Passionate woman.'

His soft laugh of triumph sent a wave of excitement through her, but there were more important things to discuss than that.

'Alain, what did you mean about something happening last night?'

'Another one of my horses was stolen.'

'Stolen? Another one? You mean there have been others?'

Gravely, he nodded at her concerned expression. 'Last night, another mare was stolen from the far field. Seth had put them there in the morning and because we were two grooms short, it was later than usual when they were brought back to the home paddock for the night. And by that time, one of them was gone. She had a foal with her, too. A colt.'

'Oh, no!' The news was serious enough at the best of times, but a breeding mare and a colt were doubly valuable. 'A palfrey, was she?'

'That would have been bad enough, but this was one of my breeding mares for war-horses. The colt would have been a destrier, worth thousands, eventually.'

'Oh, Alain. . .! Have you got men out looking for them?'

'Yes, of course, but I can't help feeling that there's someone who knows what's happening here. Last time it happened was when I was over at Monksgrange and once before when I was away from home. This time, it was just as I came back, too late to be at the stables as I usually am, last thing at night.'

'Someone who works here, you think?'

'Someone who's aware of my comings and goings and who knows which horses to go for. The first one was a yearling colt. Never a filly.'

'And never a gelding?'

'Oh no, the idea is to take one that will sire others and have value as a destrier, too. They wouldn't take a mare in foal because for one thing she might have a filly and, for another, somebody would have to know how to attend a birth. That's all time-consuming and too risky. They can't get at the stallions, thank goodness, but this is getting more and more serious.'

'What are you going to do now, Alain?' Marietta asked as they walked back across the field with their arms around each other. The pup pranced at her side, pulling at its leash to chase a butterfly.

'I'm having a horse-fair, here at Thorsgeld,' he told her. 'While I was in York, I invited several acquaintances, mostly knights who need new stock, to stay at the castle as our guests. Some dealers, too.'

'But Alain, surely that's asking for trouble, isn't it? Getting them right here so that anybody can see what you've got and where you keep it.'

'Yes, that's what it might look like, but this is not the first time I've done this. Many of the same people were invited here every year until a couple of years ago. It's time I started again. I have a distinct feeling that one of them might be behind the thefts.'

'And you think you can discover who's responsible by having them here, under your own roof?'

'I think it's quite likely, my love, but I shall need your help. Will you help me make it a grand affair, Marietta? Feasts, hunting, hawking parties? A few of them might bring their ladies, too. Would you like that?'

The idea was audacious, and to one new to castle life quite an awesome assignment, but she would like it. Yes, she would like it very much. 'Yes, my lord. Yes, that would be wonderful. When is it to be?'

'They'll start arriving on Thursday, ready for the weekend,' he said, opening the gate into the stew-pond garden. 'I hope *this* is going to be ready in time.'

Marietta stopped, dismayed by the suddenness of the event. 'Next *Thursday*? Alain, that's only a mere four days away. Why on earth didn't you tell me sooner? Four days? That's all we've got to prepare?'

He stood before her, laughing at her wifely protests of too little time. 'If you, my good wife, had not forced me to go searching deep in the deer-park, and then detained me against my will, and. . .'

'Oh, you great fool! Who detained you against your will?'

He caught the hand that pushed at his chest and kissed the palm. 'You did, little dryad in green, you lured me there and had your wicked way with me and enslaved me, and brought me back to your secret garden. . .'

'And you, my lord, have a fertile imagination. Are you going to tell me who it is you suspect of your thefts? You don't want me to speak of it, I assume?'

'No to both questions, sweetheart. Know nothing; say nothing. Just be the perfect wife so that I can boast of you, and look your most beautiful every day. We'll see what happens then, shall we?'

'I will do whatever you ask of me, my lord,' she whispered, leaving her enquiry about Emeline to the last to savour the anticipation of his certain reply. 'When shall I arrange for the return of Emeline and Iveta? Tomorrow?' She felt the coolness of the gatehouse as they walked through to the cobbled courtyard.

His answer sent an extra chill along her arms. 'Oh, they can stay while we have our guests, surely? You could probably do with Iveta's help, and you wouldn't want them to miss all the fun, would you? Besides. . . ' he avoided looking at her unsmiling face '. . .we might just find a wealthy husband for Emeline, eh?'

Marietta made no reply. She would not beg him to send Emeline home but neither would she agree that she cared two hoots about finding the girl a husband. If Emeline's last few days' behaviour were anything to go by, her conduct during the days ahead would surely change his mind.

Halting in the shadowy doorway in the corner of the court yard, he held her back against the door. 'Sweetheart, I'm home now. We're both fully aware of what a child she is, even though she looks like a grown woman. She's merely trying out her new skills, that's all. Some women have to do that—'

'I didn't!' she snapped at his excuse for the silly creature.

'No, love. If you'd been like that, too, I would not have looked twice at you, believe me. But don't you think that you and I between us can keep her under control?'

'Lock her in the stable with your stallions, you mean?'

Placing his hands across her shoulders he heaved with laughter so much that she was compelled to join in, reluctantly.

'No, lass, no. . . I didn't want to go quite as far as that. We'll save that option as a last resort, I think. Don't be concerned; I have things under control. Just trust me, that's all I ask.'

Trust you, she thought. Aye, what choice do I have? Is that really the only reason you want her to stay? What was that look all about? These were questions she could not ask; she must wait and see.

'What are you going to name this little thing?' He bent to pick up the pup with one hand and place it in her arms.

'Faith,' she said, running her hand over its smooth head.

'Aye, lass, that's good. Don't lose Faith, sweetheart.'

CHAPTER EIGHT

WITH so much to be done in only four days, there was little time for Marietta to dwell on the continued irritation of Emeline's company. At the back of her mind, she supposed that Lord Alain was right; between them they should be able to keep her from causing too much havoc. But that was only the theory.

The facts were that Emeline's havoc was being directed not at the two of them but at Marietta alone, insidiously provoking on a scale so small that any reaction to it would have appeared petty. Marietta said nothing, hoping that when the extra guests appeared they would somehow keep her sister occupied in their company. Meanwhile she went about her duties, turning as much of a blind eye to Emeline's doings as she could.

There was one thing, however, that penetrated Marietta's blind eye with all the pain of a dart; Lord Alain's assurance that she must trust him to keep Emeline under control proved not to be what she'd had in mind. In the weeks since she'd known him, he had shown far less patience with her own mild perverseness than he now did with Emeline's inconvenient whims.

Where he was fierce in his demands of her, he indulged Emeline as though making sure that she would stay for the duration of the horse-fair. Marietta would have preferred it if she had had a tantrum and gone flying off home; that would have solved all their problems. But that was now out of the question. Marietta's threat had disappeared.

'Lord Alain has asked me to stay, Marietta,' she said, glancing at her reflection in the array of gold and silver dishes on the cupboard in the hall. 'He's taking me hawking this afternoon. Will you be coming?'

Little cat, Marietta thought. Stick your claws in. You know full well that I'll be up to my eyebrows getting everything ready by Thursday.

'No, I'm far too busy. I can always find you a job if you prefer to stay and help,' she said.

'I *will* be helping,' Emeline said, 'catching herons for the table.'

Tight-lipped, Marietta turned away. The chamberlain and second steward were waiting for instructions.

After the mid-morning dinner, during which she watched yet again her husband's forbearance when Emeline childishly spoiled the decoration around the edge of a dish of saffron rice even before it had been set down, she walked away from the table alone, unable to conceal her vexation.

Lord Alain caught up with her in the narrow passageway from the great hall to the guest chambers. 'Marietta, wait!' he called.

She did not wait. She kept on walking until she felt his hand on her elbow and was hauled to a standstill. 'Let me go, my lord. I have much to do. . .'

'Wait, lass! What's all this? You've been like a bear with a sore arse for the last two days. What's got into you?'

His seeming ignorance piqued her every bit as much as his toleration of Emeline's scheming ways.

'How can you *ask*?' she snarled. 'You asked me to trust you, too. Was *that* one of your mindless questions?' She took advantage of his astonishment to pursue her mounting anger.

'Well, ask how I like it when she flaunts herself around your home as though *she* were mistress here. If you truly wanted that, why didn't you marry her as I told you you should? I never wanted this. . .it was you who insisted. Was it *both* of us you wanted then. . .was it?' With a supreme effort, she wrenched herself away and stood out of reach, fuming with resentment.

'Marietta. . .listen. . .it's not like that, truly,' he said.

'*Truly*!' she mimicked him.

'Why don't you come hawking, too? It'll do you good.'

That was like a red rag to a bull. '*Now?*' she hissed. 'Now? Just when you're about to set off. . .as an afterthought? And when you can see that I need every moment to prepare for your damn guests? I would have thought you'd be better helping me than gadding off with that stupid, scheming little. . .!'

'I *am* helping, sweetheart,' unwittingly he echoed Emeline's words, 'I am. I'm taking her out of the way. Isn't that a help?'

His last words were tossed after her as she fled along the passage. He heard the echoing slam of a heavy door, felt the shockwaves and sighed before turning back, supposing that he would have to let her win a bout, occasionally.

Marietta stood with her back to the door with the heavy bolts pushing into her, undecided whether a confrontation had been better or worse than a quick disappearance. Well, now he knew something of what she felt, though no man would ever understand why a woman found it beneath her dignity to compete for something that was already hers by right.

Cooled by the silence of the chamber, she went to sit on the bed where a pile of sheets and blankets were ready to be laid. Goose-feather pillows had been newly filled that day; the linen still had downy bits clinging to it. She picked one up and twirled it in her fingers, wondering what in God's name she was doing here.

From the half-open door into the next guest room there were sounds of maids entering, town-women brought in to help with the preparations, old biddies, but reliable and less interested in the lusty soldiers than younger lasses would have been. On the point of making her presence known, she was stopped by the slam of the far door to their chamber and their loud cackle of mirth, then a 'Shh!' from one of them.

Apparently, the instruction was not one she recognised. 'Did you see her?' she guffawed. 'Did ye not see the little hussy?'

That, Marietta thought, must surely mean either herself or Emeline. She had to know which.

'Aye. I saw her. You'd think she were mistress here instead of the other one. What d'ye think his game is, then? Does he want both of them, d'ye think? You'd have thought he'd had enough with the last one, wouldn't you? Fancy him finding another one just like her.'

There were cracking sounds of linen being shaken and words coming out in puffs as their bodies stretched and bent. 'Spitting image, isnt she?' the cackling one replied. 'Same snooty nose, too. You should hear what t'others are sayin about her. They wish she'd take her bags and go home. So do I.'

'Aye, well, it's not her nose that men are interested in, is it? It's t'other end.' They cackled again, knowingly.

'Hey, she hasn't been busy already, has she?'

'Well, if she hasn't, it'll only be a matter o' time. Here, pass me that pillow, will you? You know what it was like with the first one, there was only his lordship didn't know what was going on. He was so busy with his horses he'd no time to watch what she was up to.'

'Little tramp!'

'Now, the other, she's as nice as pie. I like her.'

'Aye, but they're only half-sis— Oh! Saints!' The woman cannoned backwards into the one behind her, sending the door crashing into the tapestry on the wall.

'M'lady. . .I didn't know. . .oh—' she clapped a reddened old hand over her mouth, struggling to remember the details of their conversation, as much distressed by the stare of the pale and silent figure on the bed as she might have been by a box around the ears for being a blabbermouth.

Curiously, Marietta felt a singular calmness, rather as though all the niggling doubts and fears of the past weeks had found a place within a much greater puzzle. Somehow, it made more sense to discover that her first impressions were, after all, correct, that he *had* been looking for a replica of his first wife, that the exclamation in the courtyard on his return had been a recognition not that Emeline had changed, but that his first wife had come back from the dead.

Why else would he be insisting that she stay? Why else would he be willing to put up with this bad behaviour except to show that, this time, he would keep her in his sights, under control, as he'd told Marietta so clearly that he could. A second chance... that's what he wanted. Two years of marriage and then her death of the pestilence; he must have been devastated, full of remorse that he'd not given her the attention she obviously craved.

Coolly, she stood and thought about the duties to be finished. 'Make up the bed in here,' she told the two astounded women, 'then check to see that the truckle beds have blankets and pillows. I don't know how many servants they'll bring, but prepare three for each room. Then come upstairs to me.' She passed them and went on in a thick mist of inner silence.

If that's what he wants, she told herself, then that's what he can have. She would not fight for her position, for she'd told him at the very beginning that marriage to him, or anyone else, was not what she wanted.

His first interest in Emeline had warned her how it was likely to be; she should have taken more heed, not been so easily persuaded by his domineering ways. Nor should she have allowed him to seduce her with barely a protest. She had been a fool. An utter fool. And now she was caught, a better housekeeper than the other one, by all accounts. But that would be no hardship.

She was in the bakehouse when the hawking party clattered into the courtyard at the end of the afternoon and, by careful determination, she contrived to appear in the hall as supper was about to commence, pretending to be unaware that Lord Alain had sent pages to look for her. Without a glance at either her husband or sister, she took a place between Iveta and Father Dylan and throughout the informal meal kept herself engrossed in their company, and those furthest away from Emeline.

Afterwards, she made a departure so furtive and hasty that Lord Alain did not see her go, and in the gentle sunshine of the evening she took tiny Faith across to the shooting-butts and leaned over one of the crenels in the high wall, sitting the pup in the space and pointing out to it the landmarks she knew so well.

Before long, Bruno joined her, padding across the grass as though on an errand. 'My lord is looking for you,' he panted.

Marietta made no move, staring out across the beautiful green valley instead and feeling a heavy thudding in her breast at the sound of his name.

'Are you coming, love? What is it, Marrie? Tell me.'

'Look,' she said without turning, 'there's home.'

He studied her with a puzzled look. 'Home? Are you homesick, love? Is that it?'

She nodded, unable to hold back the tear that plopped onto Faith's head. 'Will you tell me something? Something that might help?'

'Of course, love,' he whispered. 'What is it?'

'Tell me what you've heard about his first wife.'

'Marrie!' he rebuked her gently.

'Tell me,' she insisted. 'You must have heard something.'

'Not much.'

'What's not much? Did they like her?'

'Not the way *you* mean.' His answer was reluctant and he turned to lean his back against the wall, fidgeting with the hem of his short tunic.

Marietta rolled away from the gap to face him for the first time. 'Not the way I mean? What way *do* I mean?'

Bruno's cheeks tightened. 'She was a bitch,' he said.

She waited, expecting him to elaborate, weighing that piece of information against what she'd heard earlier. But there was no more. 'Go on,' she said.

'No, Marrie. I'm his squire. I may not say anything of my lord's business to anyone—'

'Not even to your sister? His wife?'

'No, not even to you. In any case, they don't discuss things like that in front of me. That's just what I've gleaned. All I know is that you are as different from her as it's possible to be. All the men say you're a lady.'

'They say that?'

'Yes, they don't mind me hearing that. Come on, Marrie. He'll tear me to shreds if I don't take you back with me.'

'You go, love. Tell him I'm coming. Tell him the dog is delaying me... I'll come shortly.' But not until she had walked for an hour in the deer-park and lingered in her garden on the way back. And by the time she had reached her solar, Anne and Ellie were ready to pounce on her.

'M'lady, where've you been? Lord Alain is asking for you to go to his solar.'

Then let him ask, she thought. And if he thinks I'm spending the evening in his company, with or without that clever little baggage, he can think again.

By the time he had put his head through the door

once again, Marietta was in bed and propped up against a pile of cushions. The maids withdrew.

'Where in heaven have you been, Marietta? Did you not receive my messages?' Lord Alain sat on the bed and caught the pup as it flew to his knee.

'Yes, my lord. I've been on household business.'

'What, until now? Surely everything's in hand, isn't it?'

'Yes.' She stared straight ahead, refusing to meet his eye.

'And you've got extra help in from the town?'

'Yes.'

'Then we're all ready for our guests?'

'Yes.'

'And the garden? Will that be ready to take our guests into?'

'No, my lord. It won't.'

'Not, sweetheart? Why not?'

'Because I haven't had time to attend to the planting. I was to have seen to it today, but the new plants are still in boxes and wheelbarrows.' She had passed them an hour ago and had ordered the pages to water them, quickly, before the portcullis was dropped inside the gatehouse.

'Then you shall do it tomorrow, eh? I'll get you some extra help and we'll have it ready by evening. Perhaps you'll have time to ride with me on Mist, will you? You have not exercised her for days.'

'No, my lord, I won't. Take Emeline. She'll be glad to keep you company. Let her ride it.'

She knew her peevishness had shown as soon as she had spoken, for he sighed, recognising at once the cause of her cold formality.

'I see. So that's what it's all about. And you're tired, too. Do you want me to come to bed early, sweetheart?'

'No, my lord. I would sleep alone, if you please.'

'Oh no, my lass. . .' He stood up, ready to close the argument.

'It's the time of my monthly flow, my lord. I prefer it.'

He would not deny her the right to sleep alone at such a time, though it was not what he would have wished.

'Very well, if you wish it. Sleep well, love.' He bent to kiss her but found a cool cheek instead of a warm mouth. There could be no insisting at a time like this. To Marietta's distress, he dropped the pup down onto the coverlet and went without another word.

With knees drawn up under her chin, she sat in the great bed alone, staring out towards the deepening sunset, hardening her heart against the man she knew she had come to love. She had lied; her period had been and gone before their wedding day but he was not to have known that. With any luck, she could use this as an excuse for some time and by then, he would not care, anyway. By then, Emeline would no doubt occupy his nights as well as his days.

Perversely, no matter how she tried to steer her thoughts away from the recent memory of his arms and their nights of loving, they swung back like a rudderless vessel into the path of the storm, more than once threatening to drown her in their sweetness. Now, however, they were coloured by bitterness, warped by her own furious manipulations and by the gossip of the two townswomen. Bruno had verified it; the woman had not only looked like Emeline but had been as mischievous, too. Perhaps more so.

Dwelling on the change in Emeline as an escape from a surfeit of pain, Marietta wondered at the swing from submissive child to spiteful coquette, remembering her uncharacteristic and virulent attack at Monksgrange after Lord Alain's offer of marriage, her subsequent prolonged refusal to respond to Marietta's attempted explanations. It had been there then, Marietta mused; *that* had been the catalyst.

And now, the sudden knowledge that she was desirable, brought about by Lord Alain's companions, perhaps, who had welcomed her visit to Thorsgeld with such enthusiasm; that, combined with her humiliation at not being the next Lady Thorsgeld, had produced another kind of Emeline here, under their roof. But was she a bitch, like the other one?

Wriggling down into the bed, Marietta stretched her hand across to where he should have been, stroking the sheets, the ache in her heart keeping her awake in spite of her tiredness. It was there every time she woke, every time her arm wheedled its way into the cool space where he was not.

At first light, when she knew that the porter at the gatehouse would be astir, she left a note for Iveta to find her and went round to the still-unfinished garden. How much easier it would be, she thought, if a door had been knocked out of her solar wall and steps laid down to the outside. They would have led straight into it, so much quicker than going halfway round the castle to reach it.

As the team of gardeners joined her, she laboured all morning to plant her medicinal herbs in the square plots outlined by low box heges, tall elecampane, balm, feverfew and rosemary nearest the two walls, then rue, self-heal and soapwort in the middle, and periwinkle, catmint and lavender nearer the paths. Others were placed wherever there were spaces.

Her trees, elder, bay and witch-hazel, stood at the ends of white-painted fences as focal-points, not too near the ornamental pond now teeming with new golden carp. Water-lilies were planted in here and Old Adam had laid a stone fountain in the centre that bubbled and poured from a great shell. Vervain, hyssop, bugle and betony, valerian and centaury were all found a place, some round the edges of the lawns and shade-lovers on the far side of the stew-pond.

The new dovecote in the corner was a wooden tower on a stone base, its openwork top already adorned with white and buff-coloured pigeons cooing and rattling in perpetual surprise at the goings-on, their valuable droppings now falling inside the tower, rather than on the paving.

At mid-day, she sent a message to Lord Alain, asking to be excused from the meal—she would have a picnic in the garden instead—not pausing for a moment but going from garden to orchard to supervise the planting of vines and cherry-trees against the wall, to have the grass mown and the hedge trimmed.

Returning to the garden through the prettily fenced walkway, her attention was caught by a brilliant flash of blue and red by the entrance to the stew-pond garden from the shooting-butts. Shouts and shrieks caused the garden-lads and Old Adam to look in surprise to see who intruded, breaking the peace of the afternoon.

Marietta, with hackles raised, strode up the path towards the adjoining gate and pushed it open, infuriated by the sight of two young men scooping water from the stew-pond and flinging it in sparkling arcs towards two others who held the shrieking Emeline. She laughed and twisted in their arms then ran aside, trampling over a newly planted patch of dyer's madder.

'Get out!' Marietta was in danger of losing all control, seeing nothing but the desecration of her own sacred place, the haven she had built up from nothing. 'Get out! *Out!*' She picked up a terracotta plant-pot and hurled it, screaming, at the group, hitting one lad fair and square on the side of his head. Then picking up a broom that lay nearby, she flew at Emeline, laying it about her back.

'No. . .Marietta, no!' Emeline shrieked, standing her ground. 'Lord Alain said I could come in here. . .ouch! Stop it!'

'I don't care a tinker's cuss *who* said you could! *I* say you can't. This is *my* garden. . .it's private. . .' Each phrase was punctuated by a hard thwack across their shoulders as they crouched away. 'And if you dare to set foot in here again, I'll get a cross-bow to you. Yes, you too, you whey-faced, sly, puking. . .clever little bitch! Don't think you've got the better of me. . .yet. . . you'll have to get up earlier to outdo me. . .trollop!'

'Stop, please. . .Marietta. . .don't. . .look, he's bleeding. Oh, poor. . .'

'Then go and tend him! You're a woman, aren't you? Tend him!'

Panting with white-hot rage, she flew at Emeline like a whirlwind, pushed hard at her back with both hands and propelled her through the gate at an undignified gallop. Then, keeping hold of her bliaud, she pulled the unfortunate lass round to face her, grabbing at her hair and half-veil in one fistful, her savagery now unrestrained.

'And keep your pretty unsoiled hands for those louts. . .Emeline *dearest*,' she snarled, 'and well away from *my* property! You are *not* the mistress here. . .I am! Understand?'

She pushed Emeline back, step by step, towards the wall, oblivious to the audience of squires, young knights and the Master-at-Arms who could barely be expected to ignore such an example of aggression.

'*I* will decide what our guests will do. *I* will decide what *you* do, not the other way round. And if you seek to prattle to my lord, or ogle him the way you've done since he returned, *this* is what you'll get!'

And with one mighty swing and before Emeline could guess what was meant, Marietta hit her across the side of her head with all the force she could muster.

Emeline fell like a stone onto her hands and knees, placed a hand against her head and pushed herself upright, holding onto the wall for support. She made no sound but quietly moved away, aware that she must now pass the stares of the unsympathetic older men to reach the kitchen garden and thence through the well-peopled gate-house. Her young escort had long since disappeared.

It was only then that Marietta saw how many people had witnessed her violent rage, an exhibition she had assumed was private. But only one face caught her eye among those who had lowered their bows; the Master-at-Arms was as near to a smile as he ever got, his head nodding in a clear signal of approval. Before she could turn, he had reached the gate and held it open for her, bowing respectfully as she passed through.

'Thank you,' she whispered.

In all truth, she hardly knew which way to go, so dizzy was she with spent rage and distress, so shaky were her legs, her hand stinging with the force of the blow to Emeline's head. She had never before hit anyone except a young lad, once, and Bruno in half-play. Never her sisters. Nor had she ever completely lost her temper. But never had she so consistently and sorely been provoked, nor for so long.

Holding a hand to her mouth to stifle the sobs, she saw the trampled plants, the broken plant-pot, the new water-lilies half pulled out of the stew-pond and, still too upset to cry, she stood panting in loud rasping moans as her anger flared again and simmered.

Old Adam came through from the pleasance, unperturbed, and without a word directed two of the lads to re-set the plants and tidy up while Marietta went along to the new fountain to splash water on her face and hold her wrists into its coolness.

It was then that Lord Alain came into the pleasance. Marietta was quite sure that, by now, Emeline would have told him some tale of an unprovoked attack, of a personal assault on herself, of a lad's bleeding head, and she was prepared for the full force of his wrath, even a beating. Consequently, she braced herself for his first onslaught, undeceived by his quiet approach but not willing to stand meekly and take her punishment without some contest. She glared at him with undisguised animosity as he advanced.

'That's my girl,' he said, quietly, 'that's my beautiful wild cat. I wondered how long it would be before you stopped sulking and fought back. It took trespassers on your garden to rouse you, did it? Eh?'

Still unsure of his humour, she watched to see what his hands would do, how his eyes might narrow before he struck, but there was nothing of that, only amusement and approval and an all-encompassing glance that swept her from top to bottom, making her angry so soon after the conclusions she'd been forced to arrive at yesterday.

'If you're going to beat me,' she spat, 'get on with it before the gardeners get back. I don't want an audience.' Her heart was racing now with a new threat and she held onto the wall of the fountain-pond, bracing herself.

'You think I'm going to beat you, lass? For doing what you should have done days. . .weeks ago? Nay, I can do better than that.' Without any warning—and she was too confused to anticipate—he grasped her shoulders and pulled her into his arms, closing her cry of protest with his lips and holding her painfully hard onto his chest. His kiss was like strong wine.

After the exertions of the last few moments when she had released so much pent-up anger, it would have been easy for her to soften and hold onto his supporting arms and be cradled like a child. But her pride struck a course of its own and she pushed away from him, unable to forget what she knew.

'Go!' she panted, 'go and tend your precious Emeline. *She* needs you, not me. And when she tells you she doesn't know why I hit her—'

'You *hit* her? God's truth!' His eyes danced. 'Where?'

'Where? On her head. . .where d'you think?' she growled.

'I didn't see that part. . .wonderful. . .what a woman!'

A thought occurred to her that he must have seen what happened.

'You saw? Where were you? You sent her here to provoke me, did you?'

'Nay, lass. Give me *some* credit! Up there, look.' He pointed to the windows of his solar high up next to hers, overlooking the garden.

'I heard their commotion as soon as they went in, and looked out to see what was happening. I saw you chase them off and hustle her round the corner, but I couldn't see the rest.'

'But you heard?'

'Yes, sweetheart, I heard most of it. And I saw the approval of your audience, too. It was a treat.'

'Then if you approve so much, why have you encouraged her to goad me so? Why did you not chastise her yourself instead of leaving it to me?' She pushed past him and tried to walk away but the seat was there in the corner and he would not let her pass.

'Because, my fierce woman, she is a guest here, for one thing, and I may not do that. And for another, she is *your* sister and, if anyone has to take her in hand, it has to be you. But you've been pussy-footing around her all this time as though she was made of thistledown, terrified of hurting her feelings any more. It's taken you all this time to do what you should have done ages ago.'

'How can you say that. . .how *can* you? When I told you how she'd annoyed me, you told me we'd manage her together. You didn't say you'd give in to her every whim and that I'd be the one to bear the consequences. If you'd said *that*, I'd have insisted she went home, there and then.'

'I don't want her to go home. If she asks to go home after this, I shall not co-operate She can stay put and learn to behave herself.'

'And you'll do all you can to make things comfortable for her, I suppose. . .and give way to her. . .while I do the housekeeping and. . .run round after you both. . .get off me! Take her into your bed, too, why don't you?'

She beat at him now in a frenzy of jealousy, torn between hurting herself and hurting him at the same time, all caution gone.

'Take her. . .I don't care if you bed her day and night. . .but she'll not come into my garden. . .get off! If she comes in here, I'll tear every plant up with my bare hands and throw them over the wall. I swear it!'

'There's no need to be jealous of her, Marietta. I've told you over and over that it's you I want. . .not her. Be still and hear me—'

'I won't hear you! I won't! I know more than you think I do. I'm not stupid. . .I have ears. . .it's Emeline. . .you can't fool me any more.'

He grabbed her flailing arms and slammed her back against the wall, stopping her struggles with a grip so fierce it took her breath away.

'Then listen to me, woman, once and for all. Until I can tell you what my reasons are, you'll have to go along with it. She'll stay here while we have guests whether you like it or not, and as soon as they've gone home I'll be glad to see the back of her.

'Now, I don't know what you've heard and I haven't time to find out, but hear this, and understand me plainly, Marietta. We'll have no more of this hiding and sulking. You will be at my side at every meal. . .at *my* side, do you hear? And you will play the part of mistress of the house and attend me on every ride, dressed in your finest, on every hunt and at every gathering. I want no evasions!'

'My flux. . .I cannot hunt. . .'

She had seldom seen him so angry. 'Don't lie, woman! Do what you like to me, but don't lie! You tell me you're not stupid, so give me the same credit, for pity's sake. It's not your monthly flow and you know it as well as I do. And let me make something else clear; you'll share my bed every night. If I'm not in yours, you'll be in mine. Then you'll know for certain where I am at night, won't you? Eh?'

'You can't make me. . .' She made a last attempt to flout him.

'Oh, yes, I can, my girl, I can make you do that too. You know I can.'

As if to demonstrate how easy it was, he slipped a hand round to the back of her neck and drew her forward to his mouth, holding her still just long enough for her to have moved away if she had wanted to. Teasing her lips to prove his boast, and lingering with the tenderness she had longed for during the lonely night, he let his hands fall, holding her there with his mouth alone.

'Now, my lady,' he whispered, 'you will come inside with me and do what we should have done last night. Then you will refresh yourself, dress in your brightest gown and ride your new horse with me until supper. She's getting almost as frisky as you are. Come. I'll have your obedience now.'

Silently, Marietta took his offered hand and allowed herself to be led back into the castle with all the meekness of a lamb, little Faith romping after them quite unnoticed and trailing her lead.

No nearer to making any sense of things than she'd been before, Marietta's first instinct was to obey her husband. Which was, fortunately, the pleasantest road to follow since it led her into his arms for the best part of an hour. That she had vowed never to allow that to happen again was something that lost credence somewhere along the way in a jumble of revelations and dismissals bandied about like ammunition in their earlier confrontation and which now seemed vaguely irrelevant.

Strive as she may, she could make no sense of it; it was as though he realised there was something for her to discover—at no time had he pretended otherwise—and yet felt that it was not essential she should be told. Not at this time, at least. Could she have got it all wrong? In the light of his approval of her disciplining Emeline, was it possible that he had chosen her, Marietta, because she was different? Not the same? Had she been barking up the wrong tree?

Whatever it was, she decided that, for one day, enough was enough, that she deserved some respite from the conflicts, theirs and her own. If he wanted her company enough to demand it, then her obedience could hardly be called surrender, though no one would have known the difference. And later, when she rode by his side on Mist, she adopted a mantle of serenity rather than a forced ebullience which, after her victory, might have been permissible.

She stayed near him, watching the mares and foals, observing the training of the destriers and, in the tiltyard beyond, shouted gentle encouragement to Bruno and his friends who practised with unwieldy lances against the spitefully small ring that swung in the breeze. And when the squires urged Lord Alain to show them how it should be done, she cheered with the rest when he did, and gave him the kiss that he claimed as reward.

Afterwards, she took him on a tour of every department where her skills as mistress of the household had been put to good use over the past few days, surprising him with the extent of her preparations, the detail of her planning, her forethought, her knowledge of every man in every job. At the same time, it satisfied Marietta to show him something of the work that had kept her so occupied when he had assumed that part of her absence was due to pique.

His arm stealing around her shoulders when the cook's staff, the marshal's staff, the chamberlain, the steward and the treasurer, too, all attested to her competence was a recognition that he was proud of her. She showed him the prepared guest-rooms, the supplies, the extra accommodation for servants, the lists of entertainments, the plans for outdoor food for a picnic in the garden with musicians, and several feasts.

New liveries had also been prepared for all his staff—blue badges outlined in yellow on a grey background, blue and grey parti-coloured chausses and yellow shoes—and new banners for the hall.

When they sat down to supper, they sat Iveta between them to make a fuss of her, not even asking where Emeline was. Even so, Marietta sent her a well-filled tray of food and wine and noticed that it was returned at the end of the meal, empty.

They took Iveta and Bruno to the garden after that, where all was now serene and well kept and where the lads were quietly watering the plants before sunset. The pigeons had lined up on the edges of the two ponds to take their last drink of the day, and a few late bees bumbled over the marjoram in a last raid.

Old Adam came to Marietta, ambling up the path with his hand stretched out towards her. He had known Lord Alain since he was a lad and saw no reason to stand on ceremony at this late stage.

'Look 'ere, m'lady. This is summat I were given by Lord Alain's father.'

He opened his fist to reveal a mound of tiny black

seeds. 'He brought 'em back from t'Holy Land when he were on one o' them crusades. Seeds, they are. I've 'ad 'em all this time waitin' for't right person to gi' 'em to. Now look. . .' He took her hand and poured them into her palm '. . .thou can have 'em. They're yours.'

Marietta was delighted by the honour. 'Thank you, Adam. I'll plant them straight away. Do you know what they're called?'

'Nay, m'lady, I'm not sure what proper name is, but he called 'em love-in-a-mist, 'cos they have a blue flower wi' fuzzy stuff all round, like mist.'

Lord Alain nodded wisely. 'Then we'd better find a good place to plant this love-in-a-mist, hadn't we? Do we have a place in the sun?'

'Over here,' Iveta called. 'Look, Marrie, here's a space, next to the self-heal.'

So they sprinkled the seeds on the dampened soil and pressed them down, and Iveta tied one of her red ribbons to a stick to mark the spot and to keep away the birds.

'Winged or otherwise,' Lord Alain murmured.

Marietta wondered why the first Lady Thorsgeld had not been the right person to give them to. Had it been because she took no interest in gardens?

CHAPTER NINE

THE musicians, rising to a crescendo at the end of their chorus, drowned out the words of the handsome guest sitting next to Marietta, and she was obliged to lean towards him and watch his lips to catch what he was saying.

His shoulders were turned towards her and she caught a faint whiff of some perfume from his thick well-groomed hair, and before she caught his eyes, she saw that they had already lingered on her bared neck and the outline of her breasts. More than that, while meeting hers, they flickered beyond her for a split second, to where Emeline sat further along the table.

'Until I met your husband in York last week,' he was saying, 'I had no idea he'd re-married. Did he take you by surprise?'

Ignoring the implications of the seemingly artless question, Marietta gave him more solid information to consider. 'I came to live at Monksgrange for the summer with my family in late April. It's across the valley, you know. My young brother Bruno is one of Lord Alain's squires. That's how we met.'

She pointed Bruno out to him, kneeling before one of the guests further along the table and holding the bowl for finger-washing, a towel draped neatly over one shoulder. He looked solemn and very fine in his new livery.

Her companion, Sir Bastien Symme, looked puzzled. 'I always thought that Monksgrange belonged to Bolton Priory,' he said. 'Have they let it go now?'

'Yes. Difficult times, you know. My father bought it.'

'Your father. . .would I know him, d'ye think?'

'Sir Henry Wardle. I was Marietta Wardle.'

The news appeared to distract him somewhat, for he looked up sharply at that and studied her, though Marietta thought that he saw something else.

'Sir Henry Wardle. How interesting. He owns a fair bit of land hereabouts, I suppose?'

She recognised the mildly spoken question as being more than a polite observation, for he held his head at an angle, suggesting to her that he expected a full inventory. But he was a stranger to her; such information was best kept close to one's chest. Instead of answering directly, she smiled, as though such things were taken for granted.

'Do you know him, Sir Bastien?'

'Er. . .not personally, no. But everyone knows of him, of course. Have the lay-brothers entirely left Monksgrange now?'

'Oh, yes.'

'And when do your parents leave? After harvest? You'll be on your own then, will you?' His smile caressed her skin.

Enigmatically, she replied, 'Hardly,' allowing her own glance to take in the hall packed with people. Too many questions, she thought.

When he laughed, which he seemed to do readily enough, he showed remarkably even teeth and his eyes almost closed so that one could not tell whether they saw or not. He was dark, of lighter build than Lord Alain but well-proportioned, and elegantly dressed in deep mulberry and black with far more gold jewellery about his person than her husband wore.

'And your sisters?' His eyes strayed to Emeline again before returning to her. 'Do they live here with you, or with your father?'

'Like you, Sir Bastien, they're guests here. And they're my half-sisters. Bruno and I have the same mother. . .the first Lady Wardle.'

'Ah. . .I see. That accounts for it.'

'Yes.' She knew he referred to the colouring.

'I should like to meet Sir Henry Wardle. He appears to be a fine judge of women. Perhaps he could give me some advice.'

'You are a horse-dealer, are you not, sir?'

He accepted the mild rebuke with another laugh.

'Yes, my lady, I buy and sell horses, not nearly so complicated as breeding them. Your husband is far more knowledgeable than any dealer about that side of things. The land up here can support beautiful mares, fine-limbed fiery creatures.'

Whether it was intentional or not, he made it sound as though he was speaking of women rather than horses, for his eyes betrayed the direction of his thoughts when the smile faded from them and allowed a slow search of her face that halted fractionally on her mouth.

Fortunately, she was spared the embarrassment of making any response when Bruno placed a bowl of rose-petalled water with a graceful bow and stood back to watch them dip fingers, washing away the stickiness.

On the first floor, the great solar was a conveniently pleasant chamber in the northwest tower, overlooking the kitchen garden on one side and, on the other, the stew-pond garden with the view over the great wall across the valley. Taking the opportunity to mingle, Marietta went to speak to the couple who looked slightly less at ease than the others, all of whom appeared to know each other.

'Master Geoffrey. . . Mistress Jean,' she said, holding out both hands to them.

They were young and unremarkably attractive people, plainly dressed but neat and wholesome, glowing with health. They seemed pleased to be singled out for her attention; since their arrival last night there had been little time to do more than eat and sleep. These two, the de la Dales, were employed by a wealthy breeder of palfreys and workhorses over in Wensleydale, Mistress Jean almost as knowledgeable about them as her husband and an indispensable half of the partnership.

This was the first time they had been to Thorsgeld; they had not expected such a well-attended gathering, nor such a welcome, having understood that Lord Alain was a widower. His lovely wife quite won their hearts.

'Such luxury,' Mistress Jean smiled. 'You must have had some experience to control a place as large as this.'

'Not at all. My home was the usual manor, but I was used to overseeing the housekeeping, and there are plenty of men here who know what they're doing. It's the same, only larger.'

They liked her modesty.

'And horses?' Master Geoffrey de la Dale asked. He was a shrewd-looking man, his face weather-beaten and alert.

'Not my department—' she smiled in response 'but I shall be there when Lord Alain shows you the stud.'

She knew little enough about the other guests except what Alain had told her. Sir John and Lady Isobel de Rhenne lived in an ancient manor house near York, buying and selling war-horses for local knights. He had come prepared with a list of requirements and a clerk to make notes of his transactions. They were old friends of Lord Alain and had known his father, in which case, Marietta thought, Lady Isobel might be encouraged to tell her something of the first Lady Thorsgeld. She looked approachable enough, middle-aged and comfortable.

They were the senior couple; the others, Sir Richard and Lady Mary Capestone, were somewhat younger, more like herself and Alain. Enthusiastic and quite noisy, drawing people to them like magnets, they had already begun a good-natured ribbing of both Emeline and Iveta, aided and abetted by Sir Bastien. Marietta wondered how long it would be before the one bachelor in the group claimed Emeline's company for the rest of the event.

There were plenty of other dealers who would be sleeping in the great hall with their servants, but none who expected to be entertained in the same style as these seven.

Since yesterday, they had seen very little of Emeline, and now, though she would not meet Marietta's eye, she was back in circulation with a much-reduced coterie, unaware that the young men had been warned that any repeat of yesterday's performance would see them back home in double-quick time. No white flag had been offered, either by herself or by Marietta, but no one would have suspected that sparks had flown so recently.

Lord Alain's protectiveness towards Emeline was at first taken to represent the concern of a host for a young guest. If there were those among the onlookers who wondered how Marietta felt about this overload of attention, they said nothing. All the same, there was not one amongst those who knew him well who had not made the visual connection between Emeline and his first wife.

Neither had this attention to her sister escaped Marietta's notice. In the remaining day before the guests arrived, Lord Alain had done much to assure her that her fears about Emeline were mistaken, not by direct reference but by his appreciation of herself, by his approval and, not least, by his tender loving.

As soon as the guests arrived, however, the accent changed, and Marietta was once again confused by this inconsistency, being still in the uncertain earliest days of marriage and desperately in need of reassurance now, of all times.

Had she not begun to love him, it would have

mattered less, but her heart had opened, taking in pain as greedily as pleasure. And while she longed to screw Emeline's neck like a pigeon's, who could have blamed the lass for blushing timidly when he personally lifted her upon a gentle palfrey and whispered into her ear?

Most of the assembly who noticed this pretended otherwise and kept Marietta busy with their enquiries as they mounted horses in the bustling courtyard. But Sir Bastien was the one to take most immediate advantage. Brushing aside the young groom who held his hands for Marietta's foot, he took a stand behind her, put his hands around her waist and whispered a quick 'Ready!' in her ear.

It was not until she was firmly seated in the saddle and saw who arranged the folds of her full skirt that she realised who it was. Even though a snub for such familiarity could have been all the thanks expected, Marietta did neither. It was, after all, her right to be tended by her husband and if he was otherwise engaged, he could hardly grumble at the outcome.

All the same, the man's hands on her waist had spread well across her ribs and close under her breasts, and the strength of his fingers left an imprint that tingled, even as she gathered Mist's silky mane in her hand to free it from the rein-guard.

In no particular order, the riders trooped out through the gatehouse and round the side of the castle into the stableyard, Marietta fully aware that Sir Bastien was close by her side but saying nothing to embark on a conversation and neither returning nor avoiding his frequent looks at her. And while the destriers were brought out, one at a time, and paraded before them with glossy coats shining like satin in the sun, Marietta was drawn into the general talk, though most of the guests kept their comments for their partners.

Eventually, Marietta sidled her mount across to where Emeline sat alone, and drew her to the side with a tip of her head. Emeline must have thought she was again in the firing-line for she leaned to Marietta.

'I'm not ogling him, honest, Marietta. I've hardly said a word to him.'

This was the first allusion either of them had made to their quarrel; Emeline's silence on the subject had been taken for bitterness rather than acceptance. Consequently, Marietta stared at her sister as though the denial could have been finely veiled sarcasm. But Emeline was not one to understand such sophistication. She meant what she said. 'I'm doing my best, Marrie...' it was the first time she had used the pet name for many weeks '...I didn't really want to upset you, either.' From Emeline, that was an admission not to be ignored.

Marietta realised what it had cost her. She moved closer.

'Come on up here, away from the ears.'

They moved apart from the crowd to a space by the store-rooms.

'Emmie, I don't want to fight with you,' Marietta said, keeping her voice low. 'I can't believe you're happy about this state of affairs, are you?'

Emeline's pretty mouth pursed as tears gathered. 'No,' she whispered, 'no, I'm not happy. I would have gone home when you...we...you know. But he said I must not. I wish he would let me go home now.'

'Don't cry, Em, for heaven's sake,' Marietta put a hand on her arm. 'Don't...he'll think we're quarrelling again.'

'He's not doing anything to help matters, is he?' She sniffed. 'Is he trying to make you jealous?'

'Well, *you* were, weren't you?'

'I was, yes. Because I was still mad about the whole business. But I'm not in love with him, Marrie. He scares me a bit...he's so fierce...and he doesn't laugh like my other friends. And I'm sure that he's in love with you because I've seen how he's kissed you. . .'

'Where?'

'In the garden. Does he like the idea of us fighting over him. Is that it?'

Marietta sighed. Even Emeline, not-very-bright Emeline had seen that, so it must be obvious.

'It certainly looks like that. I can't for the life of me think why he should want that.'

'Perhaps it's because you were so reluctant.' Emeline turned to her, reining back a little as the hindquarters of the horse in front swung towards her. 'You made him chase you, didn't you?'

Marietta's eyes searched him out like a homing-pigeon, alighting on his powerful black head and wide shoulders, watching as he talked, pointed, called instructions, laughed at the remarks. Proud knight. Yes, she had made him chase her. Was this a way of taking revenge for her defiance, then?

'Yes,' she agreed, 'but it wasn't coyness, Emmie.'

'What then? He frightened you, too?'

'Yes, I suppose so.' That, among other more dutiful reasons.

'Are you still frightened of him? You don't look as though you are.'

'No. Angry with him but not frightened.'

'Then why don't you play the same game?'

In all truth, the idea had flitted through her mind since the arrival of their guests but, short of some discussion and support, it had been dismissed as too dangerous. Now, coming from Emeline herself, it took on new dimensions.

'The same game?' She studied Emeline's pretty face.

She must have appeared puzzled, for Emeline frowned at her, leaning closer.

'Come on, Marrie. Don't be dumb. I know you're not used to flirting, but it's good fun once you stop worrying. I can't stop him hanging around me, I can't be rude to him and snub him like I can the squires. And we can both see how he's enjoying some kind of game, playing one off against the other. Surely you can fight back. . .like you did with me?'

'And then what. . .when I've flirted?'

'Well, then he'll be as mad as a hare and probably beat you and stick you to him like a leech. And then he'll leave me alone to get on with *my* flirting. None of the lads will come *near* me when he's around. Besides, I'm much more interested in. . .' Her eyes showed exactly where her interests lay. Sir Bastien had already edged towards them, threatening an end to their conversation. 'Come on, Marrie, he's looked at both of us as though we were fillies ready for. . .'

'Em!' she hissed, ducking her head. 'For pity's sake!'

'It's true,' Emeline whispered, now laughing in anticipation. 'You take him on for a bit, just for a day or so. It'll work, you'll see!'

There was no time to go into more detail before Sir Bastien drew alongside Marietta and regarded their blushing laughter with an air of faint amusement.

'Well, well. This is the first time I've seen you two speaking together. Will you escort me into the paddock to see the palfreys, or shall I escort you?'

'Neither,' said Emeline without looking at him. She moved away into the crowd and left the two together.

'Good,' Sir Bastien smiled at Marietta. 'That's an even better proposition.'

There was more room for manoeuvre in the large grassy paddock where the best palfreys were brought in to be trotted along the avenue of spectators. These were the best, the showiest mares, the most docile geldings, the prettiest riding-horses especially bred and trained for the most comfortable ride, for endurance over long distances and rough roads, for their good temper and patient disposition.

Laughingly, Sir Richard Capestone called out to Lord Alain, 'What I want to see is that Andalucian your lady wife rides, Alain. You're keeping both of them uncommonly dark, you old scoundrel!'

Sir Richard was more interested in the destriers and was treating the second phase of the exhibition with rather less reverence, his wife thought, regretting the attention being drawn towards Marietta and her lovely new mount.

At that moment, Marietta was well out of earshot in the company of Sir Bastien and Sir John, discussing the merits of three of the stallions they had just watched.

Iveta called to her. 'Marietta, Lord Alain wants you to go to him.'

Thinking that this was no more than a request for her company, she ambled away towards him round the backs of the riders and came up behind him, waiting some moments before he realised she was there. It was Master Geoffrey de la Dale who drew his attention to her.

'Saints! There you are. Where have you been?' Lord Alain turned sharply towards her.

'Here,' she replied, unhelpfully.

'Oh. Some of our guests want to see what the Andalucian can do. Let them see her paces, if you please. To the top of the paddock and back.'

Marietta caught Emeline's eye. 'Certainly, my lord. Mistress Jean, come, shall we exchange mounts for a while? You would like to try this one, would you not? She needs an experienced hand like yours.'

Mistress Jean's face lit up with enthusiasm. 'Oh, my lady, may I. . .really? She's such a beauty.'

And before Lord Alain realised what was happening, the women had dismounted and exchanged horses. In the light of Sir Richard's remark about keeping them both dark, this was not what he wanted, for now it would look like a verification of the jibe, and though

Mistress Jean was an extremely competent horse-woman, the visual effect was not half so attractive as Marietta's graceful figure dressed in cream and pale-blue.

What was more, when she backed silently away on Mistress Jean's mount, she found that Sir Bastien Symme was there to take up a position next to her, making her laugh at some innocuous remark. Already she was beginning to feel the thrill of danger.

Throughout the afternoon, she and Emeline developed their mutual plan, both of them deliberately staying aloof from the men who thought the game was of their own devising. Whenever she glanced towards her husband, there Emeline would be also; wherever she went, Sir Bastien contrived to be.

Surrounded by so many pleasant guests, Marietta began to relax and enjoy their company and when they rode into the tiltyard to see the young lads practise she stayed in the centre of a crowd of men, talking animatedly while Lord Alain stood aside with the ladies.

Careful not to neglect any one of them, she took the ladies into the orchard to admire the new vines and then into the garden. Although she had vowed that Emmie would not be allowed in here, their conspiracy demanded that only the two men be manipulated, not the women. To them, they must appear as friends or run the risk of revealing the seriousness of their scheme and embarrassing everyone else at the same time.

After supper, while the air was still warm, the men joined them in the garden, eager to sit with them and bask in the success of the day. Throughout the meal, Marietta had maintained a distant attitude towards her husband, seeming not to notice his warmth towards Emeline and discovering how less painful that had become when she had the attentions of a handsome man to entertain her.

Knowing that Emeline was not as interested in Alain

as she had thought her to be gave Marietta free rein to laugh merrily, her head almost touching that of Sir Bastien, coolly ignoring her husband's glance of displeasure.

Now she sank down on the grass in the enclosure where the arbour stood, watching the approach of Sir Bastien's long legs and seeing, from the corner of her eye, where Lord Alain sat with Emeline and Lady Isobel de Rhenne. Deliberately, she waved to Lady Mary and Mistress Jean to join her and though they signalled that they would, they were delayed by their deep conversation.

'Scared, my lady?' Sir Bastien whispered as he sat by her, drawing up his legs to rest his arms across. His bold stare was impossible to misinterpret.

'You think I need protection, with my husband looking on?' She looked away, but too late to hide the smile. The situation would not have been half so piquant *without* her husband looking on.

Sir Bastien did not glance towards the subject of their discussion. 'He's not doing a very good job of it, is he? Not as good a job as I would do if I were your husband of only a couple of weeks.'

Still she would not look at him, but plucked at the short grass by her side. 'Then it's as well you are not, sir,' she said, softly.

'Why?'

'Because then you would not know who to flirt with most, your wife or your sister-in-law, would you?'

'Wrong, m'lady. I always know who to flirt with most. I flirt with the host's wife. She is always the most beautiful and therein lies the most danger, the most satisfaction.' He gave this comprehensive answer time to sink in while Marietta remained silent.

So, the man was an accomplished rake. Presumably, Alain must know that, and yet he left her open to his advances while he had eyes only for Emeline. Again.

After all his assurances. Then he deserved what was coming.

She knew he studied her face but hoped he could not recognise the conflict that stirred her, provoking feelings of revenge, pain and confusion. Rejection, above all. Rejection of her company at such a time, except to show off her new mare. Just in time, the recklessness that wavered on the brink of her anger was dissipated by the arrival of the two ladies. Waving a hand to the spaces by her side, she smiled up at them. 'Come, come and join us,' she said.

'Ladies,' Sir Bastien held out a gallant hand. 'I was just asking Lady Marietta about Beckington Manor down the road, there. It's your father's property, is it not, m'lady?'

Marietta looked at him in amazement, not only because of the suddenness of the relatively uninteresting topic but also because of his assumption.

'No,' she replied, 'it isn't.'

Hoping that this would conclude the enquiry, she turned her attention to Lady Mary's lively face bordered by gleaming red hair, plaited and coiled. 'Have you left your family in good hands, Lady Mary? How old are they now?'

Deftly, almost fervently, she kept the conversation moving between her three guests, steering around their interests and away from her own as though on an obstacle course, knowing that any wandering into her doings, however trivial, would invite personal questions she preferred not to answer.

But there was to be no escape, for when Mistress Jean spoke of her magical ride on Mist, it was then only one step away from silly Dulzelina, and Monksgrange, and then her family, and then... Beckington, brought back with all the determination of a trained fighter.

Skilfully, Sir Bastien avoided asking the question he most wanted to ask, but left it to Lady Mary instead.

'This place, Beckington, is it? Who did you say it belongs to?'

'I didn't,' Marietta said, by now too far gone to care a damn who knew her business, too unused to fending off questions to know which information mattered and which did not, 'but since you seem so interested, I will tell you. It belongs to me.'

'You?' Sir Bastien looked as though he was about to fall over.

'Why the surprise?' Lady Mary asked him.

'Well, I. . .er. . .'

Mistress Jean laughed. 'Come now, Sir Bastien, surely you don't think that the only people who own property are men, do you? My husband and I are in business together. Women can do anything that men can do, you know.'

That, of course, was a signal for them all to fall about at the sheer absurdity of it, attracting the attention of the other guests.

Marietta was persuaded to explain.

'Well, it's always been passed down the female line to the first one to marry. And that's me. But it's no cause for excitement; it's in a terrible state. We're going to renovate the place any day now.'

'You've been, have you?' Though Sir Bastien flicked a lady bird off his knee with studied casualness, his question was sharply put.

'Oh, yes. Alain and I were horrified. It's been sadly neglected because we've been so far away, but now it has to be attended to. Come. . .' she spied Lord Alain walking towards them, alerted by the hilarity '. . .it's getting dark already. The midges are out, look.' They danced in tightly packed clouds in the last rays of the sun.

She would have turned to walk with Sir Bastien but,

in two strides, Lord Alain had caught up with them and taking her arm firmly in his, escorted the party back into the courtyard and then into the great hall for a last nightcap before bed. His grip was painfully tight.

Intent on releasing herself as soon as possible, Marietta wondered if she could reach Emeline's room without him noticing her absence, but the chance did not arise, for he summoned Emeline's servants to escort her away and finally, when all were gone, he followed Marietta to her solar as though to emulate the candle's shadow.

She knew what was to come. She sensed his tension.

'What is this, my lord?' She wheeled on him in anger as the door closed behind them. 'Why stick to me like a leech in the last half-hour before bedtime? Is it only now you've remembered my existence? I did not strong-arm you away from the person you've been close to all day.'

'So you admit you've been close to Sir Bastien all day, do you? Well done, my lady, that's a start. Now we can make some headway.' He walked to the door of his chamber and called to the squires who awaited him. 'Get out!' he said to them.

Marietta heard the far door close and watched as he began to undress, wondering what was in store. 'Well, of course, I've been with my guests. What did you expect me to do? Ignore them?' she said.

'Sir Bast—'

'No!' she yelled. '*All* of them! I'm not surprised you didn't notice who I was with. You've not seen anything of what I did from morn until now.'

'Yes, I have, my girl. I've seen everything you did. I saw how you got out of showing off your new mare, too. That was not well done, Marietta.' He came to stand near the window where she could see the last orange rays of the sun on his face and chest. 'You know what I expected of you.'

'Yes, my lord,' she snarled, 'and I also know it's the only time you spoke to me all afternoon, and even then it was not a request, politely couched, but a command. You think I respond to that, do you? After only a few weeks of marriage and it's come to that, already?'

'I told you to trust me, Marietta, to have faith. I know what I'm doing.'

'Oh, no. . .' She was hoarse with rage now. 'Oh, no, you don't. You don't know what you're doing to *me* at all. Insensitive. . .boorish. . .' she strode to the door, ready to go anywhere, to find a room with her maids.

But he reached out and pulled her back. 'Come back, I haven't finished. There's to be no more flirting with that jackanapes. Do you understand? No more!'

Like a wild animal, she flung his hand away from her arm.

'Hypocrite!' she yelled. 'You've known that. . .that jackanapes. . .how many years? You must have known what he's like. He actually boasted to me of going for his hosts' wives because it's more of a thrill—'

'. . .What?' He twisted round to look at her, frozen. 'What? He boasted of taking his hosts' *wives*?'

'Yes,' she hissed, bending to him to push the words home, 'that's what he said. Don't tell me you didn't know that.'

'No. . .no, I didn't know it was like that.'

'Liar!' she spat.

She thought he was going to hit her, then, for his eyes narrowed, his cheek muscles tightened and the skin of his forearms rippled as fists were clenched. She braced herself but it did not come.

'You *knew*! And yet all day, and yesterday, too, you left me alone like bait while you dallied with my sister. And then you have the *gall* to chastise me for enjoying his attentions. Well, yes, I did enjoy them. And what's more, I shall enjoy them again tomorrow. And the next day, too.'

'Marietta, let me explain. I think it's time you knew. . .'

'Take your hands off me. . .I don't want to hear any more. You are beneath contempt! Yes, my lord. *Beneath* contempt!'

She saw how, for once, his shoulders dropped and sagged, how his eyes, once hard and challenging, now emptied into bleak dark pools. This was the first time ever that she had seen that look. She had wounded him. The temptation was to say more, to inflict on him what she herself had suffered.

But she could not. The joy of hurting him lasted a mere moment; it was replaced by a longing to hold and comfort him, to say how much she loved him. But he had never spoken of love to her, only of want and desire, and she understood that whether she loved or not was unimportant to him.

'Then if you don't want my explanation, my lady, kindly explain to me what else this. . .jackanapes. . .told you about his methods. Presumably you were not talking about that when Lady Mary and Mistress Jean were with you? Or did he have designs on them, too?'

Marietta thought back to their last topic of conversation.

'We were talking about Beckington, my lord, if you must know. I'll make a full record of our topics tomorrow, if. . .'

'What? Beckington?' He pulled her back once more. 'You talked of Beckington. . .Christ! I don't believe it! Did you tell him it was yours?'

Again, she shook him off. 'Is there some law that forbids me to talk of my own property? You will not talk of it with me. He did not know it belongs to me.'

'No, little idiot! He thought it belonged to your father.'

She blinked, thrown off course a little. 'Well, what if he did? What does it matter who it belongs to?'

Instead of answering directly, he wanted to know more.

'And when you told him that you are the owner, what then? Startled, was he?'

Remembering the man's look of sheer amazement, she would have said that 'startled' was putting it mildly. But why all this fuss about something which he had so resolutely refused to discuss? 'Yes, he was startled. But only because he'd not expected a woman to own it.'

'Because he'd not expected *you* to own it, lass,' he snapped. 'And did you tell him your father had bought Monksgrange, too?'

She knew both by the question and its tone that he had the answer to that already. Tired of this conversation and totally confused by his alternating rejection and concern, it was impossible for her to know which of them was genuine, or indeed whether both were genuine, but for the wrong reasons. Reaching beneath the large curtained bed, she felt for the wooden truckle-bed, pulled it out and began to shove it across the floor with one angry foot, picking up a blanket and shaking it out.

But Lord Alain saw what she had in mind. 'You can forget that,' he said. 'You're sleeping in there.' Before she could dodge him, he had caught her in one scoop and deposited her face-down on the bed. Then, ignoring her wild struggles, he held her hips down with one hand while he unlaced the ties of her cote-hardie from neck to below the waist, something she would have found it difficult to do without the help of her maids.

'I'm not sleeping with you. . .ever again. . .no, I'm not!' she yelled.

'Come on, get this off. You can't sleep in it.'

'Yes, I can! Let me up!'

'I will in a minute, come on. . .other arm. . .but you're going to tell me what else he asked you. I want to hear what damage has been done, then I shall know how to proceed.'

'Proceed with what?'

'With my plans. Lift your hips up. . .that's better.' He threw the gown to one side and began to unpin the gold mesh cauls that held her coiled plaits to her head.

'Let me up!' she gasped, her words spitting into the bedcover.

He continued to loosen her hair with deft fingers as though he was unbuckling his own armour. 'Yes, we'll get rid of this thing first.'

'I'm not going to sleep with you!'

'What else did he want to know? Tell me!'

'About what?'

'Beckington.'

'Nothing. I told him we were going to renovate it, that's all.'

His fingers stopped their unplaiting. 'Renovate it?'

'Yes, don't worry, you know as well as I do that it's a lie, isn't it? You've no intention of putting the place straight, have you?' she growled, twisting round to look at him.

'Did you say when?'

'Oh, for heaven's sake, why all this? What does it matter? I said any day now, or something like that, because it sounded good, even though I knew it to be a lie.'

Suddenly, his hand was removed from her hips and she was allowed to roll over at last and away off the bed, wearing only a fine linen kirtle and the long waving dark brown hair like a satin hood.

'Do you want me to explain?' he asked.

He sat on the bed and finished his own undressing while Marietta stood over by the window, watching him, still boiling with anger at his treatment of her, both now and during the day. What had he meant when he'd said that he didn't know it was like that? Like what? Was he saying that he didn't know Sir Bastien was attracted by the idea of taking wives? Had he expected him to flirt with Emeline, perhaps? But how could he when *he* had hovered around her all day?

'No! I don't want any more explanations. They're worthless. I've made every effort to make your damn horse-fair a success and this is all the reward I get... your pretences! Pretend concern. Pretend ignorance of your guest's well-known lechery. You're a sham, my lord.' The lump in her throat barred further words and she turned her head so that he'd not see her tears.

On silent feet he stalked her, picked her up and carried her, now sobbing hoarsely, back to the bed where he held her to him, rocking her and stroking her hair. Still protesting that she'd not sleep with him, not ever, she listened with half an ear to his whispers that the day had been a huge success, that her planning was a miracle, that she had looked magnificent.

Tomorrow, he told her, he would not allow her to stray a hand's-breadth away from his side and, if that toadying little pipsqueak so much as looked at her, he'd geld him. For some unaccountable reason, that consoling thought brought on a lethargy so profound that sleep could be held off no longer.

For many more hours, Lord Alain lay awake, caressing her back from time to time and brushing her hair away from the hot damp forehead. She had every right to be angry, he thought. For that, and other reasons, he would not put her through such anguish again.

What was more, if he had known that it was not so much the colouring that attracted the man but the fact that he found excitement in the idea of stealing another man's wife, he would never have put her in that position in the first place. He'd been a fool. Blind. Ham-fisted. His plans would have to be adapted accordingly.

CHAPTER TEN

NOT surprisingly, Alain's assurances that he would keep her close from now on were discounted by Marietta as soon as they were uttered. After all the pledges that he would seek her, find her, and bring her back to him, then his apparent unconcern, it was not to be wondered at that even a good night's sleep failed to convince her of his sincerity.

'You will forgive me, my lord, if I don't take your word too seriously,' Marietta said, scathingly. She sat up against the pillows, watching the way the muscles of his back rippled when he ran a hand through his hair like a giant comb.

He had allowed her a justifiable anger last night, but she had better learn how far she could go. Slowly, he turned his head to look at her, showing his displeasure. 'Don't dare to challenge my word, wench,' he snapped.

Recklessly, she pursued her course. 'It's not your word that's being challenged, is it? It's your ability to protect your own wife from the attentions of a man you know to be a rake.'

'That's enough! You sail too close to the wind, woman!'

She stopped at that, still vexed and disbelieving, but not foolish enough to venture further. Pulling up the covers, she waited in sullen silence for her maids.

Iveta joined her for breakfast in her solar while Lord Alain attended to business in the hall. Usually bubbling with an account of her activities with her new friends, Iveta was now subdued, nibbling absent-mindedly at her honey-cake and watching the maids tidy the room and dressing Marietta's hair with excruciating slowness.

199

She loved Marietta's willowy darkness, the hint of full curves beneath the deep pink surcoat and palest green cote-hardie, the olive skin and luscious dark eyes. Marietta was like a golden fruit, she thought, good enough to eat. Her friend Ian had told her that she, Iveta, was like an apple, sweet like a girl but quite tough. It could have been worse, but she would rather have been a peach.

At last the maids left them alone. 'Now, little one,' Marietta said, 'are we ready to go? We're to hawk today; a picnic dinner. Will you like that?'

Iveta shook the crumbs from her yellow gown into the rushes and raised her bright blue eyes, launching without preamble into her secret. 'Marrie, I've heard some men talking about horses. Lord Alain's horses. And they mentioned Beckington Manor, too. That's yours now, isn't it? Do you think I should tell him?'

Marietta stared, not quite understanding. 'Talking where, love? Downstairs? When was this?'

'Last night.' She looked sheepish and staved off Marietta's next remark that she should have been in bed. 'Yes, I know, but it was hot and I couldn't sleep. You know how my little room faces onto the courtyard?'

Marietta nodded.

'Well, last night there was a full moon and I saw two men go into the doorway in the corner of the courtyard where the bakehouse and brewhouse are.'

'The door that leads up to these apartments. Yes.'

'Yes, that's where I thought they'd be going. Ian showed me a passageway that leads from that stairway to the granary and malting-house.'

'Yes, that's right. They're immediately above the bakehouse and brewhouse. It's where the grain and malt are kept.'

'Well, did you know that there are big wooden shutes

up there so that the grain and malt can be tipped down to the floor below? Did you?'

'Er. . .yes, I suppose I have seen them. Why, Iveta?'

'Well, after I'd seen those two men go into that doorway, I went down to the passage on the floor below this one and then along to the malting-house, and when I got to the shute, I heard them talking.'

'Men? In the brewhouse? At that time of night?'

'Yes, their voices were coming up through the shute. I could hear every word they said.'

'And who were they? What did they say?'

'I'm quite sure one of them was Sir Bastien Symme. . .the one who was hanging around you all day. I don't know who the other one was, but he seemed to know a lot about Lord Alain's horses. They were talking about a stallion called Pen. . . Pen-something.'

'Penda?'

'Yes, that's it. . . Penda. He said it was their last chance, that he dared not leave it later than Tuesday because he'd be off Wednesday morning. He told the other man he'd have to get a message to Longleigh.'

'To Longleigh? Where's that?'

'No idea. Perhaps it's somewhere around here. Could be anywhere. And then he told him to get over to Beckington, that *that* was his last chance, too.'

Frowning into each other's eyes, the two sisters puzzled over the words, shaking their heads in mutual bewilderment.

'What on earth does Beckington have to do with it, I wonder? He was asking me about it. . .seemed shocked when I told him it belonged to me. What's going on. . .?'

Her words were not so much for Iveta as for herself. 'And why does my lord get so angry when I mention wanting to put it straight?'

One thing is certain, she vowed silently, if he can't tell me what he's up to, I shall not tell him what I know, either. If he won't discuss Beckington with me, I'll keep the information to myself until I've made my own discoveries. Then I'll tell him what I know and save myself the trouble of having to ask.

Whether she had been too tired and distraught last night to hear him offer—twice—to tell her, or whether she wilfully discounted that, no one would ever know. Perhaps there were few enough ways for her to take revenge for the indignities she had suffered. If it cost him a stallion, it had cost her much more than that in humiliation and frayed emotions.

'Don't tell Lord Alain, Iveta, please. Don't mention any of this. I'll tell him myself when we have some time in private, but, for now, forget it. . .will you?'

As soon as Iveta had left, Marietta's first desire was to go along to the malting-house to look again at the great wooden shute that sloped to the floor below, but it was not to be.

With barely a knock, Emeline entered. Like Iveta, she knew little about pleasantries or preambles.

'Well?' she said. 'Did it work?'

Marietta saw no need to pretend innocence but neither did she want to complicate the issue with all that had transpired last night. As far as Emeline was concerned, it must remain a straightforward campaign to pay Lord Alain back in his own coin.

'Yes,' she said, 'I suppose you could say that it did.'

'Did he beat you?' Emeline was avid for drama, it seemed. She was prettily dressed in blue and mauve with grey-squirrel inside her long sleeve-tippets and down the edges of her surcoat. The neckline was wide, showing an expanse of white skin right up to her ears, for she wore no veil, as Marietta was now obliged to do. It would be a cool flirt, Marietta thought, who could remain unmoved by that.

But she could not portray Lord Alain as one who would beat his wife, even to feed Emeline's appetite.

'No,' she said, 'we quarrelled, but that's nothing new. He knows I'm angry with him and likely to remain so.'

'Good.' Emeline's eyes sparkled. 'Does that mean he'll make you stay with him all day? I hope it does, because I want to be free to. . .enjoy myself.' She bent to stroke Faith's head.

'Flirt, you mean.'

'Well, yes, I suppose so. Has he not told you to stay with him? You won't go off with Sir Bastien, will you?'

'I'm not going to make it easy for him, Emmie. If he wants me to stay with him, he'll have to work at it. But I'm not going to go anywhere with Sir Bastien. I don't particularly enjoy having to work so hard at double-talk. Lord Alain comes straight out with it, and I prefer that.'

He did come straight out with it. . .always had done, whether she liked it or not. Was such a man capable of duplicity then? she wondered.

Once in the courtyard, there was no time for Emeline to wonder who her escort would be; as soon as Sir Bastien Symme saw Marietta's hand being held in the vice-like grip of her husband, he made a bee-line for the fair-haired beauty in blue and mauve, lifting her into the saddle before anyone else could reach her and staying close enough to ward off other gallant young men with whom she had thought to have fun.

In one respect, it was a relief to Marietta not to have to take her flirting with Sir Bastien any further; the danger had been stimulating yesterday, but now it had already begun to pall and she was more than content to leave the chase to Emeline. On the other hand, she was by no means ready to let Alain off the hook.

Her flirtation had had the desired effect but she could not help thinking that his about-face had as much to do with Sir Bastien himself and *his* preferences as about her own humiliation. And that was not the background against which either an explanation or an apology should be made. If he thought the episode was over, he could think again.

Iveta's disclosure had also put a different colour on things since yesterday: if it had truly been Sir Bastien's voice she'd heard, then he must surely be the one Alain had wanted to entrap. But today was only Saturday and there was plenty of time to find out more before the guests departed. Perhaps she'd make some enquiries on her own account.

But today, nothing could have been further than yesterday's marked rejection of her company by Lord Alain, nothing could have been more calculated to prove how he wished to make amends, to show how he valued and cherished his wife, how he enjoyed her company. So much so that in the end they began to assume that his interest in Emeline had been no more than that of a host for a young guest, and that her resemblance to his former wife was coincidental.

Only he and Marietta knew how her polite responses to his observations were cool to the point of being icy. Only they knew that his insistence on her closeness was more enforced than voluntary. To the guests, it looked as though all differences had been resolved, but Marietta was wary enough to notice how her husband watched to see where Sir Bastien was at all times, and could not help construing this as a continuation of his vigilance over Emeline. It was an easy enough mistake, for they were together all the time.

Supper in the great hall was a merry feast, extending well beyond the music-making into story-telling, riddle-guessing, charades and blind-man's-buff where Emeline conspired to be well and truly caught by Sir Bastien while appearing to be indignant and red-faced. In the still balmy evening, they sat in Marietta's pleasance by the fountain and listened to the lute and to each other's tales then, when Iveta's yawns reminded them how late it was, Emeline took her away, leaving the others to follow as they would.

Marietta seized her chance to dart along the passage to the malting-house without being seen, while Lord Alain gave last instructions to his chamberlain about arrangements for the morrow. Intending only to look and be back in her solar before he could begin to wonder where she was, she searched the gloomy little room for the shute where the malt was tipped to the brewhouse below. In the dimness, she found it, but all was still and dark.

Through the thick malt-dust, she tiptoed on into the granary next door where the floor was white with flour. Sacks were piled high next to the square shute in the floor where they were sent, unopened, down to the bakehouse below. This floor even had a flour-covered hole as big as a coin through which one could see what was happening, but here, too, all was silent, though the warmth rose upwards from the slumbering ovens and she could not resist a guess at the number of lovers who had chosen this place for a private assignation.

Smiling at the imagery and on the point of turning away, she caught the sound of whispers; thinking that someone was coming towards her from the malting-house next door, she stepped forward to make herself seen. If it was a serving-man and his maid, they had better see her before it was too late.

But the malting-house was still empty, and the whispering, a giggling cry of half-protest, a gruff insistence, passed beneath her to somewhere under the floury boards, sounds so sharp that it was as though they came from the same room. The temptation to discover who had entered the bakehouse was irresistible, and lowering herself gently onto a hard sack of flour, she leaned towards the shute, clamping a hand over her mouth in horror as she recognised the woman's voice immediately. It was Emeline's.

'This is not the way. . .no, not here. . .!'

'Ssh!'

There was a soft thud as bodies landed on sacks of flour below the shute, a stifled yelp and protesting squeaks.

'Come on, you little tease, you've been asking for this.'

'No, don't!'

Marietta was horrified, wavering between curiosity and a desire to go down and rescue her sister. But who was the man with her? Should she calmly walk away and mind her own business? Would Emeline thank her for interfering? Was she in any *real* danger, after all?

There was a silence. Marietta slithered off the sack and knelt on the floor, placing her eye to the hole at the side of the shute. It was too dim to see much except the grey-black tones of garments, pale hands and shoulders hunched over someone who squirmed, their heads just beyond her vision, maddeningly out of reach. She could only assume that this was Sir Bastien, but there was another whose involvement could not be discounted and, so far, the voice had not been clear enough to make her certain.

'Stop, go away. I don't want. . .'

'Oh, yes, you do, my lass.' The man's voice was adamant. 'You've been eyeing me all day long, wondering if I would. . .yes, I know. Well, now you can have what you've been waiting for.'

'I was *not*!' Emeline whispered though Marietta could see how one pale hand rested lightly on the man's shoulder. 'I was not even looking at you,' she giggled softly.

'Little liar!'

There was another silence broken by sighs and the little noises that Emeline made, combinations of surprise, pretend annoyance and pleasure, and even now,

Marietta was torn by guilt at the watch she was compelled to keep.

'That's enough,' Emeline was saying. 'I have to go.'

'Not yet. I haven't started,' the deep voice whispered, teasing. *Was* it Sir Bastien's? Could it equally well be Lord Alain's? Every word he'd said could have been his.

'I *must*. . .please! I shall tell my sister—'

'Leave your sister out of it. I can take her any time I feel like it.'

'You needn't think I'm going to let you. . .'

'How are you going to stop me? Eh?'

Marietta saw her sister's hand move downwards then, to her dismay, saw the man's hand slide into the front of Emeline's gown and push away the fabric to expose her breast. She could watch no more.

With a gasp, she pushed herself away from the hole and sat back with a bump, feeling a heavy pulse somewhere beneath her jaw that vibrated into her soft kid shoes. Emeline, not yet fifteen, behaving like that with. . .with whom? That man? Or with *her* husband? Which?

The sounds of their love-making rose up through the shute, single words, a cry, then silence. Was that how *she* sounded? And which of the two men had said he could take her any time he felt like it? Sickened, confused and fearful for Emeline's safety, she tiptoed through the doorway into the malting-house and from there along the passage to the stairwell, then upwards to her own solar.

She paused with her hand on the latch, unwilling to know for certain that it was him, the man she had come to love. How was she going to bear it? Slowly, very slowly, she slipped inside where the light from the setting sun hurt her eyes after the dimness of the inner courtyard rooms.

Lord Alain stood by the window, watching her

furtive entrance. There was no warm greeting, no continuance of the gentleness that had kept her by his side all day with barely a respite. This greeting was hard and all too ready to disbelieve. 'Well, my lady? Which route did you take to get to your solar? A lengthy one, it seems.'

Marietta made no answer. The relief at having him here before her was so great that words failed her. Though Emeline was in mortal danger, at least it was not from her husband. How could she ever have doubted him?

'Well?' He looked her up and down.

'No...nowhere...I, er...' She could not tell him what she had thought nor what she had seen. It was disgraceful to watch such an intimate spectacle.

He strode forward, his mouth set in anger, his eyes dark and glittering. 'Well?' he snapped again. 'I asked you where you've been. And don't give me lies. Just take a look at yourself. Look!'

'What?' she frowned, not understanding.

'Look at yourself!' He grabbed her shoulder and yanked her forward to the light of the window. 'Look!' He nodded towards her deep pink surcoat, her shoes, her hands. They were covered with white flour.

'The granary...' she whispered.

'Who with?'

'Nobody. I was there on my own.'

'On your own? For pity's sake, woman! Don't tell me you've been rolling on sacks of flour on your own at this time of night. Between now and three of the morning when the bakers start again, there's only one thing people go to the granary for. Who were you with? That wretch who couldn't get near you today? Eh? Him, was it?' He shook her arm, making her wince with pain.

'Leave me! Let go! I was on my own, I tell you!'

Now aware for the first time of how it must appear

to him, the full absurdity of the situation changed her relief at finding him here into indignation that he should believe of her what she'd believed of him only moments ago. Yet she could not explain that she'd unwittingly spied on her sister; he would never believe that her spying was accidental, nor would she tell him why she'd gone there in the first place.

Disinclined to argue the point, Alain was quite sure that what he was seeing could not be explained in any other way, and aware of how she had balked at his restrictions all day, how she had assured him she would thwart him, just to anger him, he had no choice but to believe that this was how she had chosen to round off the episode, with a show of her self-will. With that creature!

'Well, then, my lady. . .' he went to pick up his whip from the chest, cracking its snake-like lash across the room, flicking its tongue expertly towards her feet 'in that case, you'll have time to change to the truth while you're nursing your new stripes. I'll not be as tender as he was. . .'

'Who? In God's name, Alain,' Marietta snarled, unafraid of the whip but angered by his assumption, 'do you think I'd roll around the granary with that sniggering whelp? That *toad*? I'm not as free with my favours, my lord, as you are with yours. And if I'd been in your shoes this last week, I'd have deserved to have my hide red-raw by now. . .!'

She hissed in pain as the lash stung through the fine fabric of her garments across her thighs, catching the back of one hand. Refusing to flinch, she stood rigid, bristling with the injustice of his punishment and waiting for the next cut without showing him the pain of it.

But it was as though that single lash had been an unstoppable overflow of his fury, for now he heard her words and held back, staring at her with a new doubt clouding the brilliant certainty of the moment before.

Then, without another word, he threw down the whip and left the room, slamming the door after him.

With shaking fingers and with tears rolling silently down her face, Marietta summoned her maids to help her and, without asking any questions, they salved the red weal with comfrey, shook out the clouds of flour from her cote-hardie and surcoat and made up the small wooden truckle-bed with soft sheets and a blanket and pillow from the big bed.

Curled up, silent and alone, she wept with relief that he had not been the one with Emeline and that he cared enough about her to be angry at her supposed inconstancy. Then, as reason took another turn, she wept some more because she had no idea whether it was his honour he cared more about, or her. Sleep came while she was in the middle of debating whether he would return to his own solar or to hers.

Stealthily, his feet making no sound on the floury planks, Lord Alain followed the whispering, even in the darkness. The granary was empty but still the whispering went on as he bent his ear to the dark shute to catch every word.

'I don't know,' the voice said. Alain knew it was Emeline's.

'Well, you've got to persuade him to let you go before Wednesday. I can get you out of Monksgrange easy enough, but I can't get you out of this place. It's like a fortress when the gates are down.'

'Will we have a manor of our own, Bastien?'

There were sounds of nuzzling and soft shuffling noises. Alain stared into the darkness, every sense aware, angry and relieved, too, sure that Marietta had been here where he was sitting, alone and upset with no one to confide in, unsure of his reaction to what she'd heard. Sweet, lovely girl.

'A manor, horses, servants, gowns. . .all yours. . .as long as you let me have what I want. . .now. . .'

'Not again, Bastien,' she whined.

Alain cringed at the sound.

'Didn't you like it?'

'You were rough. . .'

'I'll be gentle, then. Like this, eh? You liked that, didn't you?'

'Mmm. But we have to go. Someone will come. . .'

'In a minute. Time yet. Put your hand there. . .'

'No!'

'Go on, put your hand on it. . .'

'What will you give me if I do? A carriage and six horses, new gowns?'

That laugh. Alain knew that laugh so well; his hackles rose at the memory of the damage it had done in the past, damage waiting to be paid for. The dilemma now was that this silly baggage was in danger sooner than he'd anticipated. A fifteen-year-old virgin was hardly expected to run the length of the course at the first try. He might have known she'd be that stupid. The other one had been clever, devious, cunning. This one was brainless. Too dim even to say no. Should he put a stop to it now, for Marietta's sake?

Instantly resolved, he stood, picked up the sack he'd been sitting on, ripped open the top with his knife and shook the contents down the shute. Then he walked away, along the passage and back up the stairway to the solar without waiting to savour the yelps and indignant howls of the two lovers below He was still chuckling as he opened the door to Marietta's room.

Even at this hour, the west-facing room was not so dark that he could not see the truckle-bed with its sleeping cargo. Smiling, he undressed and pulled back the bedcovers then, bending to the form of his damp-browed wife, he picked her up in his arms and carried her to the bed.

She murmured in her sleep. 'No. . .no. . .'

'That's what I thought you'd say, sweetheart. Beautiful girl, go to sleep now. You're safe. Sleep, sweet thing.'

Everyone, except Emeline and Sir Bastien, attended mass in the small but well-appointed chapel the next morning. Perversely, Marietta had not allowed Lord Alain to make a full apology for his too-hasty assumptions last night; her wounds were too deep to be healed by a few contrite declarations, and she had gone to mass with anything but forgiveness in her heart and had come away not too surprised to feel as hostile towards Alain as she had before. It was wrong, she knew, but until he showed some consistency, it was impossible for her, in her present state, to warm to him. Loving him was one thing; liking him was altogether different.

Combining concern with curiosity, Marietta went to Emeline straight from chapel. Emeline was in a bath of steaming water.

'I needed one, Marrie,' she said, almost defying her sister to scold. 'I had to have one.'

Marietta peered into the tub. 'Water? It looks more like milk. You're not bathing in asses' milk, are you?'

'Flour!' Emeline pouted. 'Some fool left an open bag by the staircase to my room and I tripped over it.'

'By your room? Out there, you mean? I'd better find out—'

'No, don't bother, it's all been cleaned up now.'

'But who's carrying sacks of flour along here?'

'Oh, some new scullion got lost, I suppose. Wrong passage.'

'But it's in your hair, too. Emmie. Look.' She held up a matted strand and showed it to her sister, whose scowl would have frightened the devil. 'Did you fall into it head-first?'

The tightly pursed mouth showed that any retort was being held in check. Emeline scrubbed. The maids hovered nervously.

'Where did you get to last night, Emmie?'

Emeline looked discomfited. 'I was with Sir Bastien.'

'Where?'

'Oh, Marrie, you sound just like Mother. Just talking, that's all. Don't you get all nosy like she does, for heaven's sake. At least I had a day doing what I wanted to do, and that makes a change. Thing is, Marrie, I think Iveta and I have been here long enough now. It's time we were going home.' She did not appreciate the contradiction of her two statements.

'You want to go home, even though you're enjoying yourself?' Had things gone badly for her? Marietta wondered. 'You haven't been foolish, have you, Em?'

Emeline would not meet her eye but stepped out of the bath and turned her back. 'No, course not.'

'He's quite a rake, you know. He does this flirting act all the time. Did you know that?' When Emeline made no reply, she went on, gently. 'He's the kind who seduces a woman, promises her everything and then disappears.'

Emeline fired a quick barb over her shoulder. 'What did he promise you?'

'Nothing. We never got as far as that before Alain dragged me off. Maybe if I'd shown more interest I might have discovered.'

'He seems to think you *were* interested, Marrie.'

'He would, wouldn't he? Can you imagine a man like that telling you that a woman was not interested in him?'

'Huh. No.'

'Course not. Look, Em—' Marietta reached out and took her sister's hand 'perhaps you'd better tell Alain that you're ready to go now. Out of harm's way, eh? Before things get too serious.'

Emeline nodded. 'Yes,' she whispered, 'I think I'd better.'

Suddenly, Marietta felt saddened by events, by Emeline's pretty pouting face which, by rights, should have been glowing with excitement and secret happiness. She could not ask her sister what had happened; they had never been on such intimate terms where experiences were shared, but Emeline did not look as though she had enjoyed Sir Bastien's intimacies too well.

Back in her own solar, Marietta puzzled over Lord Alain's attitude towards this man. Why had he invited him to stay under his roof while knowing him to be a womaniser? Why this sudden change of attention from Emeline towards herself? Where did Alain go last night after another sudden change of mind? Had he gone to the granary and heard what she had heard? Surely he'd not wanted that to happen?

She sighed. It had been a mistake to marry him. It was not what she had wanted. She gazed out of the open window towards Monksgrange and her eyes strayed upwards towards the cave on the hillside above where she had been trapped, compelled, coerced. How different had it been for her, then?

Impetuously, she whirled round and grabbed the whip that lay coiled on the chest, strode back to the window and hurled it with every ounce of strength way out beyond the garden and over the crenellated wall into the treetops, oblivious to the sound of footsteps behind her.

'Well done, sweetheart. The fire still burns, does it?'

'No, my lord,' she whispered, putting her hands behind her to avoid his outstretched embrace. 'A healthy flame can soon be quenched by rough treatment, by lack of care. I was just admitting to myself that I made a terrible mistake.' She struggled to keep her voice level, for he was handsome in his Sunday-

best, so strong and graceful, his dark hair inviting her
fingers to push deep into its silkiness, to caress his face.

'A mistake? You mean last night?' He bent quickly
to retrieve her hands, looking sadly at the thin red line
across the back of one and raised it to his lips to kiss it.
Then he closed the window.

'No, my lord, not last night. Long before that, when
I agreed to marry you. That was my mistake.'

'Marietta, if it's any comfort to you, you did not
agree. Remember how you did everything in your
power to make it impossible. You defied everyone.
You ran away and hid, and I found you and brought
you back—'

'To *this*!' she yelled, snatching her hands away, tears
flooding anew at his reasonableness. 'You brought me
here to this. . .this. . .madhouse! Where you alternately
shore up my confidence and knock it down the next
day. Where you offer hospitality to people you appear
to dislike and rail at me when I react perfectly naturally
to their foibles. You whip me when I tell you the truth,
you ignore me one day and insist I cling to you the
next. No one, my lord, no one has ever laid a whip to
me before, not even my father, and God knows he had
reason. It was a mistake. I should have taken your
dagger. . .and. . .killed. . .killed. . .!'

'Who?' Ignoring her beating fists, he pulled her to
him roughly. 'Who would you have killed, sweetheart?
Yourself?'

'You. . .you! I never wanted you,' she sobbed, 'and I
don't want you now. I was happier without you. Go!
Go!'

She swung a free arm but it was grabbed in mid-air
and held against his shoulder. Through her angry tears
she could see how he enjoyed her storm of temper,
how he understood the fearsome contradiction of
words and emotions. Even from her limited experience

of him, Marietta knew that he would not be quelled by such an assault.

'You,' she yelled. 'I could do. . .I could!'

'Brave, wench! That's good,' he laughed, 'as long as you don't turn a dagger on yourself you can fight me any time. That shows you're still on fire, in spite of you telling me that the flame's died. Still, sweetheart. . .still! This is only a squall, not a storm. The first days are always unsettling for a lass.'

'Unsettling? I'm not unsettled. . .*you're* unsettled!'

'Yes, love. . .' he gathered her up into his arms '. . .I am indeed. So let's have a contest to see who's the most unsettled. Come with me to the butts, now, and whoever gets the most bull's-eyes out of ten wins. Eh?'

Through her rage, the idea appealed to her. 'And when I win,' she growled, 'what's the prize to be?'

'If you win, sweetheart,' he grinned, 'you can do with me what you will.'

That was an offer she could not refuse; the ideas already crowded in.

'And when I win—' he continued.

'You won't!'

'When I win, I shall take you to that bed over there and make up for two nights of lost loving. So be warned, my girl, it could take some time.'

'I shall win,' she snapped. 'Come and see.'

He was not the only one to come and see, for when it became known that the lord and his lady were to contest their skills at the butts, the entourage grew until it seemed as though half the castle were behind them. And, not unnaturally, there were many who felt that Marietta needed their support and would have been happy to see Lord Alain lose, for once.

Good-natured from the spectators' point of view but deadly earnest from the contestants' standpoint, the contest buzzed with the sounds of advice—even young

Bruno whispered in her ear from time to time as he held her arrows and checked their feathered flights.

The Master-at-Arms, knowing she could not win, soberly chose the best bow for her and applauded loudly at every score she made, but when every single one of Lord Alain's arrows landed with a soft thwack in the dead-centre of the bull's eye and when Marietta's strayed by a few fingers beyond that point more than once, the anticipation of the prize he would claim could not be held at bay.

The cheers were as much for Marietta as for the victor.

'A gallant and chivalrous knight would have allowed his lady to win, my lord,' she rebuked him, her eyes dancing with reluctant mirth.

Before them all, he opened his arms and made her come to him. 'Would he now, sweetheart? Well, this gallant and chivalrous knight wants his prize too much for any of that nonsense. Come on. Your surrender, my lady, if you please.'

'Proud woman,' he whispered into her neck, tasting the perfumed softness of her skin and hair, 'beautiful, proud, courageous woman.'

Tenderly, Marietta smoothed her fingers over his shoulders, feeling the heat and moisture generated by his vigourous loving. He had not spared her, had not taken a whit less than his due, nor had she held back or complained, having accepted his challenge willingly. It had, after all, cost her little except in pride and physical energy, and they were both instantly renewable.

'What was your prize to have been, sweetheart? Can you remember?'

She felt his smile beneath her chin. 'Arrogant brute,' she said.

'Well, can you?'

There was a pause as she sought an answer that would sting him. But a heavy drowsiness was stealing over her and the careful weight of his body on hers banished all thoughts of revenge. 'No,' she said.

CHAPTER ELEVEN

THE arbour was a delight, even before all the foliage
had closed the gaps or covered the curved roof. From
the raised floor, the four women peered through the
crenels of the great wall, fully able to appreciate how
secluded and pretty it would be by the end of the
summer, how enticing it would be to sit on the turf
benches and see without being seen.

'It was never like this before. . .oh, dear. . .!' Lady
Isobel bit back the words, aware of her indiscretion.

But Marietta took it as a compliment. 'Before I
came,' she concluded. 'No, well, it took an army of men
to have it ready for now. It was a wilderness.'

'It was a wilderness last time I came with Sir
Richard,' Lady Mary told her, honestly. 'We stayed in
the castle then, but there was no pleasance, no garden,
nowhere to walk except over by the shooting-butts. We
went hunting. . .'

'We went hunting for beds, too, I seem to remember,'
Lady Isobel retorted. 'What a business!'

'What?' Mistress Jean sat on the chamomile and
brushed a palm along its feathery fronds. 'Hunting for
beds?'

'Yes,' Lady Mary agreed, 'nothing had been prepared the way it is this time. Hardly any servants, no
bedding. It was chaotic. Isobel and I slept with some
other guests all in one bed and the men slept in the
hall.'

Marietta frowned. 'But that's. . .tch, tch! Was she not
experienced, this first Lady Thorsgeld? There are
plenty of beds in this place.'

'Experienced?' The two guests looked steadily at

each other as though to assess the lengths to which they dared go in explanation of the evocative word. 'Aye, Jayne was experienced all right. But not at running a household of this size.'

'Tell me,' Marietta said. 'Please.'

Again, they hesitated on the brink of causing offence, but their hostess was insistent. Lady Isobel twisted a heavy gold ring around her plump finger and regarded the back of her hand. 'A silly, pretty thing,' she murmured, 'thought more about her looks and men than anything else. And hunting.'

'And hawking,' Lady Mary added, staring into the sky.

'Aye, and hawking. Anywhere men went, she'd go, too.'

Marietta waited for more, then prompted, 'Were they in love, then? She and my husband? Was he sorely grieved when she died?'

Lady Isobel sighed, and told her, 'No, Marietta, anybody could see that they were not. It was not a marriage of love but of property, that's all. A childhood thing, like many another.

'And I suppose,' she added philosophically, 'that if they'd both put their minds to it, it might have grown into regard, at least. But she appeared not to care what he thought of her and it looked as though he stopped bothering. He never showed her as much affection as you show that pup on your knees, Marietta. And as for having a shooting-match with her like he did with you this morning, well, you can see now why everybody was so interested: that was a real novelty, I can tell you. Especially the end bit!'

The end bit had been her public surrender to his kiss, something none of them had ever seen before, except Emeline and Old Adam. He had picked her up then and carried her as far as the garden, taking no heed of her laughing protestations but reminding her instead of a previous time when he'd carried her and suffered her anger for his pains.

Marietta laughed, remembering the direct progress to her solar without the slightest deviation or concession to the presence of his guests. Barefaced. And he had called *her* brave.

'But surely,' she said, 'he must have been saddened when she died of the pestilence? That must have been shocking for him.'

'Pestilence? Around here?' Mistress Jean said. 'Surely not. We had it around York, but it didn't reach as far as this.'

'No, Jayne died in the same year, but not of that, I think,' Lady Mary agreed.

'Not that?' Marietta was puzzled. 'What, then? Childbirth?'

They shook their heads, unable to help, and she was bound to let the matter drop rather than dwell on the subject indefinitely.

She did, however, long to know what part Emeline played in all of this, for she had no need to ask them if she and the first Lady Thorsgeld were alike; she already knew that for certain, though she also knew that Emeline's attempts at coquetry were those of the novice rather than of the fully fledged wanton.

It had crossed Marietta's mind more than once that Emeline was being used as some kind of decoy, but that idea had been dismissed when she remembered how Alain had begun his attentions towards Emeline before their guests had arrived, not afterwards.

But he had not been in love with his wife, apparently, nor she with him, so what reason did she now have to suppose that he could suddenly have fallen in love with Emeline? The more she thought about it, the more unlikely that theory became, even when she tried to recall her other reasons for believing it. And after this morning's display, how could she doubt that indeed it was herself that he wanted?

Strolling towards the stables with her three new friends, Marietta found it difficult to keep her mind on their chatter as a new image of Alain took shape in her mind—not the devastated widower seeking a replacement for his first lost love, as she had believed, but a saddened and lonely man who had recognised in her something he had never had. And he had been prepared to whip her when he believed she'd misbehaved.

Had he punished his first wife in similar fashion? Probably not, if he cared as little about her activities as these two had told her. What a way to live, uncaring, unloved and unloving. Poor man.

The men stood in a group over by the stables, thoughtfully discussing the destriers as they were brought out to parade before them again. They barely noticed the four women slip through the gate behind them, nor were they aware how they themselves were being scrutinised every bit as closely as the stallions.

Sir Bastien Symme stood a little apart with one of the older grooms, a stocky man with massive shoulders and a shock of black hair falling into his surly face. It was the first time Marietta had noticed him among all the others and she watched with interest as the two men talked, the one languidly handsome, listening, nodding, but keeping his eyes on the horses at all times, the other lively, his eyes roaming, disapproving and contemptuous.

Marietta, attracted by a snort from one of the stable-doors behind her, went to stroke the nose of a grey who was not part of the proceedings. Turning back to the company, she saw that Sir Bastien and the groom now stood with their backs to her, close together, and before her eyes had time to move on, she saw the groom's hand dive furtively into the open leather pouch which hung on the baldric across Sir Bastien's body, grab something and pull it out, then shove his closed fist into the pouch hanging from his own belt.

The strange part of this transaction was that Sir Bastien must have felt the firm tug on his pouch, for it was not done so stealthily that it could be called a theft. Yet, the very next moment, the groom walked away, swivelling his head round to see who watched, but seeing only Marietta's back as she quickly turned and renewed her attention to the horse. The next time she managed to catch a glimpse of the pouch at the knight's back, she saw that it was firmly buckled.

'Your sister is not with you, Lady Marietta?'

Without looking, she knew who asked for Emeline. 'No, Sir Bastien, I think she may still be resting.'

'Tires easily, does she?' His smile, she was sure, indicated another meaning to the words than mere concern. 'We have a hunt tomorrow, do we not? I hope she'll be with us then. And you. . .? Do you hunt too, m'lady?'

'Indeed I will.'

'And are you as skilled at the hunt as you are with the bow?'

'You shall judge for yourself, sir.'

He took her arm and gently eased her towards the group of guests. 'It is not so easy to judge for myself, lady, when your lord and master keeps you so firmly under lock and key. Does he allow you no liberty?'

She laughed at the plaintive questions, relishing the security of Alain's powerful presence only an arm's length away. 'All the liberty I desire, sir. The lock was one of my own choosing, and the key is his to do with as he wishes. He guards me well.'

'Tch, tch! Then I am doomed to make do with your pretty sister,' he whispered. 'Too bad. I had hoped for a more exciting ride.'

In spite of herself, the hair on Marietta's head bristled. His thinly veiled reference to the episode with

Emeline was audacious and she, Marietta, was not supposed to know of it. She could scarcely contain her annoyance.

'You are referring to the hunt, of course, Sir Bastien. I'm sure Alain has something to your taste. My lord. . .' she called. 'Sir Bastien needs an exciting mount for tomorrow. What about Dulzelina?'

Lord Alain understood her message immediately. 'Oh, we can do better than that, love.' He turned obligingly to Sir Bastien. 'Leave it to me, my friend, you shall have the very finest mount. Now, if we've finished business for the day, I believe it's time for supper.' He took Marietta's hand firmly in his, smiling.

'You're looking pensive, sweetheart. What is it?' He closed the door to the solar. 'What was all that about a horse for Bastien? Was he trying it on again?'

She told him what Sir Bastien had said to her.

'Well done. You took him at his word. I can guess what he was referring to, so I'll make sure he has an eventful day on Atlas. *That* should work off his appetite, eh?' Atlas was a bad-tempered and headstrong old war-horse who was kept on only because he had been Alain's first stallion. He would leave Sir Bastien little to think of except how to stay aboard.

Marietta sat on the bed. 'My lord, I am growing concerned about Emeline. Do you think, for her own sake, that you might allow her to return to Monksgrange now?' She had made so few requests of him since their marriage and yet he was as likely to refuse as if she made them daily. Already he had refused this one only a few days ago. Beckington, too. 'Please,' she whispered, reluctant to wheedle but not knowing how else to move him.

'You're concerned, are you? Why?'

'She's not yet fifteen, my lord. That man is far too experienced a rake for her to handle, and I don't want her to run into trouble, especially here, of all places, under my care. I've played nursemaid to her for long enough now and I think my father should be the one to keep her safe, not me. Iveta...' she flopped backwards '...Iveta is different. I'd have her to live with us. She's never a problem, but I think Emeline would be happy to return now.'

Alain went to the other side of the bed and flopped backwards, too, and looked at her, upside down. 'For your peace of mind, sweetheart, I have already sent to Monksgrange to ask Lady Alice and Sir Henry to come here and take her back with them.'

'What?' Marietta sat up and leaned over his head. 'You've already asked them? When? When did you do that?'

'Last night, love. I sent a messenger. They should be here in time for supper.' He was smiling broadly at her astonishment.

'Alain, you didn't tell me! That's any moment now, and I have not had rooms prepared...or extra food... Oh, why didn't you tell me before?' She made to roll away, but he pulled her back.

'No need—' he held her across him, laughing '—they're sharing Emeline's solar. D'ye think that'll keep her safe enough?'

'Oh!' A radiant smile broke through her previous concern. 'Oh, thank you, Alain. Thank you.' She leaned over and pecked his nose, and when she would have made her escape, she found that his arms were locked about her.

Marietta would like to have had more notice of her parents' arrival but was bound to admit that this would have made no difference to the arrangements, only to her peace of mind. Everything was organised to perfection, clean rushes on the floors, more tables laid for supper, more silver and gold on view, more food and wine.

Only Emeline looked sour at the disconcerting news that they were to share her bedroom, not because she resented any threat to her freedom but, having begun to lord it over the servants, she was loath to hand over the power to Lady Alice.

Neither Emeline nor Marietta had anticipated the arrival of Sir Nicholas Bannon, though they might have known he'd not miss a chance to ingratiate himself with other landowners in the hope that one of them would discover his attributes and offer him their patronage.

To his credit, he made himself instantly affable to Lord Alain's guests and Marietta could not help noticing how sensibly he greeted her and how he appeared genuinely interested in the people around him, asking questions and, for once, dispensing with the overtones of contempt which so often concealed his feelings of inadequacy.

Instead of complimenting Marietta on her new estate or making her blush with remarks about her personal appearance, he told her what she most wanted to know, about what had been happening at Monksgrange: the state of the garden, the sow and its new litter, the argument about common land and boundaries, the rebuilding of barns. As though the short separation had supplied a lifetime of news, they talked as friends as never before, even noting with shared laughter how Lady Alice had already taken Emeline firmly in hand.

Only a day or two ago, she might have been tempted to flirt with him merely to salve her bruised pride, but now the suspicion that Alain had perhaps received enough fickleness from one wife held her back. She would play no more games. She would give her husband no cause to doubt her virtue, no reason to exclude her from his protection. She would not sink so low in his esteem.

* * *

The idea of a day's hunting brought out the best in the men; there was not one of the company who could think of anything he would rather do on a fair day in May than sit astride a bold horse and head for the vast deer-park in good company. Sir Henry Wardle was in his element, beaming across his handsome face at the antics of Sir Bastien's mount who had it in mind to be the first out of the courtyard.

'Hah!' he grinned at Marietta. 'He'll be on his way back before the rest of us have started at that rate. Is that his own stallion?'

'No, Father, it's Alain's first. He's old now, and set in his ways. He doesn't take kindly to anyone except Alain.'

'So why has he put that young buck on him? Ah! Don't tell me. It's to keep him busy, I take it; warm his backside, eh?'

He had not agreed with Lady Alice last night that Emeline's admirer was a charming young man; he knew a rogue when he saw one, even if she didn't, and had told her that it was just as well Lord Alain had invited them when he did before the young gallant got too frisky. Emeline's blushes had been mistaken for embarrassment rather than a sign of guilt, for they were not to know how their concern for her safety was already too late. She prayed they never would.

For everyone except Sir Bastien, the day was a huge success, though not without adventure. It did not take him long to realise that his request for an exciting ride had been a regrettable lapse of good sense which he would never have tossed casually in Marietta's direction if he'd known she would pass it on with such devastating effect. The massive Atlas, all bone and war-hardened muscle, had his own ideas about where he wanted to go and in which manner he wanted to get there, ideas which rarely accorded with those of his rider.

In no time at all he was in danger of overtaking the
fewterers with their straining greyhounds, and it took
all his strength and some oaths before Sir Bastien could
hold the brute back to take his place with the others.
Consequently, the ride he had so looked forward to at
Emeline's side and the planned chivalry towards Lady
Alice barely had time to materialise before he was
swept away from them like a boat on a tidal wave,
heaving and cursing under his breath, arms aching and
temper shortening.

Emeline did nothing to ease herself away from her
parents' presence, not even to see his brave chase and
his attempt at a kill. Unfortunately, his arrows went
nowhere near the hart, even as it stood at bay in a
river, for Atlas had no mind to stand still at that
moment.

For Sir Nicholas Bannon, however, whose mount
was not so wayward, the opportunity arose which was
to place him for ever in Lady Isobel de Rhennes' debt,
and that of her husband. It happened as the ladies,
following at a more sedate pace, came to a shallow
brook between steep banks which the men had taken
at a stride but which stalled the smaller palfreys until
an easier crossing was found.

Downstream a little way, Sir Nicholas called to them,
'Here, ladies! Try this. . .the bank is shallow here.' He
kept his mount in the water as they came forward,
Lady Isobel first. 'Keep clear of the hogweed, lady.'

Busily chattering to those behind, Lady Isobel took
no notice, looking neither at the hogweed nor at the
water. It was Emeline's yelp that stopped her dead.

'Lady Isobel! Lady. . .stop! Look. . .get back! Back!'

Sir Nicholas had seen it, too. A boar stood barely
hidden by the tree-like stem of the giant hogweed, its
head lowered, its mouth agape with a set of tusks that
curved upwards with terrifying efficiency. Two tiny
vicious-looking black eyes glowered at their intrusion.

'Back, lady,' Sir Nicholas yelled, 'go back to safety!'

But Lady Isobel was by now steeply inclined towards the water and could not back away, nor would her mount move on, having smelt the threatening boar and heard its grunts of anger. She was stuck on the bank, aware that the great bristling creature would not turn and flee but would attack in a frenzy of slashing tusks as able to bowl over her horse as it would a hound.

Marietta's young greyhound, sitting in the safety of her mistress's saddle, yapped, and at that moment the boar chose to charge, lowering its head and rushing in ominous silence just as the arrow from Sir Nicholas's bow hit it squarely behind one ear. The momentum of its gallop hurled the heavy body head over heels through the air, cannoning into the hindquarters of Lady Isobel's mount and sending the stricken animal plunging sideways down the bank and into the water, almost on top of Sir Nicholas and his horse.

By some miracle, Sir Nicholas managed to stay in the saddle and reach out as Lady Isobel fell, lifting her bodily off her falling horse. Pulling her across his saddle-bow, he put spurs to his stallion and sent it up the opposite bank to safety. It was the neatest bit of deliverance from certain death the women had ever seen and even before the foot-huntsmen reached them, their applause was echoing through the trees and mingling with cries of relief and admiration.

Sir Nicholas made light of his heroism, preferring to jest that he had personally organised the event in order to catapult Lady Isobel into his arms, even though the lady was no sylph. But there was no disguising the body of the boar with an arrow in its head, nor was Lady Isobel stinting in her praise and gratitude. Apart from a bruised rib and one wet foot, she was quite uninjured, only shaken.

If Sir Henry Wardle was the first that day to kill a hart, then Sir Nicholas was the first—and only one—to take a boar, becoming the hero of the day and the talk of the feast that evening, sitting between Sir John and his lady and looking, for once, self-conscious at all the attention.

CHAPTER TWELVE

DIFFERENT entirely was the picture Sir Bastien presented. He could not appreciate the jovial feast for the brooding thought that his mount had been especially chosen to serve him ill, and it was only the eyes of two very young people who noticed his early departure from the hall before the gleemen had finished their songs and the last toast had been drunk.

It was relatively easy for Iveta and her friend Ian to saunter, unnoticed, towards the mews in the late-evening sunshine, chattering about the new pups, the hunt, the adventures of the day, then to disappear inside and work their way back towards the stable end.

A ladder led upwards towards the hay loft, where the youngest grooms slept in summer on an open floor that overlooked the horses' stalls. Here, with all the audacity of youth, they lay flat on the sweet-smelling hay and peered through the stalks down to where Sir Bastien leaned against the door-frame, waiting.

Before long, they heard the footsteps approach him from the stable-yard, heard the man turn into the stable below and lean against the very same wooden pillar that held up the platform on which they lay.

They stared at each other, unable to believe their luck, but now aware that their slightest sound would be heard unless it was one which could be mistaken for the occasional thud of a horse against its stall. Simultaneously, they lowered their heads as the first words floated upwards, nodding seriously to each other as they recognised the same voice speaking to Sir Bastien.

'When's it to be, then? Tonight?'

'No, fool. I told you Tuesday, not today.'

231

'Had a good day, did you?' the voice sneered.

'Whose idea was it to put me on that bloody old stallion?'

'His. I tried to argue, but he wouldn't listen. Spite, was it? D'ye think he's getting wise to you, after all this time?'

Sir Bastien remembered the sack of flour. Few people would know of that trick unless it was someone who worked in the bakehouse. 'I don't know, but I wouldn't be too surprised if he had his own ideas. I've got to be ready and packed for this last one; I shall have to disappear for good after that.'

'You mean this'll be the last one? Nay, sir, never.'

'It will. The last.'

'What about. . .her. . .the lass? You're taking her, too?'

Iveta could almost hear his smile and the look of scorn. 'Hmph! What do *you* think, numbskull? She's a child. It's the bloody horses I want, man, not that silly bitch. She's got less sense than Jayne had.'

There was a silence at that last remark as though both men were remembering someone. Someone called Jayne.

'What d'ye want me to do, then?'

Sir Bastien's voice became urgent. 'You've got to get rid of those three, Rigg.'

'What, now? Or afterwards?'

'Tomorrow. Get a message to Longleigh. . .you'll need some help. . .hide the bodies up in the wood behind the house.'

'I can't be gone for that length of time, sir! He'll miss me.'

'If you want your last bag o' gold, you'll have to, won't you?'

'But you gave me your word. . .'

'Bah!' Sir Bastien pushed himself away from the pillar, causing the two in the hay above to duck down even lower, flat to the floor. 'My word stretches as far as your honesty, fool. Now, listen to me. . .' They walked slowly towards the stable door, out of hearing.

Iveta regarded Ian in silence to glean what she could of his reaction. This was far more serious than either of them had thought. Killing. Bodies. Those three. Which three?

'What are they going to do?' Iveta mouthed.

'Kill somebody,' Ian replied, silently.

'Who?'

Ian's mouth bunched up into a negative bow and he shook his head. 'Come on,' he said, slithering backwards, 'we must tell Lord Alain.'

'No!' Iveta grabbed at his arm to hold him back. 'No, I promised Marrie I wouldn't. She prefers to tell him herself. We must go to her.'

'Don't be daft, lass,' Ian's Scottish brogue spilled out in scorn, 'this is serious. What's the use of telling Lady Thorsgeld? She can do nothing.'

'If they're talking about Beckington again, she will. It's her property, not Lord Alain's. They said something about a wood behind the house. Well, that must be where they meant, Beckington Manor.'

Ian sat up straight and frowned at her. 'Well, why would they want to kill whoever lives there? And who's Jayne?'

'Somebody who's got a bit more sense than Emeline, by the sound of things. Could be anybody. . .' she added, innocently.

'Listen, Iveta, if Lord Alain finds out that I knew something of this and didn't tell him, he'll send me straight home to my father. For good.'

'He won't find out. I'll say I was by myself.'

'A girl? In the stable? Alone? Hah!'

'No, I could have been in the mews when I overheard. And Marietta believed me before when I said I was alone in the malting-house. . .with you.'

Ian pulled pieces of hay from her fair hair, thoughtfully. 'He musn't ever know,' he said, 'or I've had it. I shan't be given a second chance.'

Iveta tightened her lips and looked away. 'I know how to keep my mouth shut,' she said, 'you need not fear.'

'Nay, lass, don't be angry. . .I didn't mean. . .' Clumsily, he reached out and pulled her to him and kissed her on the lips, nose to nose, until he remembered that it was better to turn his head sideways. Then, drawing away, he looked down at her hands. 'You're pretty,' he said, 'much prettier than your sister.'

'I love you, Ian.'

'Aye, lass. Me too,' he replied, somewhat ambiguously. 'I'll marry you when I'm a knight. I'll wear your ribbon in my helm, and we'll live in a grand castle like this, shall we?'

She nodded with enthusiasm. 'Yes. . .oh, yes. Only. . . how many years?'

'Only seven,' he replied, nonchalantly, pulling her up.

Not until the next morning was Iveta finally able to pass on to Marietta what she and Ian had heard the previous evening, for Lady Alice's strong hand had ushered her up to bed as soon as her face had appeared around the hall door. Protests had been ignored.

Now, Marietta knelt on the window-seat, staring out across the valley and wondering what to do with the extraordinary information Iveta had at last revealed to her. The last time, she had done nothing. This time, she must act, for people's lives were at stake. Her tenants. The Fullers.

Iveta's recollection of what she had heard had lost something of its clarity during her hours of sleep. She could remember that the man had said something about 'it' being on Tuesday, whatever it was, that it would be the last, and that the man called Rigg had to get rid of those three and to hide the bodies in the wood behind the house. Tomorrow. That was today.

But why? If it really was the Fullers at Beckington they'd been talking about, why did they have to be killed? Was that what the old couple had been afraid of? The more Marietta mulled over the facts, the less the whole thing made sense except that she must protect them, whether Alain wanted her to be involved or not.

It would be no use telling him; he would fly into a rage and tell her to leave it to him. And he would do nothing, just as he'd done nothing to relieve their plight so far. She must take matters into her own hands. If the men were going to steal horses, they'd do it anyway, and if Alain had been so foolish as to entertain a man he knew to be a rogue, then surely he must be well prepared for something to happen. He would be on his guard.

But with a house full of guests, how could she go flying off to Beckington? Who could she take to give her some support? Bruno? Uncle Nicholas? Her father? Yes, that was the answer; Sir Henry would be glad to see the place.

She was mistaken. Sir Henry was her husband's ally in this and refused point blank to accompany her without Lord Alain's permission. Angry at his unhelpfulness, Marietta could only be relieved that she had not confided in him her reasons for wanting to go. Her most pressing need was to go immediately and get back to the castle before Alain discovered her absence, for her father would no doubt tell him where she was, if there was any delay. Damn these men! Why did they always know best?

Waiting until Alain and his clients were discussing business in the stable-yard and the ladies were in the pleasance, she took a horse from the ground-floor stable of the castle and shrugged off the offer of an escort. She hated this subterfuge—it was something she had never had to indulge in before her marriage—and she found it particularly distasteful and disturbing to be obliged to ask permission, to explain her reasons or to be prevented from doing what she knew must be done. Alain had been unreasonable in his attitude towards these old people and if he would not do anything for them, then she would.

The young lass, Milly, was in the herb-garden as Marietta rode up to the house and started in fright, her hand full of green leaves. Even as she dismounted, Marietta could see that Milly had been crying.

She held out a friendly hand. 'Shh! Milly, don't be afraid. You remember me, don't you?'

Milly nodded.

'Where shall I put my horse? Round the back?'

Milly strode over the untidy garden and led her along the rough dry track round to the back of the old stone house, a part that Marietta had not seen on her last visit. Here were tumbledown stables, though on one of the doors she noticed that the bolts were strong and free of rust and that horse-dung was piled to one side. They tied the horse to one of the rings in the wall.

'Who's been, Milly? Have you had visitors?'

The girl shook her head, wiping her cheek with the heel of her hand and refusing to look at Marietta. 'No,' she whispered, moving off.

Remembering John and Betty Fuller's attempts to stop their daughter speaking, Marietta took advantage of this time alone to find out what she could, and taking Milly's arm gently in her hand, she held her back. 'What herbs do you gather, Milly? Are they for the pot? Will you show me?'

Unwillingly, Milly raised the bunch of leaves, turning

them this way and that so that Marietta could identify them.

'Foxglove leaves, Milly? Is that what these are? And wolfsbane?' This was a pretty pale yellow tall-growing plant with hoods like those of the monkshood.

'Aye,' Milly said, 'bees like it.'

'And this one?' Marietta asked, by now highly suspicious. She took hold of the long stemmy plant with small white flowers. 'I don't think I know this one.'

Milly pointed to the gaping space in the limestone wall at the side of the track where the plant bushed out from between the stones. 'There,' she said, 'it's that one. Baneberry. Some call it Herb Christopher.'

'God in heaven, Milly! What are you about? These are all—'

'I know, m'lady. I know they are.' A tear rolled down her cheek.

'Milly, will you tell me. . .please. . .what are you going to do with them? One alone is enough to kill a cow. But three together. . .!'

A woman's voice came from behind them. 'Don't ask her, m'lady. She doesn't know how to tell you. She knows plenty about herbs and things but she can't put too many words together.' Betty Fuller hobbled painfully towards them, neither angry nor welcoming. 'Come on in. I saw you coming.'

'Betty,' Marietta began, still appalled by this lethal handful, 'I thought it was you who grew all the simples.'

'Aye, I meant you to. It's me what has the reputation as wise-woman but it's *her* what makes up all concoctions. I can birth women and weave spells, but it's Milly who gathers my herbs.' She gathered up the corners of her apron and held it out, inviting Milly to throw them in. 'That's it, is it, lass?'

Milly nodded and walked ahead of them to the stone steps.

'Then why. . .?'

Old Betty anticipated the question. She was still sharp. 'Nay, lady, you know better than to ask that. How many folks would've come to *her* for their potions? Eh? Her being simple. Nobody would. Me neither.'

That could not be denied. It also explained why, at Marietta's last visit, Betty had confused two relatively well-known plants and why Milly had felt bound to correct her.

The old woman hobbled off after Milly, leaving Marietta to trot after her, still bursting with curiosity about the apronful of poisonous plants. 'Tell me, Betty, please. Who are they for? Someone in particular?'

'Aye, someone in particular. Us.'

'What?'

'Us,' Betty replied, testily. 'You've come at a bad time, m'lady, but come on in just the same. I reckon if anyone has a right to know why, it'd better be you.'

Suddenly it seemed that the Fates had it in for the Fullers. If Sir Bastien and this man Rigg didn't manage to kill them, they'd manage it for themselves. Marietta began to wonder if she was dreaming.

The upper room was every bit as messy as before, though this time a layer of steam hung like a heavy cloud across the rafters, pouring from a large cauldron on the fire. The heat was overwhelming. Betty crossed straight to the cauldron and allowed Milly to remove the plants from her apron and toss them in, poking them down with a well-stained stick.

In the dimness of the room, Marietta saw that John Fuller lay flat on a pallet over by the far wall, his thin frame almost disappearing into the tattered grey blanket, his face creased with pain, his skin deathly pale and tightly drawn. One leg was bound by rags to a board, still scabbed with blood. She did not need to ask what had happened. Only how.

'Down t'steps,' Betty said, pulling out a stool and

tipping a hen off it. The creature looked affronted and stalked off. 'Here, m'lady, sit you down. Like I said, you've come at a bad time. He's not going to mend now, not with that.' She nodded to his leg. 'And he can't do nowt. And I can't. And *she* can't.' Staring at the cauldron, she sniffed and went silent.

This was terrible, Marietta thought, angered, saddened and racked with guilt that she had not defied her husband and seen to supplies for these poor wretches. That they should contemplate suicide was beyond belief. 'But, Betty, surely, why can't Milly do most of the work? She's strong.' It was a feeble thing to say. The lass was simple and not up to the task of caring for the two elderly parents in such circumstances. She regretted the suggestion.

'Aye, she's strong. She's breeding too.'

'What?' There was no need for Betty to repeat it; Marietta had heard. But could she not be mistaken? Did the lass have a lover? Had they not tried to abort it? Wise women knew about such things. Milly herself would know what plants to use: rue, lad's love, laurel, pellitory-of-the-wall.

Again, Betty forestalled her question. 'Aye, we tried to get rid of it, but it were too late. She doesn't know, you see. She can't count and she'd no idea she were breeding until it were too late. And we can't feed ourselves, let alone a bairn.'

Marietta's head swam with the bitterness of their poor lives. How could she ever have grumbled about her own woes? But the details had yet to come. 'Is John asleep?' she asked.

'Aye, Milly gave him something for his pain. It knocked him out.'

Too efficient by half, whatever it was, Marietta thought. The lass could neither count, nor measure, nor read a recipe. How many cures had she effected?

How many deaths? 'Betty, I've come to warn you of danger.'

The old lady turned her head from contemplation of her husband and swept Marietta with a glance of patent unconcern. 'Danger? Hah! There's nothing about danger that I don't already know, m'lady.'

Thinking to stir her with the fear they'd displayed at her first visit, Marietta told her, nevertheless. 'Yes, there is, Betty. There are men up at the castle who mean you harm. . .'

'Hah!' The scathing laugh burst forth like a snapping twig, dry and brittle, 'they've done all harm they're going to do, that lot. That's why they're going to find us dead, next time they get here. Hah!' She beckoned Milly to give the cauldron another poke.

Hardly able to believe what she had heard, Marietta could only probe into the implications of this and hope to come up with some facts. 'Next time, Betty? You mean they've been here before?'

'Mother. . .please. . .,' the words were whispered over Milly's shoulder, but her entreaty was disregarded.

'Aye, they've been here before, all right. Fer years they've been coming here, on and off. Devils, the lot of 'em. How do you think *she* got like that? Eh? A lover? Hah. . .hah!' Her cackling verged on hysteria.

'*Mother!*' Milly held a hand to her mouth, the tears now welling into her reddened eyes. 'Don't tell. . . don't. . .'

Marietta went to her and placed an arm about her shoulders and with the end of her veil wiped Milly's tears. 'It's all right, love, we're all women. I'm here to help you. Let your mother tell me what happened, then I shall know what to do. Don't weep, Milly, please.'

Milly stared at the veil in Marietta's hand. 'You're not like her, are you?'

This time, Marietta knew what she meant. 'No, Milly. I'm not like her. Not in any way.' She returned to the stool and leaned towards Betty. 'Betty, there isn't much time. Please tell me what's been going on. Years, you said? Who's been coming here for years? Who are these devils you speak of?'

'Thieves, m'lady. That's who. Horse-thieves. Lay-brothers from Monksgrange, and that bailiff.'

'The Monksgrange bailiff? The one who's there now?'

'Aye, Longleigh.'

'Longleigh? He's my father's—'

'That's it. Your father's bailiff. I wanted to tell Lord Alain when he asked how often he'd been used to visiting, but John shut me up. Said we'd be killed if we said too much. They used to bring horses here from all over the place and hide them here until the lay-brothers and the bailiff came to fetch them and take them up to the caves above Monksgrange. Then they'd go off to the buyers over the moor road. Clever, eh?'

'So that's it! And they used Beckington and the caves as exchange points. And you had to agree and keep quiet about it. Oh, Betty!'

'Aye, m'lady, that we did. It were no use old John there making a fuss, they just clobbered him and threatened us, and every time he protested. . .he's a pig-headed sod is my husband. . .it were poor Milly that got it,' she nodded towards Milly's back.

'Got it?' Marietta frowned. A cold shiver ran down her back.

'She were ony eleven when they first had her. Here, on the table, in front of our eyes. Lay-brothers from Monksgrange, bailiff, that filthy groom from up at Thorsgeld, too. Eleven, she were. A child. . .' Her voice broke and she clamped a hand to her mouth, holding it together while she rocked backwards and forwards.

'Lay-brothers, too?'

'Aye, them too. If Prior had found out, they'd have been sent packing, that's for sure. They were all in it together, the lot of them. An' your father never came near, not from one year to the next. Then it got like every time they came they'd take their sport with Milly, pretending like she were that simple she were enjoying it when she howled. Fiends!'

'God in heaven, Betty, was there no one who could see what was going on? What about Lord Alain? Were his horses being stolen too, at the beginning?'

Again the scathing look. 'Him? It'd be no good going to him! It were his wife who came with them. She were worse than any of them. A slut, m'lady. She were a slut!'

This was getting worse by the minute. Marietta looked around her at the dirt and disorder and began to realise how the place must have been systematically wrecked, over and over again to keep the Fullers under their brutal yoke, how poor old John had tried to defend them with his scrawny arms but been beaten, his wife and daughter humiliated, raped.

'Who did she come *with*, Betty? Why?'

'At first, she came here to meet Longleigh and that groom from Thorsgeld, Rigg.'

'You mean to help plan the thefts?'

'Nah! She weren't bothered with that. It were *men* she wanted. Men. The ony man she didn't want were her own husband. Everybody else's, but not her own. She were rotten, rotten to the core. . .filthy bitch! She'd do it here, on the table, in front of everybody. . .one after t'other, all of them, screeching and howling like banshees. . .' Her voice became harsh with disgust. 'Animals? I've never seen animals behave the way they did. At least animals get on with it in private!'

'In front of you. . .and John. . .and Milly? Saints!'

Viciously, Betty stabbed the table with one finger. 'There, in front of everybody! There, where we eat! Then they'd get Milly. And then that whore came with Sir Bastien Symme, and they'd plan how to get horses away from Thorsgeld down to our stables, and who'd collect 'em. And they'd laugh that Lord Alain never found out how he lost his horses. And that Sir Bastien, he were worse than the rest of them. He'd take Milly while he were waitin' for his woman, then he'd have *her* as soon as she got here and carry on talking business when the others arrived, still at it. I've never seen anything like it. It was like they was possessed with devils. And she'd be lying there, telling them what to do. You'd never believe it, lady.'

Marietta was dizzy with shock. She'd had warning that the first Lady Thorsgeld was man-crazy, but this was not what she had expected, a she-devil, a whore. What on earth had Alain been thinking about to marry her? Why had he not seen what was happening?

It explained much, of course, but not enough. She had already deduced that Sir Bastien had stolen Alain's wife and horses, but this put a different slant on things, a bitter-tasting, distorted, vile slant, illustrating a sequence of events she could never have imagined. Not even in a nightmare. That man. . .she had almost flirted with him herself, laughed with him; he had held her around the waist, she had put her hand into his. Monster! Her hair bristled and her throat constricted with unexpressed fear.

And Milly, poor inarticulate Milly, now pregnant.

'But the woman died, did she not, Betty? Do you know what happened?'

'Two years ago, aye. The whore died. I thought it might be better for us after that, but it didn't make a lot o' difference. They just used Milly more, that's all. Now it's best if we all die, that'll put a stop to it, once and for all.'

'Betty. . .no! Don't think of it, please. It's not the answer. It can't be. I can help.' But the words carried no conviction in her heart, for she knew she had already over-stayed her time. She should have gathered them away to safety by now and hurried back to the castle.

If they came while she was here, she'd be one more for them to dispose of, that's all. But curiosity lured her onwards. She had to know. 'How did she die, Betty?'

'It were my fault. They know it were my fault. They've threatened to have me hanged for a witch, for murder, if I don't keep my mouth shut about what they're up to. There's nothing I can do. They'll take Milly too, as my accomplice. They'll say she's possessed o' the devil.' She shook her head, forgetting that, absorbed in her pain, she had not answered the question.

'Tell me, Betty. How did it happen?'

Instead of responding immediately to the probing, she stood and, taking a large basin, stretched a greyish-green piece of cloth across it and carried it to the cauldron. Without the need for instructions, Milly scooped the limp, almost blackened, leaves out of the boiling water and heaped them into the bowl. Clouds of steam billowed upwards as Betty carried them to the table, gathered the cloth and began to twist it, squeezing more dark green juice from the leaves. This, she poured back into the cauldron.

'She got herself pregnant, didn't she?' Betty talked as if to herself. 'Get them bits o' chicken in there now, Milly, and them onions and leeks, and throw in what's left o' the barley to thicken it. It won't taste so bad.' She glanced at her husband. 'We'll get some down him first. If anybody grumbles, it'll be him! Hah! Best not tell him we're eating his one and only cockerel, had we?'

Appalled, Marietta prayed that Milly would not taste it. Poisoned broth. So that was how they were going to put an end to their lives. A last meal. Holy saints, please make something happen to prevent it.

'Pregnant?' she prompted Betty. 'Not surprising, but did she die of that, or. . .?'

'She told me to make her a potion. She had to get

rid of it, well. . .naturally, Lord Alain would know it weren't his. He never went near her. So I left it to Milly and I gave it to her ladyship when she came on't next time. Ony I gave it to her too strong, I think, cos. . .'

'No!' Milly's voice cut through the explanation like a knife.

Both Betty and Marietta watched as the lass threw the stick into the broth and strode across to the window, standing with her back to them as before. Clearly, she was agitated.

'No, Milly? What, then?' Marietta said.

Just as they feared that her words had dried up again, Milly spoke. 'It was not Mother. It was me. I knew. . .I knew what to get for a potion to start a flow. Rue, and lad's love, and. . .'

'Well, that's what you got, you silly wench!' Betty snapped at her.

'Yes, and. . .and something else,' Milly retorted, over her shoulder. 'That stuff you noticed, m'lady. . .' she turned to Marietta 'it has little black berries in autumn. They're even more poisonous than tops. It only grows up here, in the limestone. I put some of them in. That's what killed her. T'other stuff didn't have time to work before she died.'

Speechless, Marietta held a hand to her forehead. Poisoned, by this simple lass who had suffered so much at the woman's hands. 'She got back to the castle then?' she asked Betty.

'Oh, she didn't take it here, m'lady. She took it off back home, and they all thought it were the pestilence, or something. Sir Bastien took himself off with horses and didn't come near for weeks till it were all over. T'others kept away, too, then they all came back and started up again, but they wouldn't leave Milly alone, poor lass. They thought it were my fault. . .she never said it were hers. . .she'd be scared. . .'

'It didn't matter whose fault it was, Mother,' Milly

found her voice in anger, 'did it? They thought it was her own fault, but they blamed you to keep us quiet.'

Betty, clearly surprised by this coherent outburst of reasoning, simply thrust the bowl of soggy leaves into Milly's hands, ripping away the cloth and shaking the bits into the rushes. 'Here, shut your mouth, lass. Take this round to the back and throw it out. Keep it away from m'lady's horse.'

Any warning that Marietta could give about imminent danger now seemed superfluous, especially so when old John lay unconscious on the pallet, unable to move, let alone flee to safety. How she wished she had asked Uncle Nicholas to help. A poor substitute, but better than being alone at a time like this. The revelation about Lady Thorsgeld's activities with all those men, here at Beckington, her mother's property at the time, was almost too much to take in.

There were gaps in the story, plenty of those, but this was a mess of huge proportions, involving Lord Alain's property, her own, and her father's, too. No wonder that Alain felt he must bide his time. Was this why he had wanted her to leave the place alone? To catch them red-handed? If so, she had now put the cat among the pigeons and he'd not thank her for that. Not after all the planning he'd done.

'Betty—' Marietta prayed that a plan would form while she was talking '—don't eat that broth, please. Don't give any to your husband and daughter. That's not the way. . .I'm sure of it.'

'What is, then? I'll not run off and leave him here on his own and I've taken as much as I can o' their vicious ways. If they come and start again on Milly, like they always do, it'll kill her anyway. That groom were here two nights ago, and that bailiff; it were them what threw John down the steps.'

'They threw him? Oh, my God. . .I thought he fell. . .!'

'He tried to protect Milly. She were screaming and he come at one of them with a stool, but it were no use. I'm not having that happen again, m'lady. We're better off dead.'

'But the property is mine now, Betty. It won't happen again, not now.'

'Aye?' Betty's voice was heavy with sarcasm. 'I haven't noticed no great change since you were here last, m'lady.'

The accusation of neglect was difficult to refute. 'I had no idea that this was going on. . .'

What use to explain? She had tried, then she had left the subject alone to keep the peace. Her garden had come first, then guests had arrived, her hands had been full of other problems.

'I'll stay here with you,' she said, purposefully, 'then whoever comes will have me to settle with.' She looked along the table for possible weapons. 'Do you have a knife, Betty? A large one? Sharp?'

'Here, this one. This is sharp. Where do you want it?' She picked up an old worn carving knife with a blade now so narrow that it was more like a spike. 'Look here, I'll put it in here and hide it behind this great jug,' and she inserted the point up to the handle between two planks of the table where the wood had shrunk. 'There, look, you can grab at that if you need to, eh?'

'Good. And you'll not take that poison, Betty?'

'Wait 'n see, m'lady. Where's Milly got to?'

Milly had not returned from emptying the boiled leaves.

Marietta went to the window to see if she was in the herb-patch, then pulled back sharply, her heart almost leaping from her breast. 'Saints!' she whispered, 'it's that bailiff from Monksgrange, my father's bailiff. . . what's his name. . .Longleigh.'

'Vicious, he is,' Betty hissed. 'Now he's got no lay-brothers to 'elp him, he wanted more money for his part. Threatened to stop, he did.'

'He's coming up..oh, why didn't we see him coming? We could have put a barrier across the door.'

'Wouldn't do no good. They'd find a way in.'

There was no time to do anything. The door flew open with a crash and Longleigh stood silhouetted in the door-frame. He hesitated, obviously not expecting to see a visitor at Beckington for he had tethered his horse at the front, by the stone steps. 'We...e...ell.' He frowned. 'Lady Thorsgeld now, isn't it? Coming up in the world a bit, aren't we?' He took a few paces into the room. 'Come to view your property at last, 'ave yer?'

'I've already viewed it once, Master Longleigh, some time ago. And what gives you the right to walk in here, uninvited?'

For an answer, he looked her up and down, smiled at his thoughts and moved further into the room, his attitude and bearing insolent without the presence of Sir Henry at his side. A burly man, broad-chested and heavy, he had been respectful enough to her at Monksgrange on the few occasions they'd met, but so seldom that she had not picked up his name, only his dire warnings that the caves were dangerous places to be near. Demons and devils, he had told her. He had not been far wrong.

The day was warm, the stuffy room even warmer, and dark patches of sweat had formed under the sleeves of his russet woollen tunic. Meaningfully, he scratched at his groin and turned his attention to old John, still lying motionless on the pallet. 'Dead, is he?' he asked, casually. He might as well have been asking after his health.

'No...but near enough, thanks to you,' Betty snapped, moving to stop him approaching the pallet.

Longleigh sauntered across, pushed Betty out of the

way like a feather and peered down at John Fuller then, before Betty could recover her balance, nudged the broken leg viciously with his toe. John made no movement.

'Master Longleigh! Have some pity, for heaven's sake,' Marietta cried.

'He's dead.' The man straightened and turned away, unconcerned.

'Nay. . .he's not!' Betty yelped. 'He's sleeping. I gave him a potion. He's sleeping, I tell thee. John. . .John, wake up!' She went and lowered herself painfully to the floor at the side of her husband and shook him, gently at first and then more urgently. 'John. . .come on. . .wake!'

Longleigh let out a bark of laughter. 'Aye, well, we all know what happens when you give potions, don't we? Eh? You've done it again, old crone, you've done it again. Hah! Just as well to practise on your own family once in a while, eh?' He laughed, looking at Marietta as though to share the jest. His teeth were blackened and yellow and a fine line of foam showed at the corners of his mouth. Piggy eyes glinted viciously.

'Master Longleigh, go back to Monksgrange,' Marietta commanded. 'If you do not leave my property this instant, I shall see that Lord Thorsgeld and Sir Henry both know of your involvement here.'

He stopped and lowered his head, poking his face at her belligerently. 'Aye? Is that so, *Lady* Thorsgeld? Is that so? Tell your menfolk, would you? And what makes you think you're going to get out of this alive, then? Eh?' He extended one huge finger to touch her cheek but she slapped it away and moved nearer to the table.

'You've done enough harm here. Go. . .get out!'

'Where's the lass?' he said, scratching again.

'I don't know. She went out some time ago.'

'Hiding, is she? Well then, you'll have to do instead

won't you? You should know what it's all about by now.'

The breath tightened in her lungs, fear racing through every limb. 'Touch me, Longleigh, and you'll get a knife in your belly,' she snarled.

'Eh? Oh. . .!' He laughed. 'Then I'll wait till I've got some help. Shouldn't be long now. Meanwhile—' he looked at the table, then at the cauldron over the fire '—what's there to eat? I'll need some energy, won't I?'

'Broth,' Marietta pushed the word into a whisper.

'Broth?' He went to the cauldron and peered into the steam, poking with the stick at the contents. 'Who made it? Her?' tipping his head towards Betty who now lay half over her husband, moaning in anguish.

'No. Milly.' Marietta held her breath.

'Did you see her make it?'

'Yes, before she went out. I saw her put the chicken and vegetables in.'

'Chicken? Well, there's a luxury. *He* won't want any, will he? Not now, eh? Put some in a bowl, my *lady*, and I'll have some while I'm waiting for reinforcements.' He smiled again.

Vicious swine. Yes, I'll put some in a bowl for you. Gladly. Marietta could barely control the trembling in her hands, aware of the power over this man's life, power to pay him back for the suffering to this family and old John's death.

Betty lay still now, her head in her hands resting over the body of her frail husband. It was as though she was listening to what Marietta was doing, seeing it in her mind, seeing the bowl filled with barley-thickened greenish-grey liquid and chunks of vegetables and chicken, speckled with herbs. Steaming. Appetizing. Nourishing.

The stool scraped on the floor as Longleigh sat and reached for a spoon, breaking the silence after Betty's brief weeping. She turned as the bowl was set before him. 'That were for my John,' she said, resentment and anger making her voice quaver.

Longleigh stirred, then took his first mouthful, blowing as the heat caught his tongue. 'Was it, crone? Tell him it tastes all right, then.'

'He's not needing it now,' Betty mumbled, 'not now.'

Marietta could not drag her eyes away from the spoon but stood rooted to the spot as each mouthful was gobbled, each spoonful blown at and shovelled in with an audible gasp, unfaltering, rhythmic, untasted. Nothing was chewed, everything was swallowed whole until the bowl was empty. Was it not poisonous then, after all? Not enough? Slow-acting? Might it take hours? There had been no point in asking, at the time. 'More?' she asked.

The spoon clattered into the bowl, making her jump.

'My mouth. . .lips. . .tingling. . .' He rubbed at them with his wrists.

'It was too hot for you,' Marietta said.

'Too. . .too. . .hot. . .' The wrists rubbed around his throat. 'Burning me. . .burning my. . .argh!' He tore at the neck of his tunic, throwing himself away from the table and grabbing at his throat, then at his stomach. 'Burns. . .' he gasped, 'burns. . .my god. . .what has she. . .the bitch. . .help—' his body doubled over as the burning pain seared through him '—help. . .argh!' He tried to stand, kicking over the stool, his face visibly reddening and pouring with sweat, his hands clawing at the collar of his tunic, the piggy eyes now almost black as the pupils dilated. 'What. . .what is it?' he croaked.

'It's good chicken broth, meant for my John, that's what it is.' Betty rose painfully to her knees and stared full at Marietta, no trace of gladness or jubilation, no mad desire for vengeance. Rather it was as though the women took on the aspect of two mice with an aged and infirm cat, staying out of his range and watching his futile attempts to find his legs, to sight them, to do them harm while losing power, moment by moment.

Keeping out of his range, they watched him stagger towards the door, clutching first at his stomach and then at his throat. Betty was less affected than Marietta. 'Quick, m'lady, get that bowl and spoon. Hide them! If the others come, tell 'em his heart's burst, or summat.'

'Oh God, Betty, he's dying, isn't he?'

'Aye, best thing that's happened to him since he were born. The swine.'

'And John. . .your husband. . .he's. . .?'

'Gone. A life for a life.'

Longleigh smashed into the door but was pushed back hard against the wall as it opened in his face. 'Help. . .me. . .' he gasped at the man who entered.

It was Rigg, the groom from Thorsgeld. 'Stop playing games, you great fool,' he said, pushing Longleigh away. 'There isn't time for that.'

But Longleigh fell with a crash onto the floorboards and lay groaning and retching violently into the filthy rushes.

CHAPTER THIRTEEN

RIGG needed no introduction; Marietta recognised him at once as the black-haired groom she'd seen talking with Sir Bastien in the stable-yard only a few days ago, the one whose hand had delved into his friend's pouch when he thought no one was looking. The look he gave Marietta now showed that he was not surprised to see her again.

'Yes. . .' he said, softly. 'Yes, you would be here, wouldn't you? Interfering. . .nosing about. I saw your horse around the back.'

'This is my property and you are trespassing. . .' Her words went unheeded, for Rigg was staring at Longleigh who shook and moaned, his knees pulled up to his chin.

'What's been going on? How long has he been like this?'

Marietta was shaking with fright. It was her doing. He was dying because she intended him to. She must keep a grip on herself or she'd be no use to Betty and Milly, none to herself, either.

'You must have followed him here. He. . .he just collapsed. Betty thinks. . .'

Betty interrupted, 'It's his heart. I told you what it is. His heart. I've seen it before.'

'His heart? Vomiting? Don't be daft, woman,' Rigg said.

'Aye, I've seen it before, I tell thee. It's been coming on. Seen it in his face lots o' times. Too red,' she said, finally.

Still, Rigg could not bring himself to believe it. Here,

of all places. This would complicate things, as would the extra presence of Lady Thorsgeld.

'You'd better go,' Marietta said, once more moving towards the table. 'Lord Alain is sure to know you've gone and he'll come looking for you. He knows what you've been up to, you know.'

'Ah! So, my lady, you told him what you saw, did you? Well, that was not very wise of you, but I might have known you would. But he doesn't know I'm here, does he? Any more than you knew I was coming.'

'Of course I knew. Betty told me everything. . .yes, everything,' she countered, 'and Lord Alain knows exactly what you've been up to.'

'Up to? I'm not up to anything, my lady. I shall be back up at the castle as soon as Sir Bastien arrives to take the horses away and I shall deny any knowledge of it.

'The old chap's had it, by the look of things,' he looked pointedly at the grey blanket that now covered the entire body of John, 'the old crone will have a dagger in her belly, and the lass, wherever she is, well, nobody's going to take too much notice of her, are they? A half-wit? A babbling fool? And you. . .you can say what you like about Sir Bastien. . . I expect he'll be miles away by the time you get back wrapped up like old John.'

'What do you mean?'

'Mean?' His eyes moved over her lasciviously. 'Well, that's not too difficult for you to understand, is it? You know full well what Sir Bastien wants from you before he goes, and now you've made it easy for both of us. But you don't suppose he'll allow you to go yelping it all the way back to Thorsgeld, do you? I shall blame the whole thing on Sir Bastien. *You* won't be able to blame it on anybody, will you? Perhaps you should have co-operated with him a bit sooner instead of being so snotty-nosed. You had chance.'

When Marietta did not reply immediately, as he'd expected her to do, he looked more intently at the direction of her eyes and saw, too late, that she stared over his shoulder towards the doorway. He whirled. 'Sir! Holy saints, sir! You gave me a shock.'

Sir Bastien kicked at Longleigh in passing and moved further into the room, his feet making no sound on the rushes. 'That's obvious, Rigg. Presumably, if you'd known I was here, you'd not have been so eager to blame the whole thing on me, would you? I hope you're not going to blame me for *that* too, are you?' He tipped his head towards the writhing man on the floor. 'And that over there? Died peacefully in his bed, did he, or what?'

'Er. . .broke his leg. . .er yesterday. Look sir, I don't want you to get the wrong idea about what I said just now. . .' Rigg blustered, watching the handsome newcomer warily.

Sir Bastien ignored his attempted explanation and approached Marietta instead, smiling courteously.

'My Lady Marietta, you appear to be somewhat out of place here. Have these churlish creatures been offending you? Forgive them, they know no better. What he says is only partly true; I have no intention of doing away with you. On the contrary, I shall need your help now we're a man short.

'Rigg. . .' he turned to the groom '. . .get that to the top of the steps and give it a shove over the edge, will you? We can't have him making that clamour while we. . .amuse ourselves, can we? Go on, man. Get on with it!' He waved a hand imperiously at the prone Longleigh. 'What happened? You didn't fix him with one of your famous arrows, did you, lady? Or is it a stab wound?'

'Neither, Sir Bastien. Betty says his heart's burst, but I don't know.'

'Ah, well, in that case we'd better be sure. We don't want him recovering and messing up our plans, do we?'

Before Marietta could guess his intention, he strode to the door, straddled Longleigh's body and plunged his dagger up to its hilt into the man's chest. Then, carefully withdrawing it, he wiped it clean on the man's clothes and helped with his foot to push the body over the vertical edge of the stairway.

Rigg straightened and gave a puff of relief. 'That should finish him off.'

'Where are the horses?'

'Stables, sir. Behind.'

'Both of them?'

'Both,' Rigg nodded. 'Look, sir. . .let me explain about. . .'

'No need, Rigg.'

Sir Bastien half-turned as if to go inside then, with a speed too quick for the groom to anticipate, swung back and thrust the dagger upwards towards Rigg's heart, knocking him off balance and sending him hurtling down over the edge on top of Longleigh. The dagger came out as the body fell.

'There, if that doesn't look as though two men had a fight and fell, I don't know what will. Easier than I thought. No arguments, no payments and. . .' he wiped the dagger on a tuft of stonecrop and entered the room '. . .no silly tales about who did what. Eh, my lady? You didn't particularly want an audience, did you? No, you're not the kind to show off, are you? A quiet private time we'll have, just you and me. . .oh, and the old crone. . .and a corpse. Best I can do, I'm afraid. Come now, let's waste no more time.

The nightmare worsened. The heavy blanket that enclosed the darkness and would not allow her to wake, to break through, now weighed so heavily upon Marietta that she could scarcely determine what was real and what imagined. Men lay dead, one at her own hands, poisoned at her invitation. Another man was casually butchered by this suave creature who, only a day or two ago, had sat at her side.

And now he intended to possess her while his hands were still sticky with blood. A corpse lay in the same room, and a frightened old woman she barely knew, while outside. . .somewhere. . .a terrified and pregnant girl roamed about. Stolen horses waited in the stables and Alain was nowhere near. Help was a million miles away.

The incredible revelations of villainy would have been quite enough to turn her stomach, the bestiality, the indignities wreaked upon poor people, without any further events. She had made the decision to stay and help to protect them without knowing the consequences and yet, if she had fled, both Milly and her mother would have been dead by now, if not by these men's hands, then by their own.

The horrors must be shut out. This beast must be dealt with by her alone. She must win. She was Alain's. He loved her courage; he had said so, often. It must not desert her now. She prayed. Holy Mary, help me.

Seth waited until Lord Alain had finished speaking to two of his guests in the courtyard, standing respectfully to one side until he was noticed.

'You'll not regret it, Mistress Jean,' Lord Alain was saying, 'they're thoroughly reliable. Three of my very best—in fact, I wouldn't be ashamed to ride 'em myself.'

Mistress Jean smiled. 'I'm tempted to keep them for myself, Lord Alain. But look. . .isn't your head groom waiting to speak with you?' She nodded towards Seth.

Lord Alain swung round, 'Seth, ah, what news, man?' They moved apart, not willing to be overheard.

Seth's whisper was urgent. 'As soon as you'd left the yard, my lord, he took Penda and Apollo down the lane instead of to the croft. He had a horse waiting there, did you know?'

'No. Then what? Off, was he?'

'Aye, my lord, off across the fields. Short cut to Beckington, I reckon. One horse on each side of him.'

'Didn't waste any time, did he? Good timing, too, just when we'd finished business and he knew he wouldn't be missed. Right, saddle up and I'll be with you straight away. Thomas!' he yelled to the young page who crossed the courtyard with a jug of ale in each hand. 'Put those down and run to the Master-at-Arms. I want him here, fast. Fast!'

The lad placed the jugs on top of the mounting block and flew through the gate-house arch as though demons were after him.

'Where's Lady Marietta?' Lord Alain asked Bruno. 'She was supposed to be here to take the guests in. Have you seen her, Sir Henry?'

'Not for several hours, my lord. She asked me if I'd go to Beckington with her, but I refused to go without your permission. Didn't want to override your wishes—'

'Beckington Manor? She asked you to go with her? Did she say why?'

'No.' Sir Henry looked thoughtful. 'She didn't give a reason but she would surely not have gone alone without your approval, would she?'

'Oh, yes, she would, Sir Henry. Did she always rely on *your* approval?'

'Nay, you know the answer to that, my lord.'

'Bruno! Go search our apartments and the garden. See if you can find her.'

The chaplain hobbled over to the group and caught at Lord Alain's arm before he strode off. 'My horse,' he said, pointing to the courtyard stable, 'my horse was taken an hour ago. I've been waiting for someone to bring it back, my lord, I was about to go off on a visit. . .'

'Damn the girl, she must have taken it! Did nobody see her go? For heaven's sake. . .is everybody blind around here? Master, there you are! I want twelve men ready to go with me. Now. Here. Lady Thorsgeld's gone to. . .'

'Aye, my lord.' He ran to the gatehouse where the garrison were roused, his voice bellowing loud enough to wake the dead. Horses and soldiers began pouring into the courtyard; swords were buckled on, Lord Alain's stallion was brought in, then Sir Henry's; others followed.

Bruno appeared with Sir Nicholas at his heels. 'No, my lord, her maids say she's still not returned.'

Lord Alain snarled at him in anger. 'What the hell is your sister doing, going off without my permission? She knows damn well I don't want her to go near the place.'

Feeling the sting of injustice, Bruno's caution slipped. 'She's *your* wife, my lord, not mine!' Automatically, he ducked as the back of Lord Alain's hand swung at his head, then dodged away to collect his horses.

The blow was delivered more in frustration that Marietta had not only spoiled his plans to catch the men red-handed but had put herself at risk, also. A side-effect more dangerous than the theft. The secondary plan to discover more about his wife's death had had to be abandoned when he'd seen how close Emeline had come to danger.

Marietta had drifted close to danger, too, due to his carelessness, and now she had sailed right into it, probably because she thought he'd be too busy to notice what she was up to. Headstrong, proud lass. But this was sheer disobedience. What could have possessed her?

'Yes, you young whelp! She's my wife, as you say. And it looks as though I shall have to remind her!'

Seth came running back through the gateway. 'My lord. . .it's as you thought. . .he's been followed. About ten minutes ago. . .while I was here with you. . .Sir Bastien. . .'

'Ah! He followed? Was he alone?'

'Yes, my lord. He took the road.'

'Well, something's going according to plan, anyway. Good, Seth. We're ready for off. Don't worry, we'll get 'em. Pray God we get my wife back unharmed, that's what *I* care about.' He swung up into the saddle and turned to catch Sir Henry's eye. 'Come, Sir Henry, we'll retrieve your daughter yet again.'

They rode cross-country in a tight pack, keeping to the trees, then spreading out as they neared Beckington, encircling the house stealthily to cut off all escape, finally moving in like a tightening band. They found it strange to see no men preparing to leave, to hear no voices. Only horses were at the back of the house; the chaplain's, Sir Bastien's and another from Thorsgeld. So, Marietta was still there.

Silently, Lord Alain motioned to Sir Henry, Sir Nicholas and Bruno to follow him round to the front of the house, but their caution was arrested when two crumpled bodies lay across their path, one almost on top of the other.

'God's wounds! That's my bailiff. . .Longleigh!' Sir Henry exclaimed, 'What's he doing here?'

'Not a lot, Father,' Bruno said, flippantly. 'But why is his face purple, I wonder, and his eyes wide open? Was he stabbed?'

'This one was. This is my groom, Rigg—' Lord Alain looked up towards the open door at the top of the stairway '—and it looks as though they met their match. Come, we must find Marietta.' He darted round to the steps and bounded up them, two at a time, blinking into the foul dimness of the room at the top.

If the room had been a mess on his last visit, now it was a shambles of smashed stools, broken pottery, wooden bowls and implements everywhere, blood-soaked straw and, almost under the table, the figure of Sir Bastien Symme bent double, clutching his ribs and moaning, speechless with pain.

Over by the wall, the corpse of old John lay covered with a blanket, and Betty, staring blankly and registering no surprise, sat by his feet, rocking gently back and forth. There was no sign of Marietta.

'Mistress Fuller,' Lord Alain called to her. 'Betty! Where's Lady Thorsgeld? Where is she?'

'Dead,' whimpered the old woman, 'all dead.'

'Dead? Lady Marietta?' He turned on Sir Bastien like a wild animal, yanking his head back by a handful of hair. 'You've killed her, swine? Where is she. . .what have you *done*?'

'No. . .God in heaven. . .mercy!' he moaned. 'No, she's not. Argh! The woman thinks you mean. . .mean Jayne. . .argh! My lord, oh, have mercy, let me go, I'm wounded. She stabbed me and fled. . .ah, I'm bleeding.' His face, contorted with pain, was ashen, his well-cut tunic was stained darkly with blood that seeped through his fingers. His face, too, was bloody as though there had been a struggle, though clearly he had suffered worse than the victor.

Lord Alain had no mercy, shaking him like a rat. 'Where? Where. . .you filthy, lying whoreson? Where is she? Tell me or I'll throw you down on top of the others, cur! Where?'

Almost unconscious now, Sir Bastien moaned. 'No. . .no. . .she ran off. . .I don't know where, she ran oh. . .stop. . .leave me.'

'Did you harm her, rape her?'

'No. . .no, I swear I did not. . .' He fell hard onto the

floor again as Lord Alain threw him down, his head making a sickening thud. He lay still.

'Sir Henry, will you stay and find out what you can here? Sir Nicholas and Bruno, come! We must find her. God knows where to start looking.' This was nothing like he'd expected. Three men dead, another lying mortally wounded, old Betty now fast losing her wits, Marietta fled. But where was the girl? He doubled back into the room, 'Betty! Betty!' he shouted. 'Where's your daughter? Did she go with Lady Marietta?'

Betty shook her head, her face still a blank. 'No. . . o. . .o.' she crooned, 'she's dead. All dead. . .'

'Oh, for pity's sake!'

'She's out of her wits, my lord,' Sir Nicholas said. 'Take no notice. We'll find her. Marietta wouldn't just run away, would she? Perhaps it was the girl who ran off and Marietta's looking for her.'

Bruno agreed. 'Yes, there are woods behind here, and high rocks. There has to be an explanation. Marrie wouldn't run away without a good reason. She knows our voices. . .' they tripped down the steps '. . .we can call. She'll hear us, my lord.'

'Yes, you're right. Pray God she's not harmed. Come.' He stopped briefly to speak to the Master-at-Arms then, still calling to him over his shoulder, he broke into a trot behind Bruno and Sir Nicholas and, on foot, entered the dark shadowy woodland.

Dazed and covered with blood, her legs trembling and shaking with fatigue, Marietta wandered upwards through the thick elders that sprouted like arms out of the rock face, providing foot- and hand-holds for her to cling to. Panting with the effort of the climb and with the even more arduous effort of containing her terror after the most recent events, she searched through the trees for a sign of the drab grey kirtle that Milly wore, calling softly, for she had no energy to do otherwise. 'Milly, where are you? Milly, don't be afraid. . .it's me. Milly.'

The silence was like a drug, tempting her to sit on the mossy boulders and give in to its embracing calm, to lie under the green canopy and sleep, forget, obliterate the chaos in her mind, to do what Milly had no doubt done and lose herself in the peace as an antidote to the awful events down below her.

But the lass had to be found, for her nightmare had lasted years, not less than an hour, and her reaction was sure to be proportionately greater, especially as she had less to live for—no protection, no loving, no means of sustenance and a bairn on the way. One that had been forced upon her. Poor wench. She must be desperate. Frantic.

Another push through the high brambles, another torn cheek and then she saw her. 'Milly, don't move! I'm coming. I'll help. . .you're safe.'

Milly was sitting poised on the edge of a sheer drop where the limestone cliff, topped by hawthorns, rose out of the woodland. Her legs dangled over the side and, on her lap, the bowl of soggy black leaves was hugged by bramble-torn arms. Wild eyes stared ahead, recognising nothing.

'Don't move, Milly, I'm coming,' Marietta called, wondering how she could sound so confident about a move fraught with difficulties. But if Milly had managed it, so could she, and after watching one of her shoes hurtle downwards over boulders and into a giant bramble, she managed to reach the shivering girl without alarming her or sending her leaping away in fright.

Talking all the time, Marietta crawled along the deeply fissured rocks and sat by her side. Then, very carefully, she took hold of the bowl with its noxious contents and slowly eased it away from her. 'Let me have it now, Milly. You don't need it, you're safe, they've all gone. Dead. They can't hurt you any more.'

It was not the meaning of the words that soothed Milly's fear but the sounds of gentleness and calm instead of her mother's harshness. It was the feeling of warmth and sympathy to which she responded and the knowledge that, somehow, she was being understood. Without moving, she listened to Marietta's voice in silence. And when Marietta wondered if she had heard any of what had been said and took her hand to hold it warmly in her lap, Milly clasped it and allowed it to stay there.

'You're not like 'er, are you?' was all she said.

'No, Milly. I'm not like her. I'm nothing like her.'

She heard a horse neighing in the distance and wondered whether that could be Alain come to find her or whether it was only one of those already there. And how would he find her? How would he know where to look? How was she to get poor Milly, who had carried a bowl of poisonous leaves here, alone, to eat them and put an end to her life, away from this place? How long could they wait for help to come?

'Do you want to come back down with me now, Milly?'

Milly shook her head.

'They've gone. The men are all dead now.'

'You're saying that. . .saying that. . .to get me. . .'

'No, Milly. I mean it. Rigg came, and then the others—' she was about to explain, but Milly would have none of it.

'No!' She bunched up, ready to spring away, but Marietta held onto her hand.

'All right. . .all right, stay here. Lord Alain will come and he will lead us down. You'll come and live with me, Milly, at the castle.

The wide eyes turned to Marietta at last. 'Live? With you?'

'Yes, with me, at the castle.'

'Not my mother. . .and father?'

'Just you, unless you want them. . .?'

'No. . .no! With you. Live with you.'

'I shall look after you.' She was not to have known, at that moment, how valuable her invitation would be in keeping the poor wench by her side until help came.

Each moment seemed like a lifetime during which questions came and went, mostly concerning Alain and his first unfaithful wife. His attitude to her, Marietta, led her to wonder how he would regard this interference into his affairs and into her own property here at Beckington after his express command that she should wait on his approval. He would be angry, no doubt. She had disobeyed him. He would have every reason to beat her.

Strangely, her concern was less for herself than for him. She could understand how he must have felt, betrayed in his marriage by a woman whose appetite for men knew no bounds. Insatiable. No wonder he was so intent on lying claim to *her*, having seen her unequivocal dislike of the idea of marriage. Undoubtedly, that was an over-reaction on his part, but understandable.

They heard the calls first, faint and muffled by the wind in the trees, then two voices, then three. 'Marietta! Marietta!'

The hand she held in hers squeezed tightly, the tattered body stiffened in fear and Milly seemed to shrink. Her eyes widened, but she made no move.

'Stay with me, Milly. I'll call to them. You'll come with me.' Then she called, feeling the girl's trembling as the invisible net tightened on her. 'Here!' she yelled. 'We're up here.'

'Marietta!' It was Alain's voice.

'Here, Alain! Up here!'

There was a silence as they tried to pinpoint the sound, but Milly could bear the tension no longer. Any man's voice was a threat. Pulling at Marietta's hand, she scrabbled backwards, slewing her captor round in an effort to escape.

'No. . .Milly, stay with me. . .please, come back. . .!'

The voices returned. 'Marietta, where are you?'

'Milly. . .no..stay.' Marietta heaved on the girl's wrist, lost it and made a wild grab at the hem of her kirtle. Pulling her down into a heap, she threw herself on top of the girl's body in a tangle of skirts and legs and, in combined anger and desperation, rolled her face downwards, ignoring her cries, and straddled her hips, holding her shoulders to the bare rock. It was the only way; they were inches from the cliff face. Now, with all the air left in her lungs, she screamed, 'Here! Here, Alain! We're here, on the cliff!' Tears of desperation rose with her cries.

She heard them shouting to each other, heard the crashes as branches were broken, then Alain's voice again. 'Where? I can't see you. . .'

Exhausted, she fell on top of Milly. 'I'm here,' she muttered into the girl's neck. 'I'm here and I want to go home. Come and find me.'

'On the cliff, my lord—' it was Bruno's voice '—up on the top.' Then the shouts were behind them, close at hand, calling, whoops of discovery, panting and grunts of effort as the men scrambled over towards the two prostrate bodies. 'Here, my lord. She's here!' Bruno yelled.

'Oh, holy saints, no. . .Marietta!' Gently, hands lifted her upwards, pulling her off Milly and hauling her backwards into the comfort of two strong arms. 'Blood. . .she's wounded. . .sweetheart, speak to me. . '

'Alain,' she said, 'take me home.'

'You're wounded, sweetheart. Where are you hurt? Show me.'

'No, not badly. This is not my blood, it's. . .oh, Alain.' As relief poured through her, the enormity of what had happened flooded back again, threatening to drown her joy in the dark memories of terror and conflict.

'Don't cry, my love, you're safe now. Safe. I'll take you home.' He held her close to his chest, smoothing her wild hair and searching her eyes for signs of pain. 'Did he wound you, sweetheart? Did he. . .?' He could not say the word to her for fear she would tell him the worst.

'I fought him off. Is he. . .did you find. . .?'

'We found him, and the others. He won't survive, but tell me what this lass is. . .she's not dead, is she?' He looked up at Bruno and Sir Nicholas.

'No, my lord. Swooned.'

'Thank heaven,' Marietta said. 'She's in far worse shape than me. I had to sit on her to stop her running off. Carry her down quickly before she wakes. Look. . .' she pointed to the bowl of wet leaves '. . .she came up here to eat. . .oh, saints in heaven, the broth. . .don't let anyone eat it!'

'Sweetheart, what are you talking about? What broth must not be eaten?'

'It's poisoned, Alain—they were going to poison themselves when I got here. That's why I had to stay. . .! Oh Alain, quickly, the men must not sample it. It's in the cauldron over the fire.'

'They won't,' he assured her. 'I know it.'

Sir Nicholas and Bruno lifted Milly. 'We'll take the maid down between us, my lord,' Nicholas said.

'Good. Come on, my love, we'll wait for the other explanations till later. Put your arms around my neck. Lost your shoe, did you? Hold on. Gently now.'

He lifted her safely into his arms and carried her easily over the rocks while she nestled her head into his neck and closed her eyes to relish the feel of his arms and the closeness of his body, the warmth of his skin and hair, even the smell of his sweat.

He chided her gently as they went. 'This is a habit

I'm going to have to break you of,' he murmured,
kissing her damp forehead, 'or I shall be spending the
rest of my life searching for you and bringing you back.
Shall I put a leash on you? Eh? Shall I?'

'I didn't run away from you, my lord,' she replied. 'I
had to find Milly. She took the leaves to empty them
away but she didn't come back and I suspected she'd
gone off to eat them.'

'Why ever should she want to poison herself?'

'She's pregnant, my lord.'

Alain stopped dead in his tracks. 'What? How? I
mean. . .who?' When Marietta didn't answer, he understood. 'That swine?'

'It could have been. It's a long story. I think you'll
have to hear the whole of it before you understand
what the family have been through.'

'Then it will wait, sweetheart, until you're safe home
again.'

Down below, at Beckington, the men had already
begun to clear away the evidence of carnage which had
greeted them a little while earlier. The stolen Penda
and Apollo were already on their way home, the
murdered men were wrapped and slung over horses—
only old Betty could not be moved.

To Marietta's confusion, the men broke into spontaneous applause as the three men and their prizes
emerged from the woodland.

'Blood? She's wounded, my lord?' Sir Henry's face
registered alarm as he took her hand. 'Did that
fiend. . .?'

'No, Father, I'm all right, really, no more than a few
bruises. Is. . .is that man still alive?'

'No, Marietta, he died only a short time ago. Was it
you who stabbed him?'

She nodded, her lips tightened, remembering the act.

'That's my brave, fierce woman,' Lord Alain whispered to her, settling her before him on the wide

saddle, 'my courageous tigress. Well done, my beautiful girl. More than a match for any man, eh?' Tenderly, he tucked her into his arm and held her close.

'Where's Milly? She must come too.' She turned her head to look, but Milly was already on Sir Nicholas's saddle.

'Yes, sweetheart, everything shall be just as you want it now. The place is yours and you'll be allowed to say what happens to it, and the Fullers. We've held off for long enough, too long, to wait for that monster to give us the evidence we needed. I'll send men down to see to old John and his Betty. They'll be tended, don't worry. Home now.' He kissed her.

Home. She had never realised how sweet the sound could be.

CHAPTER FOURTEEN

THE feast, originally meant to be a farewell to the guests on the last day of their visit, was a celebration that paid little heed to the multiple deaths of the day, only to its more than satisfactory conclusion.

Rested, bathed and tended with loving hands, Marietta's fears that Lord Alain would be angry at her interference in the affairs of Beckington were quickly dispelled by his attention to her superficial wounds. Bruises and a few nasty scratches claimed as much sympathy as a broken limb would have done while Alain did his best to assure her that she had saved them all a great deal of trouble by defending herself so proficiently. Sir Bastien deserved no less.

But Marietta wondered, as he soothed her guilt, whether he was aware of Sir Bastien's part in the affairs of his late wife, not merely as a lover, though that would have been serious enough, but as a man of bestial habits who repeatedly raped a defenceless girl and terrorised her parents.

Later, after the feast, and once more alone together, she sought to broach the subject in a roundabout manner, asking him how badly his plans had been spoiled by her involvement.

Half-naked in the warm solar before the sun disappeared completely, he sat on the pillows of the great bed and pulled Marietta backwards into his arms.

'Come to think of it, sweetheart, very little. The reason I didn't want to make it look as though we were about to renovate the place or move the old couple out was because I suspected something of the scheme when we saw horse-dung there, and tracks. And a newish bolt on the stable door. I knew the old couple were not telling me the truth and that they were scared stiff of something, so I decided to let things take their course. In fact, I tried to make things easy for the thieves to steal again; your father being away from home helped, too.'

'You knew about Longleigh, then?'

'No, I didn't. I'd no idea your father's bailiff was involved, even before Sir Henry bought Monksgrange, but I was fairly certain that the caves in the hills above were being used as staging-posts for horse thieves. Do you remember when we saw the dung there, too?'

'Yes, and I told you I'd heard travellers in the mist? Were they horse thieves?'

He took her face in his hand and turned it to his so that she could see his laughing eyes. 'They, my sweet runaway girl, were horse thieves.'

'Taking your horses?'

'Taking my horses while there was a heavy overnight mist and my back was turned.'

'But I saw Thorsgeld Castle above the mist that morning.'

'The mares and colts were in the lower pastures,' he whispered.

'And you were at Monksgrange.'

'And I shall expect compensation, my lady, for their loss.'

'Were they very valuable?'

'Very, *very* valuable.'

'Oh, I have little to pay with. You'll take payment in kind, will you?'

'That was what I had in mind.' His hands caressed.

'Would more information do, instead of what you had in mind?'

'What information?'

'That the lay-brothers who worked at Monksgrange before my father bought it were also involved.'

His hands stopped their exploration. 'The lay-brothers? From Bolton Priory? Are you sure?'

'Yes. They breed horses too, you know.'

'Yes, but not destriers for war. Palfreys and draught horses.'

'Nevertheless, they went to Beckington to collect horses for Longleigh and take them on up to the caves.'

'Who told you this, Marietta?'

'Betty Fuller.'

He paused, taking in the implications. 'What else did she tell you?'

'That your groom, Rigg, was involved, too. Did you know?'

'Only recently I discovered that. I knew that one of the men in the stables was up to something. It had to be someone who knew where the horses were going to be at any one time, but I didn't realise it was Rigg until I saw him with Sir Bastien. Then I knew. Thick as thieves, right under my nose.'

Marietta had it in mind to tell him what she'd seen and what Iveta had heard, but there was nothing to be gained by that. It could not be used in court now, it was too late. Come to think of it, it was too late to tell him anything except those parts that would help her understand him. But she had opened the door to her source of information and she knew he would ask.

'What else, sweetheart?'

Instead of answering him directly, she asked a question of him. 'Will you tell me, Alain. . .?'

He sensed her reluctance and knew what was to come. 'What is it you want to know, sweetheart?' he said into her hair. 'About my first wife?'

'Yes.'

'You have a right to know. I've treated you harshly, and unfairly, too. It was all part of a plan to discover more about what happened two years ago, but it went wrong because I misunderstood the facts and so I don't understand any more than I did before. It serves me right for abusing your trust of me. All I discovered was that he...that man...was as evil as ever, and that I nearly lost you as a result of my stupidity. And I discovered that you are as unlike her as it's possible to be, and I thank God for that.'

His voice dropped to a whisper in her ear and his arms pulled her closer as though to cushion himself against the pain of discussing past events.

'Why did you marry her? Was it arranged?'

'It had been arranged since we were both fourteen, to bring property to my family and connections to hers. It was seven years before we were married and I'd heard rumours that she had already broken our betrothal vows by associating with other men. But I thought it was jealous talk and I took no notice. I was busy winning my spurs and squiring. I couldn't believe it. She was so fair.'

'Like Emeline?' It was the same question she had asked her father.

He sighed. 'You knew, then?'

'I knew that much, yes.'

'And that's why you were so insistent I was for her, rather than you? Because you thought I wanted a replacement?'

'Yes. Partly.' She turned and kissed his bare shoulder.

'Nothing could have been further from the truth, sweetheart.'

'But she was fair, and you married her.'

'Yes, I married her, thinking that whatever I'd heard would be changed, that she would settle down and be the perfect wife. But she didn't, and she wasn't, and there was little I could do about it, except lock her up in here and keep her captive. That was not the solution.'

'Was there a solution?'

'No. None that I knew of. I was young and I suppose I did not pay her enough attention. It was a marriage we both drifted through and such marriages need careful nurturing to make them blossom. I hadn't the sense to do that, and she ran wild in a place like this, with men everywhere.'

'But she died, two years ago.'

He nodded and shifted her round to sit in the crook of his arm, taking a strand of her hair to wind around his fingers. 'Yes, love. She died.'

'Do you know how?'

'That was something I hoped I might discover during the last few days. But I didn't. All I know is that she came home one day from a ride, went to bed and became violently ill, and by the time I'd sent for the wise-woman from the town, it was too late.'

'There was no enquiry about the manner of her death?'

'No, it was the year when the pestilence took so many of those officials who attend to such things, and it was easier and less painful to write it off as the same thing, though it didn't seem to me to be the same in every respect. No one else here caught it.'

She quailed at telling him, but he wanted to know. He had said so. 'You knew that she and Sir Bastien were lovers, Alain?'

'Is that something you deduced over the last few days, or did you learn it some other way?'

'I had already worked it out when Betty confirmed what I had thought.'

'What does that old crone know about it?' he asked, sharply.

'More than you'd think, my lord. She told me about it today.'

'What? What did she tell you? Tell me what she said.'

She took his hands in hers and held them, anxious

not to hurt him more than he had been already but knowing that, if he wanted the truth, it was a risk she would have to take. So she repeated, after all, the story of what Iveta had heard of the threat to the Fullers and how she herself had decided that she must risk his displeasure by warning them. They were her tenants, she said, and what would have been the use of telling him when he had not wanted to speak of Beckington?

He said nothing to that. It was too true to deny.

She went on then to describe how she had found the Fullers on the verge of taking their own lives, at Betty's insistence, and then the full story of how they, and Beckington Manor, had been used for Lady Thorsgeld's evil pleasures, horse thievery and torment by all the men involved.

'Lay-brothers, too?' Lord Alain was incredulous. 'And Rigg...and Longleigh? All of them? Good grief, I can hardly believe it!'

He was as appalled as she knew he would be when she told him of the attempt at abortion—always a risky business, with as many failures as successes—of how Betty was not reliable with the correct herbs, of how Milly always made the potions and how, on that occasion, she wreaked her vengeance on the woman who had so brutally assisted in her torment.

'Merciful heavens! I had no idea,' was all he said. 'No idea.'

Choosing her words carefully, Marietta told him how she herself had contributed to Longleigh's death, not by stabbing as it had seemed to the men, but by poison. Then she broke down and wept, for she had been responsible for two men's deaths that day, and as much as Alain insisted she feel no guilt for defending herself against the one, two souls in purgatory weighed heavily on her conscience.

He allowed her to weep; few women ever killed one man in a lifetime, let alone two in one day.

'You killed in self-defence, sweetheart, not in cold blood. They deserved everything they got. They were beasts, and they would have had *you*, and killed you, if you had not got them first. I'm proud of you.'

He kissed her tears away. 'You have courage, and beauty, and intelligence. I was wrong to have taken advantage of you over this business. You were hurt, I know, and confused, and I was set on seeing my plan work so that I could catch that beast and hang him.'

'What...what was your plan?' She snuggled her damp face against his chest and ran a hand softly across the undulations of his muscles and ribs, delighting in the firmness of his skin and the hardness below it.

Alain laughed softly. 'If you're going to do much more of that, tigress, you're going to have to wait some time before I can remember.' He placed a large hand over hers. 'Which do you want first, proof of my irresponsibility, or proof of my love for you?'

Love? That was a word she had never heard from him until now. She tipped her head back to look up at him, meeting his dark eyes with wonder. 'Love for me?' she whispered. 'Is that what you said, or was I dreaming?'

For an answer, he lowered her backwards onto the pillows, spilling her luxurious dark hair around her like a rippling sea. 'I made so many mistakes in my first marriage,' he told her, 'you'd think I would have learned a few lessons in what women need from a man, love, security, respect. Few men bother with that, but I don't intend to spend my life without love, Marietta. I've tried it, and it's a barren place. And yet, when I fell in love with you the first moment I saw you...'

'No, Alain, you forget—'

'Hear me, wench. I do not forget. You lay on the ground, yelling at me to leave you alone, taking a swipe at me...' he smiled at that, making her blush '...and I couldn't keep my hands off you. And when I fell in love with you, as I said, something warned me to have a care. I'd been caught once. I dared not tell you I loved you, only that I wanted you and that I would have you.

'So we got off to a bad start, didn't we? With not a little help from your dear stepmother and half-sister. And for some reason, there never seemed to be a good time to tell you that I've loved you like a madman since that time you fell off that stupid horse.'

Tenderly, she caressed his face, but he caught her palm and kissed it. This was something she had never thought to hear. 'I thought. . .my father said you liked my courage. . .and my looks. . .and I was not very flattered—' she smiled at him, shyly 'but I thought of you day and night. I think that must have been love, too. Do you think it might have been, Alain?'

His grin broadened. 'I think it might have been, darling girl. And now? Has the feeling gone, after all you've suffered at my hands, or is there still a bit of it left?'

The temptation to punish him rose in her like a bubble about to burst with the first huff of laughter, so she held the expression of it in her eyes while she reverted to the question he had still not answered.

'Tell me what this grand scheme was first, then I'll decide whether you shall know of my love for you or whether I shall keep it to myself for another hour or so.'

'I could get it out of you in less than an hour, woman.' He lowered his head to hers and took a kiss that confirmed his boast.

'I know you could, brute, but allow me to keep you in suspense for a little while longer. It's a delicious feeling.'

'Very well, but I believe you must already have drawn some conclusions about what I was trying to do.

It was when I saw Emeline here at the castle and realised how much like my first wife she was.'

'But you must have noticed it before, surely?'

'Only distantly, love. Here, at Thorsgeld, she seemed to have bloomed. It's strange, but in *this* setting, where *she* had been, the resemblance seemed to be more pronounced, and it occurred to me, at that moment, to use her to trap Symme. It was not so much that he'd had my erring wife that rankled, but that he'd made a fool of me by taking my horses, too. And yet I'd been unable to prove anything. No trace.

'In my innocence, I thought it was merely the blonde good looks that he was attracted by, so I had to do what I could to keep Emeline from bolting back home after her arguments with you. And the surest way of doing that was to be nice to her. I'm afraid it looked bad, sweetheart. Didn't it?'

'Yes, it looked *very* bad,' Marietta said, remembering the pain. 'But go on. You wanted her to stay while you got Symme here and saw his reaction to her. Is that it?'

'I thought he'd be sure to make a bee-line for her, especially if he thought she was what I wanted.'

'Ah, I see. So you made it look as though she was yours.'

He had the grace to look shamefaced. 'Yes, sweetheart.'

'And that was why you kept her by you, to entice him.'

'Yes. I know it was putting her in some danger, but I thought there were enough of us to keep her safe. And I thought, foolishly, that somehow if he showed an interest in Emeline, it might help me to find out what happened to cause my first wife's death and, at the same time, give me some idea of how he was taking my horses. I had an idea about Beckington by then, and the caves, and I knew that if he was with Emeline for much of the time, she would blabber to me about what he was up to.'

'Especially if you kept being nice to her,' Marietta snapped.

'Yes, my love, except that I didn't realise that he was more interested in you than in her...no, don't protest, it's true. It was men's wives he preferred, not particularly their colouring. You discovered that and told me. Remember?'

'Yes, I remember. So then you had to switch alliegances.'

'Sweetheart, no. It had already got out of hand. That day when I kept Emeline by me, I expected that he'd hover round like a frustrated wasp, trying to get her away. But he didn't. He stayed at your side instead. It was one of the worst days of my life. That's why, by the end of the day I could stand no more of it and pulled you away. That's why I was so angry and unreasonable. I realised I'd put you in danger and discovered that my plan was flawed from the beginning. I'm sorry, sweetheart: forgive me.'

'You thought I'd been with him the next evening, didn't you?'

'Yes, I saw you covered in flour. I was livid.'

'You cared enough to beat me. Did you beat *her* when she misbehaved?'

'No, sweetheart, she was not worth the effort.'

'Alain...'

He caught her to him and buried his head in her throat, moving his mouth over her in a wave of remorse that broke loose over her lips.

'Sweetheart, I'm sorry. That I should harm you after all you suffered.' He told her then what had happened, how he had gone to the granary and tipped flour over the lovers and Marietta hooted with laughter and told him how Emeline had still been trying to get rid of it the next morning. It had sobered her down too, she said, for the lass was by no means as ready for Sir Bastien's forceful advances as she had thought she was. By that time, she'd been ready to go home.

'Alain, did that man. . .did he. . .you know?'

'Sweetheart, I don't really know. It's possible, but only time will tell if it had any effect. Say nothing. Just pray that she doesn't have to pay the price of her foolishness, or mine.'

'I think I might ask her.'

'Will she tell you?'

'Mmm. . .mmm. . .we've come to a better understanding over this you know. She discovered she needed my help and I found I needed hers and now we've called a truce; she learned a lot while she's been here.'

'Especially how not to fool about in your pleasance,' he teased her. 'Are you going to become the wise-woman of Thorsgeld Castle?'

'Yes, I am. And what's more, I have a new assistant. Milly's going to be very useful to me. You'll allow her to stay, won't you?'

'After all that's happened, sweetheart, I would climb up to the moon and reach it down for you if that's what you want. You have only to ask.'

Marietta thought that that was the loveliest offer anyone could ever make. She wrapped her arms about his neck.

'Thank you. I won't take advantage of that immediately, my lord, but I do want some of that loving, please.'

'You shall have my loving until you cry out for me to stop, but first, dearest love, there is something you're going to tell me, is there not?'

Teasingly, she frowned and pretended puzzlement.

'Stop teasing me, wench. I've waited long enough to hear it,' he growled.

'Ah, now I remember. I love you, Alain. I love you

desperately. . .' She got no further with the long-awaited endearments, his lips stole the words from hers and added his own when they stopped for breath.

'I didn't want another wife like her, sweetheart, believe me. I saw you and knew by your very first resistance to me that you were as unlike her as it's possible to be. You fought me off, you ran away, you tried to talk me out of it, you wanted none of me, did you?'

'My body wanted you. My heart wanted you. But. . .'

'But what? Courage? It let you down, did it?'

'I felt sure I was second best, and I was angry and insulted.'

'Sweetheart. . .ah, my fierce, proud woman, second-best never. You're the brightest star in the sky. The only one I want, ever. Love me now. Love me and let's start again, shall we?'

'No more misunderstandings. No more schemes.'

'I swear it. I love you too much to risk your scorn again.'

'Then let's forget. . .'

He took her offer and locked her into his arms as the light slowly faded from the room and a cooling breeze brought the faint scent of rain through the open window from the west. And when she gave herself, utterly and completely, her thought was that, if this was the difference it made to their passionate loving, it had perhaps been worth striving for. If she had given up when she had thought of doing, she would never have known this, the bliss of complete freedom from doubts and nagging fears.

'About those fierce sons and wild daughters,' she whispered.

Alain lifted his head in the dim light and studied her face. 'You like that idea, do you, after all?'

'Mmm.' She smiled. 'Shall we start with the sons?'

'He'll be magnificent,' he whispered, 'truly magnificent.'

The day of the guests' departure was cool and misty-moist with a layer of low cloud hanging into the valley bottom, shrouding the road to Monksgrange. But none of this dampened the hearty farewells and shouts of advice, laughter and parting shots as groups, augmented by newly bought horses, made their way out of the courtyard. Marietta had made new friends; they had promised to visit again before summer was over.

Sir John and Lady Isobel's retinue was augmented by more than horses, though. Since the hunting adventure when Sir Nicholas Bannon had saved her from a wild boar, Lady Isobel had so much taken a fancy to Marietta's uncle that she had persuaded her husband to take on a new Horse-Master, a younger man who reacted quickly to danger and was strong enough to serve them as a retainer should. Sir Henry Wardle needed little persuasion to let his brother-in-law go; it was what he had hoped would happen this many a year and Lady Alice agreed, Nicholas must seek advancement further afield.

Lady Alice's smile was genuine enough. 'We shall miss him,' she simpered, hoping that the words, at least, would have a genuine ring. 'The girls, especially.'

Emeline turned her eyes towards Marietta and pulled a face. 'Which girls do you think she means, Marrie? Not me, for sure. There's nothing I shall enjoy more than not having his advice thrust at me all the time. He's as interfering as Mother. That wild boar was a godsend.'

The new friendship between the two half-sisters appeared to be founded on conspiracy, but neither of them saw any harm in that and Marietta took the chance to offer a suggestion along the same lines. 'Emmie, would you miss Iveta very much if I asked

Lady Alice to allow her to stay here with me at Thorsgeld?'

Emeline's face lit up. 'Perfect!' she breathed. 'Then I can have the maids to myself!' It was a typical response.

From the castle wall in Marietta's garden, they watched and waved as the winding retinue snaked down through the mist into the valley towards Monksgrange, savouring the strange emptiness of the green place which, until today, had thronged with their guests. The sun now spread its bright light through the whiteness, promising warmth after the rain, twinkling on the leaves that covered the arbour and catching the glossy white coat of the greyhound pup that sniffed and pranced at a stalwart frog beneath the box hedge, yapping at its stoicism.

'Look,' Marietta said, snuggling closer to Alain, 'we shall be able to take her hunting soon. It's time she was. . .'

'Time enough for that, love. But look over there, at your assistant.'

She followed his gaze towards the end of the garden where Milly, now clean and white-coiffed with a basket at her feet, snipped and tidied the herbs and flowers in the beds, totally absorbed and at peace. 'I shall care for her, Alain, and her babe, and her mother. Is there a cott somewhere nearby where Betty can live, where I can keep an eye on her?'

'No need, my little protector, your father is finding her a place in his village where Lady Alice can watch over her. He insisted. She was Lady Alice's tenant, after all, and they both regret not managing Beckington as they should have done. We'll soon put the place to rights. We'll make it our next task, shall we?'

'Oh yes, it could be such a pretty place, with some attention. And the garden's complete now, Alain, come and look.'

She led him to the corner of the herb-plot next to the self-heal where, after the overnight rain, tiny green shoots had begun to push their spears through the soil. 'See. . .' she bent to touch them '. . .it's the love-in-a-mist that Old Adam gave us.'

Alain pulled her up into his arms and held her gently, smiling at the aptness of the name. 'He must have known, the old rascal. Love-in-a-mist. Perfect.'

Historical Romance™

Coming next month

LADY DECEIVER
Helen Dickson

Miss Cordelia Hamilton-King was tired of the frivolous life, and wanted—horrors!—to work. She refused her influential father's help, and became Miss Delia King, secretary, at Stanfield Hall in Norfolk. That one small deception caused havoc.

Captain Alexander Frankland, newly restored to his ancestral home after the war, had connections with the Hamilton-Kings that Delia, in her growing love for her employer, knew nothing about…

A COMFORTABLE WIFE
Stephanie Laurens

Miss Antonia Mannering had made plans, and Lord Philip Ruthven featured largely. They had been childhood friends, but had not seen each other for years. She knew Philip was popular with the ladies, but he had never married any of them. Wouldn't he now be ready to set up his nursery? If she could prove to him that she could run his home, not disgrace him in Society, and be a *comfortable* wife for him, surely he would be prompted to propose to her—that she might fall in love had never occurred to her!

'Happy' Greetings!

Would you like to win a year's supply of Mills & Boon® books? Well you can and they're free! Simply complete the competition below and send it to us by 31st August 1997. The first five correct entries picked after the closing date will each win a year's subscription to the Mills & Boon series of their choice. What could be easier?

ACSPPMTHYHARSI

_ _ _ _ _ _ _ _ _ _ _ _ _ _

TPHEEYPSARA

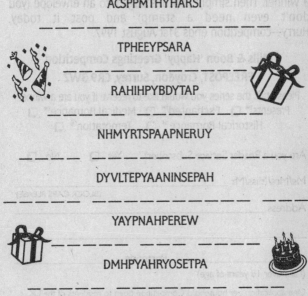

_ _ _ _ _ _ _ _ _ _ _

RAHIHPYBDYTAP

_ _ _ _ _ _ _ _ _ _ _ _

NHMYRTSPAAPNERUY

_ _ _ _ _ _ _ _ _ _ _ _ _ _ _ _

DYVLTEPYAANINSEPAH

_ _ _ _ _ _ _ _ _ _ _ _ _ _ _ _ _ _

YAYPNAHPEREW

_ _ _ _ _ _ _ _ _ _ _ _

DMHPYAHRYOSETPA

_ _ _ _ _ _ _ _ _ _ _ _ _ _ _

VRHYPNARSAEYNPIA

_ _ _ _ _ _ _ _ _ _ _ _ _ _ _ _

Please turn over for details of how to enter ☞

How to enter...

There are eight jumbled up greetings overleaf, most of which you will probably hear at some point throughout the year. Each of the greetings is a 'happy' one, i.e. the word 'happy' is somewhere within it. All you have to do is identify each greeting and write your answers in the spaces provided. Good luck!

When you have unravelled each greeting don't forget to fill in your name and address in the space provided and tick the Mills & Boon® series you would like to receive if you are a winner. Then simply pop this page into an envelope (you don't even need a stamp) and post it today. Hurry—competition ends 31st August 1997.

Mills & Boon 'Happy' Greetings Competition
FREEPOST, Croydon, Surrey, CR9 3WZ

Please tick the series you would like to receive if you are a winner

Presents™ ❑   Enchanted™ ❑   Medical Romance™ ❑
Historical Romance™ ❑   Temptation® ❑

Are you a Reader Service Subscriber?   Yes ❑   No ❑

Ms/Mrs/Miss/Mr _____

(BLOCK CAPS PLEASE)

Address _____

_____

_____ Postcode _____

(I am over 18 years of age)

One application per household. Competition open to residents of the UK and Ireland only.

You may be mailed with other offers from other reputable companies as a result of this application. If you would prefer not to receive such offers, please tick box. ❑

C7B

mps MAILING PREFERENCE SERVICE